YOUR DREAM FOR ME

YOUR DREAM FOR ME

Alison Schaffir

To Mom, by favorite fan. To Dad, my favorite editor. And to Noah, my favorite critic.

Praise for Your Dream for Me

"Schaffir captures the sheer fun and passion of the emotional roller-coaster that is high school. 'Your Dream for Me' has humor, heart, romance, and characters to relate to and root for. Scarlett is the friend everyone needs. You're in for a treat."—Julia DeVillers, bestselling author of *How My Private, Personal Journal Became a Bestseller*

"Alison Schaffir's debut novel captures the delightfully awkward feeling of what it means to be a teenager. It's a light-hearted story of friendship, family, fashion, and first love that deserves a round of applause."—Sarah Ainslee, author of *That Wasn't in the Script*

"Thoroughly entertaining and heartfelt, *Your Dream For Me* is a poignant story of strong friendships and having the courage to ask yourself who you want to be. It's impossible not to root for Scarlett, whose genuine, spirited voice gives readers plenty of food for thought, as she navigates her junior year of high school. Her experiences are raw and relatable, and through her struggles and triumphs—stitched together with humor and heart—we can all begin to unpack what our dreams are...for ourselves and for those we care about."—Leah Dobrinska, author of the Mapleton novels & the Larkspur Library Mystery series

"Alison Schaffir creates a relatable, realistic journey through the changing complexities of both romantic and friend relationships in

Your Dream for Me. Experience the emotional turmoil of teen-hood through Scarlet's eyes as she navigates her junior year of high school, learning some of life's most challenging lessons. Tender moments and anxiety-riddled twists drive this hard-to-put-down dramatic tale."—Micki Bare, author of the award-winning middle grade novel *Society of the Sentinelia*

Chapter One

I spot the door slightly ajar. From inside, light streams out, casting a faint glow along the linoleum floor. I can feel it beckoning to me, like there's a magnetic pull drawing me closer.

Looking in both directions, I confirm that there are no onlookers. I glance down at my watch to confirm the time: 6:52 a.m. Most students don't arrive until at least 7:15. Lucky (or unlucky) for me, my car is getting inspected, and my mom offered to drop me off before an early work meeting today. So, with extra time on my hands, I thought I might as well explore the theater costume shop.

Moving cautiously, I twist the door handle and slide across the threshold. Once I've made it to the other side, I gaze around the room.

"Wow," I breathe.

The shop is empty and quiet. As I enter, I notice costumes from past productions displayed proudly on mannequins. The walls are lined with colorful swatches of fabric and elaborate props that make me feel like I'm a performer at a circus. I marvel at the cutting tables, stitching stations, and storage spaces. *A designer's paradise.*

Skimming my hands over the costume material, I smile to myself.

It's no surprise that I would find comfort here. After all, my dream is to become a fashion designer one day. I've doodled in sketch pads, created Pinterest boards, and cut out magazine collages since I was a little girl. I've even watched *The Devil Wears Prada* more times than

1

I can count. Somehow, I admire Miranda Priestly's powerful editor-in-chief character, even if she scares the living hell out of me. There's something I find exhilarating about the fashion world—the glitz and glam, the grit and the guts. I know becoming a fashion designer isn't an easy road, but it's a journey I'm committed to, especially one that I'm ready to pour my heart into once I get into my dream school: Fashion Institute of Technology.

As I continue to explore the shop, I see a costume that calls out to me in particular. It's a red, sparkly flapper dress—one that looks like it would have been featured prominently in a show like *Chicago*. My parents both participated in musical theater when they were younger and have exposed me to shows over the years, so I'm familiar with a number of them. It's a shame that I never inherited their singing or dancing genes, though. That's why, as much as they've tried to convince me otherwise, theater has never been the path for me.

As I stare at the dress, a mischievous idea pops into my head. I glance both ways again to make sure no one else is here. Then in one fluid motion, I pull the dress off the hanger, lift it over my head, and shimmy into it, still fully clothed. I don't consider myself a rule-breaker, so I wouldn't normally do this. But gosh darn it, it's a Monday morning, and I need to add some spice to my life. I twirl around to stare at my reflection in the full-length mirror propped across from me. Twisting back and forth, I begin humming "All That Jazz."

"Come on, babe. Why don't we paint the town?" I croon. Doing a full spin in the shimmering red dress, I imagine myself as the vaudevillian Velma Kelly, plotting her husband's demise. It makes me feel powerful and alluring. For a moment, I'm absorbed to the point where I forget that I'm in a high school costume shop. I'm transported to the 1920s jazz era. I'm about to sing the next line when suddenly, I hear a rustling from behind me.

"And all that jazz," someone chimes in from behind me.

The blood drains from my face. I don't know what's worse: the fact that I'm being caught in the act in this outfit or the fact that someone is witnessing my off-key singing voice, which sounds more like a dying cat.

As I spin around, I pray that it's a custodian, or any impartial third party who can keep my little spectacle a secret. But standing in front of me is a male student who looks to be about my age. And not just any male student—one with beautiful blue eyes and dark, glossy hair. He's wearing a gray cotton shirt, and his arms are crossed in a way that accentuates his athletic build.

"Great song choice." He smirks as he watches me with curiosity.

I place a hand over my heart, still trying to catch my breath. "Please don't tell me you've been here the whole time."

"Oh, don't worry. Just enough time to watch your opening number."

I don't know whether to laugh or cry. I'm not sure who this guy is or why he's here, but I feel the need to justify myself. "I'm not a theater kid, if you can't tell."

"You could be one. You seem to have the chops for it," he says.

Maybe it's his piercing stare, or the fact that I was just caught breaking into the costume shop, but I feel light-headed. All I want to do is get out of this stifling dress as quickly as possible. "Hey, could you look the other way for a second?"

I know I'm fully clothed, but I still feel exposed taking off this red dress in front of a total stranger—especially one that's making my heart rate speed up the way it is.

"Sure," he laughs. "I'll even close my eyes, if that makes you feel more comfortable."

I know he's probably joking, but it brings me a sense of relief. "Thanks," I murmur. I reach my hand to the zipper in preparation to pull off the dress, but the zipper won't budge.

"Shoot." I breathe as the panic begins to set in. "It's stuck."

3

This has got to be the worst Monday in the history of Mondays.

The guy removes his hands from his eyes. "Want me to help you with that?"

I would put up a fight, but I have no choice. I made my bed, so I might as well lie in it, too. "Yes, please."

He comes up behind me and reaches for the zipper. My body freezes as he brushes a strand of hair away from my neck.

"Stay still," he whispers as he tampers with the zipper until I hear it click. He glides the zipper down my back. The gesture causes a chill to run down my spine.

"There we go. That wasn't so bad, was it?" He looks at me with an earnest expression.

I tug the dress off and place it back on the hanger to return it to the rack. "Please, just promise me you won't tell anyone about this, okay?"

"I promise I won't tell anyone," he says, "but maybe you should tell me your name—just so I know who I'm not supposed to be talking about."

He's smooth...I'll give him that. Still, I rationalize that I'm probably not going to see this guy again anytime soon, so it really doesn't matter. "You know, it's probably better if I don't." I brush past him without responding to his question, keeping my head cast down. "Thanks again for the help."

As I exit the costume shop, I glance back one more time. He's grinning at me. "You're welcome."

I feel like my cheeks must match the color of the red dress I was just wearing. The hallways are picking up with students now that class is almost about to start. Wanting to forget this entire situation, I veer off into the adjacent hallway and go to find my best friend, Macie. After all, she's taking theater as an elective this year, so she's the one person who will find humor in this. As I approach her locker, I see her curly strawberry-blonde hair from behind.

"Macie, you'll never guess what happened." I tap my best friend on the back. I always meet up with her before school starts.

"What happened, Scar?" Her hazel eyes light up as she grabs her water bottle from her locker.

"I was poking around the costume shop just now, and this random guy caught me trying on one of the dresses."

She laughs and shakes her head. "Look at you getting into mischief. At least it could be worse. You don't have to face your doom performing a monologue in the third period for Mr. Walsh like I do."

My heart goes out to her. Though she's not a performer, Macie chose to sign up for an elective theater class when the semester started in September. Originally, she had registered, thinking that the class would be a joke. But it's turned out to be more work than she'd bargained for. From what she's told me, the exams are awful, considering each student is required to perform a three-minute monologue in front of the entire class. And this happens to be the last theater exam before Winter Break, which means it will weigh even more heavily on her grade.

I put a hand on her shoulder. "You're going to be great. How bad can it be, right?"

"As long as I don't faint on stage or have a heart attack during my performance, I'll consider it a success."

"Atta girl." I flash a sympathetic smile.

"Look." Macie points behind me. "It's Liam!"

I turn just in time to spot Macie's recent friend from the swim team, who also happens to be in her acting class. He's walking in our direction, sporting a retro corduroy jacket and faded dark-wash jeans. I don't know him as well as she does, but Macie seems to have built a good relationship with him. And a friend of hers is a friend of mine.

"As if seeing you at practice every day isn't enough already," she teases to Liam, "I can't believe we both have to survive this same Acting Technique class, too."

"I know. This exam is going to be killer. At least I'll get to make ridiculous faces at you during your monologue."

Macie sticks her tongue out at him in return. "Well, gee—thanks, Liam," she retorts. "If you do anything to mess up my monologue, I might have to get on stage during yours and trip you."

Liam puts his hands up in the air, as if signaling a peace declaration. Then he turns to me. "Scarlett, you should come to the mini theater during third period. Anyone is allowed to sit in during the monologues."

Now that Liam's mentioning it, I realize that there's nothing I'd rather be doing than watching Macie recite a theater monologue. I'm not passing up a chance to witness my best friend act in front of an audience. Macie sure carries the athletic gene when it comes to swimming, but acting is far from her strong suit. Plus, third period happens to be my free period.

"I have Study Center then." I grin at Liam. "I will totally be there."

Liam does a silent fist pump as Macie groans.

"At least now we'll both get to make fun of you during your performance too, Liam." I chuckle.

"Don't get too excited," Macie interjects. "He's actually one of the more convincing performers in class."

"Well, aside from Nathaniel Wilder," Liam says. "It's like he came straight out of a movie from Cannes."

"Nathaniel…who?"

There's a particular ring to the name in the way it rolls off of Liam's tongue—the type of name that once you hear, you can't easily forget.

"You'll understand after his monologue," Liam continues. "He just moved here this year, but he's already building a reputation as a legend in the theater department."

"He's a sight to see," Macie confirms.

I'm intrigued by the way Liam speaks the name with a hint of reverence, as if this "Nathaniel" is some sort of wizard with magical acting powers. For some reason, I think back to the guy I met in the costume shop this morning. After all, he asked for my name, but I realized I never got his name. Still, I doubt he could be who Liam is referring to.

The name rings over again in my ears. Whatever his gift is, I'll find out soon enough.

Chapter Two

I wasn't able to get out of Study Center until the end of third period, so I'm just now slipping into the theater. Quietly, I scan for the first available seat and slide into a middle row, hoping not to draw too much attention to myself. When I look out in front of me, I'm surprised to find Macie waving at me. She motions to the girl finishing up on stage and mouths, "I'm next."

On the left side of the theater, I notice the majority of the class goofing off, failing to pay close attention to the current monologue. On the other side of the theater, Macie is sitting alone, except for one other guy seated next to her. I squint in the darkness, trying to recognize him. Though I can't make him out from behind, I see that his leg is fidgeting back and forth near the aisle.

As the girl finishes, the audience gives a mild round of applause. I watch Macie rise from her seat and approach the stage. The spotlight accentuates her sharp cheekbones, and she twirls a piece of her curly hair.

Macie mumbles a quick introduction, and then walks closer to the front of the stage. I take a deep breath, sending her a silent affirmation as she opens her mouth to speak.

The moment the first words leave her lips, my face curves into a knowing smile. I recognize the monologue. She's performing a scene from *Ferris Bueller's Day Off*—one of our favorite 80s movies to watch together at sleepovers. I listen as she imitates Ferris Bueller faking sickness to his parents in order to get out of school for the day. With each word she speaks, she grows more confident, her stage fright evaporating. I'll admit my best friend has more skill than I originally gave her credit for. She finishes her last line theatrically, bowing before the audience.

As the monologue ends, Macie's class claps in an enthusiastic round of applause. I flash a thumbs-up sign in her direction, breathing a sigh of relief for her. Meanwhile, she descends the stairs, joining the rest of her classmates on the other side of the theater.

With a heavy sigh, I begin to push myself up from my seat.

Yet, out of the corner of my eye, a movement piques my interest. The guy who had been sitting next to Macie stands up from his chair. I watch as he mounts the stairs at a leisurely pace, approaching the stage with a graceful stride. Once he's reached the center, he rustles a hand through his coffee-brown hair and turns to face the audience, gazing out with his alluring blue eyes that I realize I've seen before.

"Last, but certainly not least, we have Nathaniel performing for us," Mr. Walsh, the school's drama teacher who is sitting in the front row, announces.

Nathaniel. The recognition sets in. Not only is this the name of the "legend" that Liam had referred to earlier, but this is the same guy who caught me snooping in the costume shop just hours ago. Wanting to avoid being spotted, I slink down further in my seat to remain discrete. I guess since I'm already here, I'll stay to watch this last performance. If anything, I'm curious as to whether his monologue will live up to his reputation.

Nathaniel faces forward and glances out into the audience again. I notice him scan the room slowly—almost as if he's searching for a specific target. Then, my heart stops. Nathaniel's eyes land directly on me.

He probably can't see me, I reason to myself. After all, the lights are dimmed. And further, actors are instructed to focus their attention toward the center of a room all the time.

"I'm going to be performing an excerpt from Oscar Wilde's *The Picture of Dorian Gray,*" Nathaniel says.

As I prepare to hear his monologue, I shake myself out of a momentary trance. I know what Liam said—but how talented can he really be? I fold my arms together and wait for him to start.

Once silence descends upon the auditorium, Nathaniel opens his mouth and begins:

> *"Harry, imagine a girl, hardly seventeen years of age, with a little flower-like face, a small Greek head with plaited coils of dark-brown hair, eyes that were violet wells of passion, lips that were like the petals of a rose."*

My jaw drops at his opening lines. The words ring through my ears like a symphonic choir. I almost imagine him speaking straight to me, as if his words were meant for me. After all, my seventeenth birthday was only a couple of months ago. I do have distinctly dark brown hair. The passionate eyes and petal-like lips? Those are debatable. Still, the passage feels too coincidental. It's almost as if Nathaniel Wilder had predicted that I would be sitting in this exact spot right now—like he chose this excerpt for my ears alone.

His voice hypnotizes the theater, and he captivates the audience with his gestures and powerful inflection. When I turn my head, I notice that every previously distracted student is now transfixed on the stage, focusing on his performance.

> *"But an actress! How different an actress is! Why didn't you tell me that the only thing worth loving is an actress?"*

Nathaniel concludes theatrically, waving his hand up for dramatic effect. For a moment, the entire room falls silent, as if absorbing the aftershock. Then, cutting through the stillness of the air, a resounding applause fills the theater. I find myself clapping along with everyone else, mesmerized by the performance of a guy that I only met this morning.

His script may have denoted an actress, but all I can think to myself is one question: *Why didn't you tell me the only thing worth loving is an actor?*

I feel the chills pulsing through my body as the lights of the theater are flipped on. Before I know it, Macie is running up to me, flinging out her arms for a hug.

"Scarlett!" she exclaims. "Thank you for being here. It really eased my nerves knowing that I could look out into the audience and see you sitting right there."

If Macie could see me, that means that Nathaniel Wilder was actually aware of my presence. Which means he probably recognized me from earlier today. I suddenly feel more exposed than before.

"Of course," I reply, not quite giving her my full attention. "What are friends for?"

I spot Mr. Walsh shaking Nathaniel's hand on the other side of the theater. Nathaniel flashes a smile to him and then joins Liam. Collecting their backpacks, they begin to head toward the exit along with the rest of the class.

Macie and I trail behind. I vaguely listen as she chatters about how nervous she was, how relieved she is that her monologue is over, and how she never wants to take another drama class again.

"Mhm." I nod, still keeping an eye on Nathaniel as we head out of the theater and back toward the main hallway.

"I just hope I get a decent grade, you know," Macie babbles. "I mean, I know I wasn't the best person in the class, but I feel like I did better than expected, don't you think?"

"Yeah." I watch as Nathaniel and Liam head for a different hallway. Just as they are about to vanish out of sight, Nathaniel turns. His eyes meet mine for a second, before he whips his head back around. Liam and Nathaniel disappear around the bend.

As the oxygen returns to my lungs, I realize that Macie is still waiting for me to respond.

"Sorry," I murmur, "I just got distracted for a second." I give her shoulder a squeeze. "You were great." I flick my eyes to the hallway where Nathaniel had vanished. "And get this, Macie. That guy, Nathaniel, that Liam was talking about—he was the one I ran into in the costume shop this morning."

"You're kidding, Scarlett."

I lean in closer to her. "I know, right? Liam wasn't lying. He's got quite the talent."

Macie laughs. "Yeah, I guess so. He's a talented actor, that's for sure. I just don't get why everyone puts him on a pedestal." She crosses her arms. "I mean, he's just a normal guy. The girls in our class act like he's a celebrity or something."

"It's weird that I've never seen him before today. I feel like our school's small enough that I recognize most people. Or at least have heard of them."

"Well," Macie pauses, "he only moved here a little while ago. Liam seems to like him, though. They've become closer through this theater class. You know guys and their bromances."

I chuckle, but inside, my mind whirs, fishing for more information on the enigmatic Nathaniel. Now, I can't stop playing his performance in my mind.

"Well," I divert from the subject, not wanting my interest to come off as too apparent, "I'm glad you gave me the excuse to sneak out of Study Center to see your performance. I wish I didn't have to go to my next class."

Macie laughs. "I have to say, your timing couldn't have been any better if you had tried."

I wave at her, as I spin in the other direction. Once she's out of hearing range, I whisper under my breath, "Tell me about it."

I'm not sure if I say it more for her sake or my own, still reeling from the events of the past few minutes. My timing couldn't have been better in more ways than one.

* * *

"Will you promise to design a dress for me one day when you become the next Vera Wang?" Macie asks.

She's sprawled out on my bed, toying with one of my plush pillows that have an Eiffel Tower on it. My room is decorated like a classic designer's studio, inspired by my future career aspirations. I have coffee table books with brands like Prada, Dior, and Louis Vuitton on the covers. On my wall, vintage Vogue posters hang above my boutique desk. In the center is a bulletin board where I keep my latest designs and sketches, next to a full-length linen-covered mannequin. Of course, the irony is that I can't afford to shop these brands right now, except for the rare special occasion. I mostly shop at Fashion Fwrd, the local retail store I work at. But they say dress for the job you want one day, so my parents let me dress my room accordingly.

I turn back to her in amusement.

"You mean if I become her one day," I correct her.

"No, I mean when," she emphasizes.

I smile, grateful for her confidence in me. With Macie's busy swim schedule and my retail job, we're rarely able to hang out after school. Especially with homework and studying, and college prep work. Usually, our time together is reserved for the weekend movie nights and sleepovers. But today is a unique day where both of our schedules lined up, so I was excited that I could invite her over. After her stressful monologue earlier this morning, I'm sure she could use some time to unwind. And with Winter Break right around the corner, we both needed a distraction from tedious exam studying this week.

"Scarlett." She sits up and glances at the bulletin on my desk. "Your sketches are amazing. You really should share these with the world."

My parents got me a sketchbook two years ago for my birthday, and I've been using it ever since. Sketching has become my creative outlet whenever I'm stressed or overwhelmed with school. In my free time, I'll sit and brainstorm new designs with bright colors and playful proportions. My hope is that one day, I'll be able to start my own clothing line to inspire other girls to feel bold and confident in their clothing. For now, I've been pinning my sketches up on my bulletin board as inspiration.

"Hey, I can do a few sketches in a notebook, but I can't swim a 200-yard medley in under two minutes like you can." I've watched Macie during her swim meets before. She's like a bullet gliding through the water.

Macie shakes her head. "You know swimming isn't my end goal, like design is for you. I just want to do it competitively in college. And maybe some coaching here and there."

"You're so good with the kids when you lifeguard during the summer."

Her face lights up. "Yeah, I like working with the kids. That's why I think I want to go into early childhood education."

"Miss Macie has a nice ring to it." I imagine her in the front of a colorful classroom, teaching letters and numbers to bright-eyed students.

With college on our minds, we've been thinking more about our futures and what our majors will be one day. The thought is both scary and exhilarating.

As I watch her, Macie hops off of my bed and walks over to my angled white bookcase. She picks up a framed photo of her and me when we were younger. It's one of the two of us in our softball gear with our arms slung around each other.

"I can't believe we've known each other since Little League days in third grade. We've been best friends since the beginning."

It always makes me smile when Macie refers to me as her "best friend." There's pride in the way she proclaims it—that I mean that much to her, that our friendship is grounded in such a solid statement. It's a title I don't plan on giving up anytime soon.

Whenever Macie comes over, she seems to treat my room like a museum, observing my photos and objects like artifacts that have deep meaning behind them. She continues to examine the contents of my shelf, and I watch as she pulls out another framed photo, one of my parents from before I was born. "Your parents are so cute." She shakes her head. "You said they met in a musical in college, right?"

"Yes, and I'll never be able to compare to that."

Of course, my parents have a disgustingly adorable meet-cute story. My mom directed a production that my dad happened to act in. They hit it off, started dating, and the rest has been history. Thanks to that musical for bringing them together, I get to exist in the world. Unfortunately, it's unlikely that I'll have a theater romance the way they did. They've tried to coax me into trying it, but they know I've never been one for the spotlight, which is why I'd rather stick to something more behind-the-scenes, like design. I get too nervous in front of an audience. I'd rather just be a girl behind a curtain.

I sigh. "It's too bad I don't have a musical bone in my body, so I won't be finding someone that way."

Macie walks back over to the bed and sits on the edge.

"Hey," Macie says, "I never thought I'd be taking a theater class, and yet I'm doing it as an elective this year. Never say never."

I contemplate her words. It's true that I could sign up and participate in theater this year if I wanted to. I've always been curious about the world of the performing arts, especially after the costume shop incident today, and my parents seemed to love it in their youth. Still, with my retail job and all of the responsibilities that come with junior year, fashion needs to be my focus.

I point to my laptop to change the subject. "Hey, let's finish watching the movie from the last time you were over."

We make our way to my bed and lie back against the headboard as I put the laptop between us. The last time Macie and I had a sleepover, we decided on *Back to the Future* as our 80s movie of choice.

"I can't believe we both fell asleep last time. Especially during the Enchantment Under the Sea dance. The best part."

I press the play button on the screen and watch as George escorts Lorraine to the dance, and Marty fights to make sure his parents end up together.

"Why don't they make dresses like they did in the 1950s anymore?" Macie sighs. "Look how beautiful Lorraine's dress is. With that pretty peach overlay collar and the lace belt."

I laugh. Of course, Macie's focus would be on the details of the costume design and not the action unfolding in a thrilling sci-fi movie. My kind of girl.

"Is that the type of dress you would want one day when I become the next Vera Wang?" I ask. "A retro 50s dress like Lorraine wears in the movie?"

"Yes. A vintage swing dress, just like that. With a fit bodice and a flared skirt."

I make a mental note. "Okay, first, I'll need a sewing machine. I've been asking my parents about getting one for forever. Then, I'll need to learn how to sew, and then I'll make you a custom dress just like that."

Macie claps her hands together. "The perks of having a designer best friend."

I groan. "I need to get through this Exam Week, and then the holidays, and then I'll work on adding you to my ultra-selective list of clients."

"Okay, I'm honored. I can't wait, Scar."

I return my attention back to the screen just in time to see lightning strike the clock tower. My mind wanders back to the costume shop I had stumbled into earlier and all of the unique designs. Macie's words about theater ring through my head: *Never say never.*

Chapter Three

Today is the last day before Winter Break, and I decide to leave the cafeteria early, so I can get some extra study time before my European History exam. My grades have always been important to me, and with college applications coming up next fall, I want to finish off my first semester of junior year strong, especially during Exam Week.

I make my way out of the cafeteria into the cold air, feeling the wind whip against me. I pull my scarf tighter around my neck, burrowing my face to block the breeze. Approaching the side entryway of the main building, I reach for the door. But instead, the door swings out by itself. Suddenly, my body freezes...and not because of the chilly weather.

Standing in the doorway, with one arm outstretched, is the person I've only met once before, and the last person I could expect to see: *Nathaniel Wilder?*

My heart skips a beat. When I look to my left, I notice Liam is propped up against the opposite side of the entryway. "Hey, Scarlett." *There's no turning back now.*

Nathaniel's staring at me curiously with his aqua-blue eyes. The intensity in his expression causes me to dart my eyes back to Liam.

"Hey, Liam," I manage. I wonder if Nathaniel recognizes me from my embarrassing moment in the costume shop the other day, and if so, now he knows my identity. I still can't believe he caught me singing to myself while trying on a red flapper dress.

When I turn back to face Nathaniel, I'm surprised to see he's smiling at me. "Scarlett," he repeats, as if digesting the name. The way he accentuates both syllables carefully sends a ripple of chills down my spine. "So, that's your name."

He definitely remembers me from our first encounter.

"I'm…" Nathaniel reaches out a hand, like he's about to introduce himself. Before I can get a hold of my tongue, the words come out.

"Nathaniel, isn't it?"

The surprise on Nathaniel's face is apparent. How do I explain the fact that I already know his name?

I motion back to Liam, hoping to recover from my slip-up as best as I can. "Liam mentioned you. Apparently, you have quite the reputation around here," I joke. At least, he'll be flattered by the compliment about his acting skills.

Nathaniel continues to stare at me, lifting a brow in question.

The direct eye contact makes me feel uneasy, as if I need to explain myself further, "As in your acting, I mean. People seem to speak highly of you."

A silence fills the air.

"Not that I talk about you, in particular, or anything," I ramble. "Just what I've heard from other people. Not that I *specifically* listen for things about you."

Wow, I wish I knew when to shut up.

I open my mouth one last time, feeling flushed and defeated. "Just that I saw your monologue from the audience during your exam," I sigh, "and it was really good."

At this point, I just want to burrow underneath the ground and hide away.

When I have the courage to look back up, Nathaniel's smiling—he's actually smiling—at me. "You liked it?"

At least he's not running in the opposite direction from me, like I thought he would be. I ask the question that's been weighing on my mind since his performance. "How did you choose that monologue?"

Nathaniel leans his body back against the wall. "We'd actually just finished reading that novel in AP Lit," he pauses. "For some reason, the passage spoke to me in particular. I think the way it talks about false appearances—how you can think you've fallen for someone you barely even know. Like how Dorian loved the fantasy of Sybil, rather than the person herself."

I hadn't guessed he'd put that much thought into it. Ironically, the situation he described hits a little too close to home for me.

"Well," he shakes me from my thoughts, "I'm really glad you liked it and that you were there to see it."

I know he probably means he's appreciative of an audience in general, not me, specifically. But for a moment, I feel light-headed.

"I'm glad I was there to see it, too," I say.

All of a sudden, I am knocked back into reality. The bell rings, signaling five minutes left before class. Students begin bumping past me as I realize that I am still standing in the middle of a doorway.

"Well," I sidestep over the threshold, "I guess I should get out of the way. I don't want to start a traffic jam."

I glance over my shoulder one more time, murmuring a quick, "See you guys later."

Without waiting for a response, I begin walking to class when Nathaniel's voice stops me from behind.

"It was nice to see you, Scarlett." I turn to see him waving at me.

He remembers my name.

I'm already in over my head.

* * *

"Scarlett...Wait up!"

I see Macie weaving down the hallway to catch up to me a couple of periods later. There's only one more exam left to go before the start of Winter Break, and I could not be more excited.

"How'd Psych go?"

"Brutal," she groans. "I've got carpal tunnel from this one—non-stop writing, all by hand for the past hour and a half. My fingers need an ice bath right now."

"Well, you might be able to set something up with the wrestling team."

"Very funny," Macie nudges me. "Let's stop by the PTA booth downstairs. I hear they're giving away free hot chocolate."

I nod enthusiastically. The perfect drink to power through these last few hours of school. We veer off of our normal path, heading for the nearest stairwell. I'm about to turn to Macie when all of a sudden, I stop. At the bottom of the stairwell, about to make the ascent to the second floor, is the same person I spoke to in a doorway so recently. The dark, tousled hair. The crystal blue eyes. What are the odds I would see him, not once, but twice in the same day? Our school is small but not that small.

I dart my eyes back to Macie and think about my recent run-in with Nathaniel. I have no idea why he and Liam had been hanging out there, apparently waiting to hold doors open for people. I decide that if, by circumstance, I have the opportunity to talk to him again, I'm going to ask him that question.

Zoning back into reality, I take a deep breath and take a second peek. I should get ready to say "hi," again, just in case. After all, he'd said it'd been nice meeting me—that means something, right?

Now, I really sound crazy in my head. He's probably told every stranger ever that it was nice meeting him or her. I'm no exception to the longstanding form of etiquette.

When I spot him again, he's not alone. Walking next to him is a girl with a heart-shaped face and sleek, auburn hair. Nathaniel is immersed in their conversation, speaking with animated gestures. The girl places a hand on his shoulder and giggles.

Jealousy hits me like a splash of water to the face. He has a girlfriend. After all, what did I expect? That a guy who seems too good to be true actually could be true? And even if he is, he hasn't already been taken by some too-good-to-be-true girl?

I feel silly for spending the past few periods thinking about him. And even more so—assuming that one conversation, if I could even call it that, would carry any weight with him, like it did for me. After all, I barely know the guy.

By this point, we've almost crossed the stairwell. Nathaniel seems too engrossed in his storytelling to notice me. I turn my head away, disappointed in myself for my naïve hopefulness.

I look back at Macie on the stairwell, doing my best to seem invested in our conversation as I rack my brain for something to say. "Macie," I go with the first thing that comes to mind, "when do you leave for your vacation again?"

Macie's face lights up. "This weekend," she squeals. "I can't wait to be on the cruise ship. I can almost feel the sun rays and warm ocean breeze right now."

Phew. By now, we've passed them on the stairway, and I've accomplished my mission of acting preoccupied. I'm still spinning from our almost-encounter as we reach the bottom of the stairs.

"I'm so jealous of you," I grumble once we reach the PTA table. "It sure beats working extra shifts at Fashion Fwrd and hanging out at home, like I am for Winter Break." My vacation, unlike the excitement of Macie's, will probably be boring and uneventful.

We both reach for paper cups, steaming with warm hot chocolate.

"Speaking of Winter Break, I know what might cheer you up." Macie waves a finger in the air. "Come to the swim team's New Year's Eve party with me when I get back." She reaches for a cup sleeve to place her hot chocolate in. "Please don't make me go alone."

My ears perk up at her request. *A New Year's Eve party?*

For once, I won't have to spend another New Year's Eve alone with my parents, drinking bubbly apple juice and falling asleep as soon as the clock struck twelve. I'm grateful for Macie's swim team liaison when it comes to parties. Working retail has its perks, but it also tends to isolate me from our school's social scene, considering I don't have much time left to socialize.

Without having to think twice, I nod. "Count me in."

"Maybe we'll both find cuties to kiss at midnight this year," she flashes me a mischievous grin.

I chuckle and then take a sip of my hot chocolate. At least this will be the best way to get over my interest in a guy I don't even know. Sure, he can quote some words from a novel—so what? Maybe, a little New Year's Eve party is exactly what I need.

* * *

Later that night, I'm sitting across the dinner table from my parents, pushing around roasted chicken and mashed potatoes on my plate. "I think my exams went well. I'm just relieved the first semester ones are over. It'll be nice to have a breather."

"Scarlett, we know how hard you've been working," my mom sends a sideways glance to my father, "and we have a little something for you." Scooting back her chair, she reaches for the cabinet behind her and pulls out a large, neatly-packaged present in her hands. "We thought it would be the perfect way to kick off Winter Break."

My parents are generous, but they don't usually bestow random gifts upon me for the sake of it. "But Christmas isn't for a couple more days.

You want me to open that now?"

"We know it's a little early," she says as she closes the cabinet with her foot, "but we thought you might be able to start getting use out of it sooner."

I'm not one to turn down gifts, regardless of the occasion. I nod eagerly as my mom brings me the present. It's big and heavy, and I can see her straining to carry it. She sets the gift down on the table with a thud.

"Go ahead," she urges. "Merry early Christmas." She returns to the seat next to my dad and gives his hand a squeeze.

With anticipation, I tear away the packaging to uncover the box underneath. When I see the picture on the label, I can barely contain my excitement.

It's a sewing machine. My parents got me my very own sewing machine. I've been wanting one for ages, but I know how expensive they can be.

"We know how passionate you are about your fashion dreams. And how hard you work on your sketches. We thought maybe you could start turning them into a reality," my mom says.

"Are you serious?" I run around to the other side of the table to give them hugs. "I have the best parents in the world. Thank you. Thank you!"

I can't wait to text Macie about this. She'll flip when she hears that I'm one step closer to designing my own clothes. Of course, I'll need to start small and practice first. But maybe one day, I can finally make her that 50s dress she's dreaming of. I clap my hands together. Speaking of Macie, the New Year's Eve party she invited me to comes to mind. I guess that now would be as good a time as any to bring up the question to my parents.

I take a deep breath and put my fork down next to my plate.

"Hey, Mom, Dad. There's something else I wanted to ask you about."

"Sure, sweetie. What is it?"

"It's no big deal," I downplay my question as much as possible, "but Macie invited me to a swim team party on New Year's Eve. It should be low-key—just a couple of friends hanging out." I shift at the table. "Can I go?"

My dad lowers his round tortoiseshell glasses at me. "A New Year's Eve party?"

"I think that sounds like a nice idea," my mom responds. "You deserve to go out and have some fun, especially after such a rigorous semester."

I breathe a sigh of relief. My mom tends to be the more lenient one, advocating in favor of my social endeavors. My dad, on the other hand, is a bit more cautious.

"Well, I guess that would be alright." My dad furrows his brow. "Are you sure you don't want to celebrate with us? We already bought noisemakers."

I smile, entertained but unwilling to surrender.

"I appreciate it, Dad. But I'm sure they'll have those things at the party. I mean *gathering*. It's really so small that it's not even worth calling a party."

My dad flashes a weary smile. "We understand that you don't want to celebrate with your old 'rents." His mouth forms a hard line again. "No alcohol, right?"

"No, Dad. Don't worry." I put a palm in the air to reassure him. "No alcohol."

To be honest, I have no idea what the party will consist of, how big it will be, or how wild it could get, but I have to convince him it will be nothing but wholesome fun.

"Normally, I would call the parents first and check to make sure that's the case. But I trust you. And Macie." He pauses. "If there does happen to be alcohol there, you'll leave immediately, correct?"

"Correct," I confirm. "And don't worry. Macie and I are completely trustworthy."

My dad nods in support.

At his approval, I give myself a silent fist pump. I really shouldn't be this relieved that my parents are letting me go to a normal high school party, but I'll take what I can get.

"May I please be excused?" I chew a final bite of my dinner. I'm itching to bring my new gift up to my room, so I can take it for a spin. "I can't wait to open up my sewing machine."

My parents nod, and I grab the box, visions of elaborate clothing designs dancing around in my head. Carrying the machine, I bring it upstairs and set it down on my desk. I type out a text to Macie.

Look what my parents got me as an early Christmas gift. Hope you're soaking up the sun on your cruise. I snap a picture of the sewing machine box and send it along with the message.

Wow, look at that! A fashion star in the making. Miss you & can't wait for NYE! Her response pings back almost instantly.

Grabbing a pair of scissors, I cut open the box and pull the sewing machine onto my desk, setting it down carefully in front of me. I rummage for the instruction manual, but as I reach for it, its weight is heavier than I expect.

When I pull it out, I see that the manual isn't just a small guide—it's a large packet with pages upon pages of instructions. I turn to the first page and immediately become overwhelmed. On the cover is a diagram of the twenty-six different parts of the sewing machine, along with lengthy text instructions about machine basics, maintenance, and troubleshooting. Between terms like "bobbin-winder," "needle clamp screw," and "thread take-up lever," my brain gets fuzzy just from looking at the complex words on the page.

Releasing a sigh, I sink into my seat. Even with YouTube tutorials and Wiki How-To's, I have a feeling that learning to sew is going to be harder than I had expected. I wish I had someone who could physically teach me how to use the machine, but neither of my parents has ever used one, and our local fabric store doesn't offer classes during this time of year. Maybe becoming a famous designer is going to take longer than I thought. I push the sewing machine to the edge of my desk. One day, I'll learn how to sew using a machine properly. One day, I'll make Macie's dream dress a reality. It's only a matter of time.

Chapter Four

The rest of the holiday week flies by in a blur. My mom and dad surprised me with more coloring pens for sketching on Christmas Day. I worked on some new fashion designs and hung them up on the bulletin board in my room. I even made some extra money working the holiday shift at Fashion Fwrd—though the hours were long and the lines were practically out the door. My week wasn't nearly as exciting as Macie's week, which she documented by sending me photos of her lounging on the deck of her cruise. But even grueling shifts and cranky customers couldn't dampen my mood. Instead, I've been focused on what the highlight of both of our breaks will be: the swim team New Year's Eve party.

Finally, the night of the event is here, and I'm looking at my reflection in my bathroom mirror, applying a swab of cherry red gloss to my lips. The color is bright and bold—two of the qualities that I aspire to have in the coming year. Thinking about my New Year's resolution, I decide that this is what it will be. I am going to propel myself brightly and boldly into the future. I am going to take chances and open myself up to whatever my life has in store.

Yes, this is exactly what I will do.

I'm applying one more coat of lip gloss when I see a text from Macie that she is here. My heart skips a beat as I grab my purse. I round the corner and glide down the stairs with a little hop in my step as I reach the first floor.

"Have a wonderful time." My mom enters the foyer. "Gosh, what I would do to relive my high school days."

My dad comes over to stand next to my mom. "I hope not too much." He wraps his arms around her. "The high school days were before you met me."

I laugh at his sappy display of affection before reaching for the door handle.

"I'm sleeping over at Macie's tonight," I remind them. "I'll call you if I need anything."

"Alright then," my dad says. "Be safe. Have fun. And we'll see you next year." He gives me a wink.

I beam as I head out the front door and make a dash for Macie's car.

When I get closer, I see she's waiting out front for me. I rush up to meet her, and we both squeal with excitement as we pull each other in for a hug.

"Hey, girl, hey," I grin.

She squeezes me. "I missed you."

"Tell me everything." We release each other, and I open my car door as Macie swings around the other side. I slide into the passenger seat. "How was the trip?"

"Scar, you would have loved it." Macie backs out of our driveway and drives down the street. "The cruise had an unlimited ice cream bar, live shows at night, and a water slide that wrapped around the side of the boat. It was heaven."

"Sounds more relaxing than my vacation," I sigh. "And thanks again for inviting me tonight, Macie. You don't know how happy I am to have actual plans for New Year's Eve this year."

The truth is that I've been to small gatherings with friends through-out my years of high school, but I've never been integrated into the "party" crowd. Will this be a huge rager with tons of guests? Will we play cliché basement games like Spin the Bottle and Seven Minutes in Heaven? Will partygoers get trashed and spend the night throwing up in bathrooms, like in the movies?

Or am I just letting my imagination get the best of me? For all I know, it could be a quiet evening surrounded by new friends.

We pull up to the curb of the house, I assume is for the swim team party, and Macie cuts the engine.

"I don't really know what to expect," Macie admits. "You know I usually haven't gone to these types of swim parties in the past, but I'm glad you'll be here with me tonight."

"I'm so ready for this new year to begin," I state triumphantly. "Let's do this."

At the same time, we hop out of the car and begin trudging up the path toward the front door. Taped to the door is a note letting us know that the party is downstairs.

"I guess we can just let ourselves in then," Macie says as she turns the handle.

I hear the soft thrum of music and steady chatter of voices below us, and Macie motions to the stairway leading to the basement. Following her lead, I descend the stairs carefully. As the space comes into view, I notice groups of people dispersed throughout the room, mingling with each other and bopping along to music. Some carry red Solo cups in their hands, while others munch on snacks near the bar—what seems to be a typical high school scene. Macie tugs at my sleeve, pointing to where a group is standing in the corner. "Let's say 'hi' to the hostess."

As we approach, she taps a girl on the shoulder with wavy, caramel hair and a shimmery tank top. "Jasmine," Macie gains her attention, "thank you for having us."

The girl spins around. When she recognizes Macie, she reaches out to give her a hug. "Macie. So glad you could make it. Help yourself to snacks and drinks. By the way, some of the guys brought beer if anyone wants any." She motions to a table in the corner.

My dad's words ring in my ears, as does my promise to leave if alcohol is present. Still, I can't help but wonder what the harm is if I'm not actually drinking it. After all, the last thing I want is to get hammered tonight. I just like the idea of alcohol being available. It makes me feel as if I've reached a new level of maturity—like I could drink if I wanted to. That I have the choice to do something rebellious, and no one is here to stop me.

We both thank Jasmine and turn to make our way to the snack bar. Macie reaches for a can of beer and hands one to me. "Here, Scarlett."

I should decline. After all, I'm already breaking the rules by being here. I can only imagine what would happen if my dad found out I was drinking, too.

Then I pause. It's just one can of beer. What's the worst that could happen? I'll need to prepare my liver for college at some point, and I've got a full stomach. "I guess a little wouldn't hurt. And I am sleeping over at your place tonight. Why not?"

Taking the can from her hands, I pop the tab open, releasing a pressurized fizz. Slowly, I put the can to my mouth. The bitter carbonated liquid slides down my throat, making my lips pucker. It's not the most pleasant flavor, but I still hold the container in my hand proudly, feeling like a real adult for once in my life.

"Oh my gosh." Macie points to a guy in the corner. "I see Ashton over there. He was in the Caribbean over Winter Break, too. Let's go ask him about his trip." She grabs my arm.

As much as I want to meet Ashton-Who-Vacationed-In-The-Caribbean-Too, I also want to check out the snack selection first. I'm always in the mood to munch. "You go ahead." I reassure her, "I'll meet up with you in a sec."

Macie nods and makes a beeline for Ashton.

Meanwhile, I head toward a bowl of peanut M&M's I see on the counter—my favorite type of candy. As I go to grab a plate, I feel an arm bump into me.

"Sorry," we both mutter at the same time.

I look up and then freeze, making direct contact with a clear blue set of eyes. I blink as I stare back at none other than Nathaniel Wilder. *So much for new beginnings with the New Year.*

Nathaniel places a finger to his chin. "Scarlett, right?"

For a split second, I give myself a mental pep talk, as if I'm a coach about to send a boxer into the ring: Nathaniel Wilder is here in front of me. All I have to do is muster up an ounce of confidence and appear cool in front of him—unlike the day I made him help me with my dress in the costume shop. I think about my bright and bold New Year's resolution I made earlier.

I can do this.

The boxer within me puts on her gloves and walks into the ring. I return my attention to our conversation and flash a smile. "I'm impressed you remember." That was smooth enough, right? "I didn't know you'd be here tonight."

Nathaniel motions over to a group of guys playing beer pong on the other side of the room. "Liam invited me. I've been hanging out with the swim team because of him."

Wow. I had thought this New Year's Eve party would help me stop thinking about Nathaniel. I didn't realize it would lead me to find another connection with him.

"Are you on the swim team?" Nathaniel asks, bringing my attention back to him.

I shake my head, suddenly hoping that he doesn't prefer girls who can swim. "I'm not, but Macie is. She's always my ticket to the swim crowd. I can do a pretty fast backstroke, though."

With a bemused grin, Nathaniel looks to the bowl of M&M's I was about to take from. He reaches for the scooper. "Want some?"

I try to calm myself, even though I'm buzzing with energy.

"Yes. That would be great," I respond.

Nathaniel gingerly scoops a handful of M&M's from the ceramic bowl and pours the candy pieces onto my plate.

"Good choice." He scoops another handful for himself. "Peanut M&M's are the best." He pops a blue M&M into his mouth.

Don't you dare focus on those lips, I think to myself a second too late.

"Down to play some foosball?" He motions to the empty table next to us.

I'm grateful for the distraction from where my mind was going. "You're on," I say. "Just to warn you, I've had some practice."

We assume our positions across from each other at the table, gripping the handles in preparation. Nathaniel grabs the plastic ball from the side compartment and returns his eyes to me.

"Are you sure you're ready for this?"

"Really, I should be the one asking you that question."

I'm surprised at myself. Who knew a little foosball could bring out my inner competitive side? Or rather, the person standing across from me at the foosball table.

Nathaniel tosses the ball in, and we both begin rotating our handles. I'm competitive enough with a regular opponent, but with this game, I am more determined to win than ever. I feel as if it's vital to demonstrate my capability—like the state of this party, and all of the New Year's Eves to come, and the future direction of my life's course are depending on it.

Letting my hands take over absentmindedly, I look up at him from across the table, thinking back to our last encounter in the hallway.

"So, what were you and Liam doing standing in the doorway the last time I saw you guys? I just thought it was funny, you know."

Propelling the ball forward again, he smirks. The ball bounces off of the goal and back toward the center of the field. "Sometimes, Liam and I like to hang around and people-watch. There's a lot you can tell about people based on body language. I've always found it interesting to observe. Especially since I've gotten into theater."

I'm intrigued by his answer. How much can he tell just by reading body language? And more importantly, how much can he tell about me in particular?

"If you say you can read body language," I ask, "then what does my body language say right now?"

I'm nervous about his response. I can already be self-conscious enough as it is, but when it comes to Nathaniel Wilder, his scrutiny might be the death of me.

Nathaniel releases the handles he's holding and crosses his arms. "It says you're..." he draws out his response, like he's purposefully prolonging my suffering, "It says you're...a tough foosball competitor."

He's teasing me.

My mouth curves up into a smile. I deflect his gaze, returning my attention to the game. "That I am."

I flick the ball forward to start again when—

"Scarlett?" Nathaniel whispers. "Guess what time it is."

Partygoers are gravitating toward the TV on the other side of the basement. With Nathaniel Wilder, I've lost all sense of time. For all I know, it could be morning right now.

He points to the TV. "The ball's about to drop. It's almost twelve."

"Wow," I say. "Where did the time go?"

"Come on. Let's watch the countdown."

I follow his lead, pushing past the spectators to get a good view. As we find a spot near the TV, my nerves grow. Am I actually about to watch the ball drop with Nathaniel? An hour ago, he was simply a distant crush—someone I wasn't sure when I would talk to again. And now, he's standing a foot away from me on New Year's Eve, very much within my reach.

34

I'm aware of what people do once a clock strikes midnight on New Year's Eve. And I hope, more than anything, that Nathaniel is on the same wavelength. I can practically feel him behind me, only a few inches away. The swim team chants loudly, counting down backward toward zero, and we join in. The seconds tick away one by one.

Finally, the glimmering ball in Times Square reaches its base. The room explodes with the sound of poppers and noisemakers as everyone breaks out into a resounding "Happy New Year!" I glance around, watching people embrace and celebrate enthusiastically. My eyes stop when they reach Nathaniel's. He's staring at me with an intensity that makes my heart want to stop beating in my chest. All other noises seem to fade into the background, as if someone's pressing the "mute" button on my hearing. Time seems to slow to a snail's pace.

He steps forward until we're only a few inches apart.

"Happy New Year, Scarlett."

The world around me fades, and it's just him and me at the moment. He's so close to me that I can practically feel his body heat, even though we're still not touching. I brace myself for what I hope is about to come, lowering my eyelids and leaning my head forward. This is it. This is everything. This is the moment that I will kiss Nathaniel Wilder for the first time—

"Happy New Year, girl! I was looking for you!"

My eyes jolt open as Macie wraps her arms around me. She's jumping up and down, suffocating me with her hug.

With a heavy heart, I untangle myself from Macie's grip, hoping to recover myself. When I look back in Nathaniel's direction, I see that Liam has moved in to talk to him. Tearing my gaze away, I return my attention to Macie, but I notice something's off. She seems to be swaying from side to side.

"Are you okay, Macie?"

"What are you talking about, Scarrr?" her words slur slightly as she speaks. "I'm totally f-fine."

"Oh my gosh. Are you...drunk?"

Macie leans into me for support. She cups her hand to my ear, as if she's about to tell me an important secret. "Okay, Ashton may have poured a bit of his flask in my cup."

I don't even know the guy, but I already distrust him. "He brought a handle with him?"

"Just for him—and a few of the guys," she giggles.

"Macie." I run my hand through my hair. "We're supposed to drive back home tonight with your car."

Macie blinks her eyes, then casts her head down as the realization sets in. "I-I'm sorry. I wasn't thinking about that."

I reach out my hand. "I've only had one sip of my beer. I'll take your keys from you."

"Really, I've got this." She holds them up above her, refusing to hand them to me. "I'll be fine to drive. Just give me a few minutes to sober up."

"Not on my watch, you're not." With a fast swoop, I snatch the keys from her hand.

"C'mon, Scar," she pouts. "You're no fun."

I let out a humorless laugh. "And right now, you're a little too much fun for your own good." My dad's warning rings through my ears. "I think we should go home."

I glimpse over at Nathaniel one more time. He's talking with Liam and some of the swim guys who have moved this way. Out of the corner of my eye, I spot another recognizable figure. It's the auburn-haired girl Nathaniel had been talking to on the stairwell. She's chatting with one of the other guys on the swim team, caught up in conversation.

I think back to my irrational jealousy. Maybe, I was overreacting when I thought that she and Nathaniel were an item. She could just be a mutual friend he knows through Liam. Either way, it doesn't matter now. More than anything, I want to go over and say goodbye, but I'm not sure exactly how to. I don't want to interrupt the conversation, and I can't abandon Macie right now. So reluctantly, I link arms with my best friend and lead her to the basement steps, using the banister for support. Once we're about halfway up the stairs, I let go of her.

"Leaving so soon?" I'm about to take the next step when a voice startles me from behind. Twisting my head around, I'm surprised to see Nathaniel making his way up the stairs. He stops when he meets me face-to-face on the staircase.

He actually came to say goodbye? What I would do to stay at this party with him for longer.

Meanwhile, Macie continues to trudge up the stairs without me, unaware that I've been detained.

I sigh regretfully, "Macie and I should get going now. But thanks for tonight. I had a lot of fun, you know, competing against you in foosball." To be honest, I have no idea how many goals either of us scored. Tonight was a win in my book, regardless.

I lift my hand in a wave. I assume he's about to do the same, but instead, Nathaniel reaches out and pulls me into an unexpected hug, wrapping his arms around me tightly. I melt into his touch, resting my head against his chest.

When he pulls away, I'm left breathless, practically spinning in circles. "Goodnight, Scarlett," his voice is warm. "Happy New Year."

And boy, is it one happy New Year.

I try not to squeal as I race up the last steps to catch up to Macie. I feel like I could run a marathon, jump off the high dive at the Olympics, and then do a triple-back handspring.

I'm practically jumping up and down as Macie and I make our way down the front steps. A cold wind whips against my face, but I don't care. Considering how flushed the rest of my body feels right now, the chill is refreshing. I shepherd Macie inside the passenger's seat and then make my way around to the other side.

The streets are completely empty as we coast slowly back to Macie's house. I make a conscious effort to focus on the road, because my mind is having trouble concentrating on anything besides that hug right now. As we reach Macie's street, I activate the left blinker and turn into her driveway. I take a deep breath as I park, suddenly remembering the real heart of the problem.

"Crap, are your parents still awake?"

Macie opens her eyes groggily and shakes her head. "No. They should be in bed by now."

"Jeez, I really hope so," I implore. "If they are awake, just try to act as normal as possible and head straight for your bedroom."

We get out of the car, and I punch in the code to the garage door. After all, I know it by heart, considering this is practically a second home to me. I turn the doorknob quietly. When I peek my head into the house, the lights are off.

"C'mon, let's go." I pull Macie inside and steer her in the direction of her room. We climb up the stairs and make our way down the hall. Once we reach the door, I marshal her inside. Suddenly, the hallway light turns on.

I freeze in my tracks. Mrs. Young is in her nightgown, leaning against the door frame.

"Scarlett. Is that you?" She lets out a yawn and then rubs her eyes.

"Mrs. Young." I attempt to quell my surprise. "We were just getting back from the party."

She stretches her arms. "I must have fallen asleep waiting up for you to get home. Did you girls have a good time?"

"Yup." I force my lips into an artificial smile. "Couldn't have asked for a better way to ring in the New Year."

"Good. I'm glad." She squints her eyes, furrowing her brow. "Where's Macie?"

"Um…" I rack my brain for a response. "She really had to use the bathroom. Said she might be a few minutes," I chuckle nervously.

Mrs. Young blinks at me for a minute. "Oh. Well, I guess I'll just ask her about it in the morning. Glad you girls had a good time."

"Thank you. Goodnight." With that, I wave to her and retreat slowly, slipping behind the bedroom door.

Phew, that was a close one.

As I enter the room, I notice Macie is sprawled out on her bed, but she's still as a statue. I make my way over to her, the knot in my stomach growing. How much did she have to drink? Should I have told her mom? I bend forward and rest my head on her chest, listening to her breathing. Staring at her face in the dim light, I exhale.

She's going to be okay.

I place the bathroom trash can next to her and fill up a cup of water, just in case. Once I've gotten ready for bed, I crawl into my own sleeping bag and finally allow myself to digest my life's drastic change within a mere few hours. My ears are ringing, my body is shaking, and my brain is fuzzy from my time spent with Nathaniel.

Is this actually real life? Out of all of the fish in the sea, what are the odds that Nathaniel Wilder would pay attention to this one fish in particular—*me*? I want to scream out, dance around the room, and do jumping jacks.

The foosball. The ball drop. The hug.

Did they all really happen? My eyelids droop, and I finally succumb to the exhaustion. As I'm on the brink of losing consciousness, I think about how, for once in my life, reality feels better than my dreams.

I just hope that this reality isn't a dream, after all.

* * *

"Ow," Macie moans.

I turn the lamp on and rub my eyes, still sleepy, as I make sense of my surroundings. Macie is lying on top of her bed, still fully clothed from the night before. I'm in my sleeping bag on the ground next to her. The events from the night before come back to me in a rush. I think back to the party and driving Macie home.

She lifts her head from her pillow and massages her temples. "Is this what a hangover feels like?"

"I wouldn't know," I admit. "I've never had one."

She sits up, her hair messy and her mascara smeared on her face. She looks like a pretty raccoon. "Well, if you ever feel like your head is throbbing and you're spiraling from vertigo, then that's kind of what it feels like."

"How pleasant. I'll remember that for the future."

She pushes herself up off of the bed. "Ugh, I'm thirsty. And so hungry."

I laugh. "I left you water on the nightstand."

Macie turns and sees the cup of water I set out for her the night before. "Bless you." She reaches for the plastic cup and gulps down the water quickly. "You're too good to me."

"Hey, just looking out for you. You scared me—I've never seen you drunk before."

"Scar, I'm sorry to put you in that situation. I didn't mean to let it get that far. That party was really fun, though."

It was a fun party, I'll admit. And I wished we could have stayed longer. I think back to the way I convinced her to leave so abruptly. *Was I being unreasonable?*

"I was just looking out for you. I want to make sure you're safe."

Macie's well-being will always be a priority to me. After all, she's like a sister.

She chuckles as she pulls her hair up into a bun. "I know you're always protective of me. It's one of the qualities I love most about you—that I always have a bestie who watches my back. But we only have a year and a half left before college. I'm going to need to be a big girl and learn how to handle myself at some point."

"I don't want to think about that." I sigh. "I can't imagine what it will be like when we both go to new schools one day. It's just going to be so different."

When I was little, I used to have a bigger group of close friends, but a lot of them moved away or changed schools when their parents got new jobs. Because of that, Macie's really all I have. She's the only one who's stuck it out with me since the beginning. I can't imagine her leaving me, too.

"We'll have texting, FaceTime, and social media," Macie says. "We'll still talk all the time and visit each other. Nothing has to change. But let's not think about that now. Let's just live in the moment and enjoy our junior year."

She's got a point. We have so much time, and I don't have to think about that just yet. I should take a step back and let her have her fun.

"You're right. Just be safe, okay? I don't want anything happening to you. You literally make high school survivable."

She grins. "Same to you."

With that, she stands up and stretches. "Now, like I was saying before, I'm starving. Can we please make pancakes?"

"Only if they have chocolate chips and powdered sugar on top."

"Deal."

Macie and I whip up pancakes in her kitchen. I ladle the batter onto the griddle while she uses the chocolate chips to make designs on them. Thankfully, they turn out to be a solid hangover cure, and by the time her parents get back from grocery shopping, they don't suspect a thing. After breakfast, I say goodbye to the Youngs, and Macie drives me home. When I walk through the front door, my parents are waiting for me.

41

"Hey, hon. How was the party?" My mom is stationed at the kitchen counter, flipping through a magazine.

I drop my sleepover bag on the countertop. "Party was fun. Nothing too crazy. Just hung out in a basement with Macie's friends from the swim team." I shrug, hoping I sound nonchalant. "Pretty anticlimactic, actually."

"Well, glad you had fun."

My dad walks around the island counter. "Look what came in the mail for you." He slides a white envelope in my direction. "It's from FIT. Looks like they sent you an admissions pamphlet."

I grab the envelope. On the cover, "Fashion Institute of Technology" is featured in big, bold letters. Underneath, I see a subheading about how FIT is one of New York City's premier public institutions, an internationally-recognized college for design, fashion, and art. I turn the cover to see a group of students with an FIT flag in the background. On the other side, a group of models are wearing elaborate outfits while walking down a runway. The inside flap shows a skyline view of Manhattan with the twinkling lights of the city.

My dad rests his hands on the counter. "No swim parties every weekend for you, okay? If you want to get into FIT, you have to keep those grades up. Study hard. Do well on the SATs. Get strong recommendations. This is a really important year for you."

I wrinkle my nose. "I know, Dad. Trust me, I do."

"Discipline is the name of the game. No distractions. And once you get into FIT, we'll be able to visit you in New York all the time. We'll see Broadway shows every weekend." My dad begins singing the tune of "New York, New York" in the style of Frank Sinatra.

I can't help but wonder if he's more excited about me getting into FIT for him or for me. I appreciate his enthusiasm, but I don't want to put too much unnecessary pressure on myself. I can hardly think past next week, much less years into the future.

"Don't worry, Dad. I'm going to make it happen."

He gives me a nod of approval.

My mom rounds the corner. "Let her have her fun. It's high school, after all." She turns toward me. "Scarlett has the rest of her life to figure out what she wants to do. Give her time to explore."

"That may be so," my dad crosses his arms, "but it's necessary to build the foundation now. Start with the building blocks and then layer on the rest. That's why it's important for her to keep working retail, like she's doing now. If she demonstrates her dedication and commitment to a job over an extended period of time, then colleges like FIT will be impressed."

I grab my sleepover bag, so that I can gracefully make an exit.

"Speaking of, I'm going to go upstairs and get the work done that I've neglected for most of this break. You know, so I can get good grades, pass my classes, and eventually get into FIT one day."

"That's the spirit," my dad responds.

My mom swats his shoulder playfully with her magazine.

Shaking my head, I make my way out of the kitchen and trudge up the stairs to get to my room.

Geesh, the pressure is on. It's too bad that it's a lot more fun to think about New Year's kisses than to think about studying.

Chapter Five

"Hey, stranger."

I spin around from my locker to see Macie standing behind me with a grin on her face. It's the first day back at school after Winter Break, and I'm already at the point where I'm ready for another one. I stayed up past my bedtime last night doing homework and catching up on class assignments that I had put off.

"How does it feel to be back?" she asks me.

"Like I'd rather not be back."

Macie clutches her books to her chest. "Speaking of Winter Break, I know I told you the next morning," she says, "but thank you again for having my back the night of the party. I'm not sure what I would have done without you."

"You would have done the same thing for me."

Macie's face suddenly curves into a grin. "On another note, there was something else I wanted to talk to you about."

My heart flutters in my chest. For some reason, my mind circulates back to Nathaniel. Does she know something I don't? Has he talked about me at all since the party? Are she and Liam working on some kind of scheme to bring us together after that night?

As hard as it is to believe, I haven't actually mentioned any of the New Year's Eve events to Macie yet. Since the night of the party, I've been keeping my feelings to myself. For some reason, I can't muster up the courage to outwardly voice that I like Nathaniel. My biggest fear is that I'll scare him off by admitting my interest in him. What if declaring my feelings makes me somehow less desirable? What if the thought of a relationship sends him running? What if I had misread the signs, and he doesn't actually like me back as anything more than a friend? As much as I'm itching to disclose my inner turmoil to Macie, I keep my mouth sealed, at least for the time being. After all, she's close with Liam, and Liam's close with Nathaniel. My confession could easily make its way back to him.

"What is it?" I ask nervously.

Macie claps her hands together. "Winter Formal is coming up. You know how much I love school dances."

I breathe a sigh of both relief and disappointment. *Just Winter Formal. What I should have expected…*

"We should buy our tickets," she continues, "and go dress shopping."

Macie is always one step ahead when it comes to school dances. Every minuscule detail matters to her, even though the dances are nothing more than sweaty teenage bodies jumbled together in the high school gymnasium for three hours.

"Okay, let's do it." I nod in agreement.

"And we can go with the swim team. That would be more fun than going just the two of us, don't you think?"

The swim team. Maybe Nathaniel will be in the same group, too. This would be the perfect opportunity to continue where we left off at New Year's. With the darkness of the gymnasium and the blaring music, I might have the bravery to finally make a move.

Yes, this is very good news.

"That sounds great," I confirm. "Count me in."

"Yay," Macie exclaims, "I just geek over school dances."

"I think you're the anomaly at this high school."

"Maybe this will sway you." She wags a finger. "Guess what the theme is."

Before I even have a chance to guess, Macie continues. "It's Winter Wonderland. I'm sure they'll have hanging snowflakes, teardrop lights, tulle—the whole works."

"You are way too excited about this," I laugh.

"It's in my nature. I can't help it," she winks.

And I can't help but think that maybe Winter Formal will be just the opportunity I never knew I needed.

* * *

"Macie, don't you like this one?" I joke as I fish out a bright neon green dress with glaring rhinestones covering the bodice. It's two days later, and we're brushing past the endless rows of dresses mashed together on metal rods in our mall's department store. I swear—it feels like a jungle with foliage so thick, you'd need a machete just to get across. We could have looked around at Fashion Fwrd where I work, but they don't sell formal dresses, so this was the next best option.

"Scarlett, you could easily sketch something more flattering than this," she grimaces. "This is an insult to my fashion sense."

I don't disagree.

All of a sudden, my eyes fall upon a black dress with lace sleeves that is—dare I say it—*tasteful*. Capturing Macie's attention, I gesture in the direction of the dress.

"Wow. Leave it to you to find the one fashionable dress in this store," she applauds as she pulls out the tag. "You know you have to try it on, right? It looks like it would fit you perfectly. And it's a steal."

"Well, if you insist." Snagging the dress from the rack, I motion to the fitting rooms. "Let's go."

As we near the fitting rooms, I stop.

Walking out in front of me is someone I recognize. Squinting to get a better view, I realize it's the pretty auburn-haired girl—the one who had been talking with Nathaniel on the stairwell before break. She has a dress slung over her arm and is making her way toward us. I move out of the way to let her pass. After all, she doesn't know who I am.

I'm about to keep walking when she looks at us.

"Hey, girls." She makes direct eye contact with me. "Wow, you look really familiar."

I turn to face her, caught off guard by her words.

She taps her chin, like she's trying to put a finger on it. Then her eyes widen as the light goes off. "You were at Jasmine's party on New Year's, weren't you?"

I'm surprised that she recognizes me, considering we weren't even introduced that night. Still, I'm flattered that she remembers me, and further, that she's going out of her way to make conversation right now. "Yes, I was," I say, smiling.

"Quite a fun party wasn't it?" she says, flashing a set of pearly white teeth. I'm guessing she's one of those girls who bypassed the perils of puberty—the type who's never had an awkward phase in her life. What I would do to be her.

"Sure was," I grin. "I think everyone enjoyed themselves."

"Well," she continues, "some of us more than others, at least...."

I chuckle at her comment and send Macie a sideways glance. "Some of us?" I still can't get over the fact that she's even acknowledging me. Until this point, I've always thought I was invisible to those of a "higher" social status.

She shrugs with a giggle. "Like, I don't know, you seemed to be having a pretty great time."

"Me?" This girl doesn't even know who I am, much less what I was doing at the party that night. Not that I was doing anything of particular interest in the first place.

"Tina..." Macie interjects, and I realize they must know each other.

"Well, I don't mean to pry," she prefaces, almost like she has the complete intention of prying, "but it looked like you were getting a little comfortable there with Nathaniel Wilder." She directs her words at me.

My mind immediately goes blank. I look at her in bewilderment, taken aback by her comment. Stammering, I muster up a response, "I…we…you must have me confused with someone else."

"I don't think so. I saw the way he ran up the stairs after you to say goodbye." Her voice grows more accusatory, "That was you, wasn't it?"

I rustle a hand through my hair, absorbing the realization that Nathaniel and I had attracted an apparent audience during the hug. "Oh, that?"

This conversation suddenly feels like an interrogation where I'm admitting guilt. For some reason, this girl now exudes an air of intimidation that makes me want to keep my distance.

"Oh my gosh. You're not his girlfriend, are you?" I put my hands up in defense. "Because if so, I can promise you that nothing happened between us."

This would explain her intrusive questioning. I remember how flirty she was with Nathaniel in the hallway that day.

"Not exactly."

The air returns to my lungs again.

"But I'm definitely working toward it. He just doesn't know it yet." She winks in my direction. "I don't know if he's mentioned it to you, but we're actually both playing leads in the spring play. And those leads happen to be love interests." She smiles tauntingly, as if she knows she's hit me right in the gut.

This must be how she and Macie know each other—through the drama department. I absorb her admission. She and Nathaniel are playing romantic leads together? Just when I think I might have a sliver of a chance, someone has to step in and crush it. Macie hadn't been joking when she said other girls seem to put him on a pedestal. I shake it off and attempt to suppress the self-doubt in my head. Who does this girl think she is, anyway? She can't stake a claim on Nathaniel like he's a piece of property.

Once I get a hold of myself, I speak as calmly and evenly as I can. "You may be playing romantic leads together, but it's called 'acting' for a reason, right?"

Her Cheshire Cat smile turns into a rigid line. I can see the conflict on her face as she attempts to regain her composure. She wasn't expecting me to fire right back at her.

"Well," she responds, "it certainly won't be acting on my part. And once I spend enough time with him—which I will—it won't be acting on his either."

"You seem awfully confident there, but I think you might be overestimating how easy it would be to gain his attention."

She folds her arms in front of her. "I mean, a girl like you did it for a night, so it can't be that hard, right?" Her words cut me like a knife. "I just wanted to warn you not to get too attached."

I'm left speechless—blinking back the mist forming in my eyes.

Tina suddenly flashes an artificial smile. "Hey, I'm just looking out for you. We girls have to stick together, right?"

I would laugh if I weren't on the verge of tears right now.

"Well, anyway," she smiles, as if this were just another typical conversation, "good luck with the rest of your shopping, you two." Scanning me, she lands on the dress I'm holding in my arms. "Hope the dress fits."

With a wave, she turns and saunters away from Macie and me. My jaw hangs open as I watch her exit the fitting rooms and vanish out of sight, without so much as a second glance back.

"What the hell was that?" Macie gasps.

For a second, I had almost forgotten she was there. "I honestly couldn't tell you."

"Nobody talks to my best friend that way," Macie fumes, balling her hand into a fist for emphasis. "I ought to give her a piece of my mind the next time I see her in the theater."

I manage a faint smile. I may be boiling internally, but I remind myself to remain calm. After all, the best revenge is not letting a petty girl like that get to my head.

"Well, on a more important note," Macie turns toward me with her arms crossed, "what in the world happened between you and Nathaniel at that party?"

I realize that Macie still doesn't know much about that night, considering the state she had been in and the fact that I had been too nervous to tell her.

"It really was nothing," I attempt to play it down.

Macie scoffs, "If you've got a girl like Tina wound up, it's not nothing."

I turn toward Macie. I finally confide in her about the night's events—from the foosball to the ball drop, to the hug on the way out. The only part I omit is the almost-kiss. It's still too tough to think about what might have been.

When I finish, Macie gasps. "Holy crap, Scarlett. How could you not tell me about this? Especially during our sleepover." She claps her hands together. "You and Nathaniel—this is so exciting."

As the words leave her lips, my brain goes into panic mode. I know how quickly gossip at our school spreads. And the last thing I want is for rumors to be buzzing about the two of us when we hardly even know each other. Rumors could be the kiss of death, even if there is the slightest chance of something more with Nathaniel.

"Wait, Macie. It was an amazing moment, don't get me wrong, but that's all it was. A moment. Nothing else is going to happen between the two of us, okay? You have to promise me that you won't say anything about it to anyone else."

"Okay, okay." She purses her lips. "I promise I won't say anything about it to anyone else."

I let out a cathartic sigh. "Thank you. Now, I'm going to try on this dress."

With my black dress slung over my arm, I push open the door to the first available fitting room. Tina mentioned that she hoped my dress would fit. I'm hoping it will, too. Preferably that it fits in just the right places.

That way, while she's busy having eyes for Nathaniel, Nathaniel won't be able to take his eyes off of me.

* * *

After my encounter with Tina at the department store, I realize how little I know about my theater crush. Of course, I've painted a picture in my head of the person I envision him to be: this well-respected actor who's built a name for himself in the theater department. I do know some basics—that he moved here this year, that he's a competitive foosball opponent, and that he can recite some poetic words by an Irish novelist. But besides those details, he still might as well be a mystery to me. If I'm going to have a crush on someone, I should at least do a little research to substantiate it first. Maybe it's time to see what all of this hype is about.

Taking a seat in the swivel chair at my desk, I spin toward my laptop and type in my password. Glancing behind me, I make sure the door to my room is closed, just in case my parents decide to walk down the hall. Then like the detective I am, I log onto Facebook and go to the search bar to type in Nathaniel's first and last name. His profile pops up when I see that Macie and Liam are mutual friends with him. I click on the profile and hold my breath.

When his profile picture appears on my screen, I almost have to look away. I know his pictures are public, but I feel like I'm intruding—almost like he was on me that day in the costume shop. Nathaniel's wearing a blue button-down shirt, and he's sitting on a park bench. His arm is outstretched as he looks away from the camera, smiling into the distance. He looks relaxed and happy, like the photographer captured him in a carefree moment. Right now, I almost feel like he's sitting here with me—not like I'm looking at a digital screen.

I click into his timeline photos and look back further. He's tagged in pictures from past productions at his old school. Professor Harold Hill in *The Music Man*. Danny Zuko in *Grease*. It looks like he used to participate in improv and choir classes over the years, too.

I shake my head. How does someone become comfortable in the spotlight, singing and dancing in front of a full crowd like that? I can't help but think of the irony. There he is: a guy who loves to perform on stage. And then there's me: a girl who prefers to be behind it, designing clothing out of the spotlight. He seems to have no problem with attention, and I'm a girl who avoids it at all costs. Maybe the two of us are polar opposites.

I go to click on another picture.

"Hi, honey."

The sound of my mother's voice startles me. I jump in my seat, turning just in time to see my mom slip into my room.

"I wanted to drop off your laundry."

Reflexively, I grab the top of my laptop and clamp it down before she gets any closer. Of all times to come into my room, she chooses this one.

"You couldn't have knocked first?"

My mom laughs as she walks toward me. "Why—do you have something to hide?" She flashes a mischievous grin. "Were you talking to someone special just now?"

I wish that were the case. Unfortunately, my mom gives me too much credit. If only she knew I was doing more stalking than talking.

"Nope," I brush off her comment. "You just startled me, was all."

My mom points to the sewing machine on my desk, which hasn't been touched since I first opened it during Winter Break.

"You still haven't used your new sewing machine. It's a shame it's building up cobwebs on your desk. I thought you'd be creating a new wardrobe of clothing by now."

"I know, Mom. The instructions are a lot more difficult than I thought they would be. I think I need to sign up for a class at the fabric store or something once they're being offered again. I just wish I had an instructor who could teach me."

My mom nods. "I'm sure they'll have more classes in the spring. We can look into it together."

I think back to the costume shop I stumbled upon the day I first met Nathaniel. I envision the beautiful fabrics: the prints, the patterns, the textures.

"Mom, what made you decide to do theater when you were in school?"

My mom's eyes light up. I know she would love nothing more than for me to follow in her footsteps. "Why? Are you thinking of joining?"

The more I think about it, the more intriguing of an idea it sounds. Still, I should probably set her expectations. "I don't know. I was just curious."

"Well, I may be biased, but I think that there's no better outlet than theater. It's all about freedom of expression. Creativity. Confidence. You know, your father and I could coach you. Give you pointers. If you're really interested."

I laugh. "If I ever chose to participate, it'd be more behind-the-scenes than being an actual cast member. But I appreciate your enthusiasm."

"Well, honey, I'm fully in support if it's something you want to explore." She stands up from the edge of my bed and moves the laundry basket to my dresser. "I'll let you get back to, you know...*not* talking to whomever you were talking to." She winks at me.

If only my social life were as lively and exciting as my mom imagines it. I tap my nails on my desk until she's walked out of my room and closed the door. Speaking of a social life, I decide to text Macie to confirm the plans for this weekend's dance.

Can't believe WinFo is almost here! Let me know the deets.

I'm way too excited. She messages back. *Come over to my place around 6 on Saturday for pix with the group before we leave for the dance.*

I give her message a thumbs up. Once I'm sure my mom is out of hearing range, I open up my laptop and quickly exit out of Nathaniel's profile.

Too close of a call.

Hopefully, after this weekend, I'll be able to spend actual time with him, and not just through a social media screen.

Chapter Six

"One. Two. Three. Smile!"

A slew of parents flash cameras in our direction, temporarily blinding us. I blink away the spots in my line of vision. The night of Winter Formal has finally arrived, and the group is standing in Macie's foyer taking pictures before we leave. I haven't been able to stop thinking about the dance all week long. Taking group pictures is always fun, but I'm even more excited to get to the main attraction.

"Okay, okay. We've had enough of this torture," Macie groans. "Mom, I think you have enough pictures to last you a lifetime."

Mrs. Young comes over and pinches Macie's cheeks before releasing her. "It's not every day I get to watch my sweet girl go to Winter Formal. One day, you'll thank me for being such an avid documenter. You never know when the nostalgia will hit."

"Maybe one day," Macie says, "but not today."

Mrs. Young tucks her camera away. "Alright, I'll stop cramping your style. You girls have fun, and be safe."

Blowing a kiss in our direction, Macie's mom makes her way for the door.

"Ditto to what Mrs. Young said." My mom comes up from behind me and pulls me in for a hug. "I think I have enough pictures to fill an entire album. You girls have a blast."

I snicker at Macie as we watch my mom walk to the front door. "Our moms are the worst."

"The worst, but we have to love them for it." Macie grins.

I look around the foyer expectantly, my eyes wandering from person to person in the swim group, scanning for a particular target. I lift my head one more time before returning my attention to Macie.

"Macie, where's, um, Liam? Isn't he coming in this group, too?" Internally, my question is meant in reference to a certain someone, but I'm still hesitant to say his name out loud. I can't help but notice neither of them is here for pictures before Winter Formal.

"Oh, Scar, I was meaning to tell you that Liam texted me. They're meeting up with a few friends but should hopefully be able to make it to the dance later." Macie laughs. "Typical Liam to wait until the last minute to tell me."

My face falls as I look at her. I was really hoping they'd be going in our group. Macie notices my change in expression.

"I know—I'm bummed they're not here right now, too." She rests a hand on my shoulder. "But don't worry; there will still be plenty of other options to dance with when we get there." She gives me a seductive wink.

"Macie. You're the worst."

"The worst, but you have to love me for it," she grins. "C'mon, let's go."

* * *

Once we've checked in with the parent chaperones at school, Macie grabs my hand and hauls me in the direction of the dance. Her grip is tight enough that I don't object, as we push open the double doors. With anticipation, we enter into the darkened gym.

Who knew the gym could look this good? Shimmery white curtains line the walls, and glittering blue snowflakes dangle above us. Tulle has been decoratively draped around the room, accentuated by sparkling lights suspended from the ceiling.

"Wow," I marvel at the scenery. "This is beautiful."

"See." Macie gestures around the space. "Now, you understand why I love school dances. Magical, isn't it?"

"I can't argue with that. It sure is…."

Or at least it *was* until I look toward the center of the room.

The breathtaking illusion of Winter Wonderland is shattered when I notice the dance floor. Rather than a graceful foxtrot or a sweeping waltz that one would associate with the elegant decor, my fellow classmates seem to be preoccupied with…an alternate form of dance.

I stare at my peers as they dance against each other, partaking in the term associated with my generation: grinding. I turn away and attempt to focus my attention back to the decorations. The loud electronic dance music pulses from speakers located around the room, making my ears vibrate. I look back at Macie to make sure she's still standing next to me.

"I just don't get it," I shout over the thrum of the music. "Why does our generation enjoy that kind of dancing?" I can barely hear myself with the noise in the background.

"I hate to break it to you," Macie whispers into my ear, "but our generation can be wild." She grabs my hand. "Let's go dance."

I hope she means "regular" dancing.

Before I can protest, Macie once again pulls my hand, dragging me into the crowd. As we push our way toward the middle, I notice the density increase, like we're moving from Earth's mantle to its core. We continue to shove past the tightly packed bodies until we've found a pocket of space to dance. Glancing left and right, I recognize a few of Macie's swim teammates dancing near us. Macie raises her arms up, shimmying gracefully from side to side. Meanwhile, I try to mirror her movements, feeling more like a jellyfish than a dancer.

I peer around the room again. While a part of me feels highly out of my element, another part feels a small pang of jealousy. I'm secretly curious what it would be like to emulate the people around me. How do others make it look so normal? Where do they first learn it? I wouldn't know where to begin, even if I wanted to.

I'm so preoccupied with my own thoughts that I fail to notice the transition taking place in the group around me. Out of the corner of my eye, I spot Ashton come up behind Macie. He places his hands casually on her hips and mirrors her movements.

Immediately, my mind goes into overprotection mode. I remember how he had poured more alcohol in Macie's drink the night of the New Year's Eve party. It gives me an unsettling feeling about him—especially when his actions involve the person I care about most.

As I look up again, I notice Macie lean her body back against him, swaying to the rhythmic beat. Others in the group begin dancing with each other, too—altering from bouncing around casually to something more intense. And now, I'm the only person in the group without a partner to dance with.

I push my way over to Macie, leaning into her ear. "Macie, you don't have to do this," I plead, referring to her dancing with Ashton.

"Loosen up, girl—I'm having fun." She calls out over the music.

"But what about New Year's Eve?" I huff between gritted teeth, trying to maintain a discrete voice. How does she know she can trust him? After all, we had both suffered the consequences of Ashton's actions that night.

"Relax. We're just dancing."

But I'm not so convinced. "C'mon. We can find you a different guy to dance with."

"I promise, Scar, I'm fine," she counters indignantly. Then, a mischievous gleam appears in her eyes. "But I hadn't even thought about you."

She whispers in Ashton's ear, and he releases her.

Breathing a sigh of relief, I'm glad that Macie is done dancing with Ashton. "I was just about to...."

But she puts a quieting finger to my lips before I can finish my sentence. "Wait here. Don't move."

Before I know it, Macie is dragging a random guy over and guiding him toward me.

"Scarlett, this is Gavin. Gavin, Scarlett."

"Don't worry, girl," she leans into me, "What kind of friend would I be if I didn't find you someone to dance with, too?"

Oh, some kind of friend, alright, I mutter to myself as Macie bounces back over to Ashton.

I stare, mortified at this so-called "Gavin," unsure of what to do or say. I've never even met him before. I don't know if I want to dance with a stranger in that way. To be honest, I'm not sure if I'll ever be bold enough to move in that way. Call me an old soul, but I'd rather take a guy out to coffee first before dancing against him like we're at a nightclub.

"So, do you want to dance?" Gavin asks nonchalantly, as if it doesn't matter to him either way. It feels like this is some impersonal business transaction, and I'm just a stock he's deliberating whether to trade or not. I stand motionless, at a mental crossroads. Say "no," and face the embarrassment of having to dance alone for the rest of the night. Or say "yes," and lose my dignity of feeling like I even have a choice.

"I...um," I stutter, fishing for the right words to say. Eventually, feeling slightly obliged by the situation, I nod.

I start swinging my hips separately, hoping this might be what Gavin has in mind. But to my alarm, he wastes no time bringing his hands to my hips and pulling my body back against his, guiding mine to match his rhythm. My muscles tense at the unfamiliar touch. I try to mirror the beat of the music as Gavin tightens his grip and sets the tempo. I look straight ahead, unsure of what to do with my hands and the rest of my body. I feel more like a robot swaying back and forth rather than a person attempting to dance.

I snicker to myself. How can two people share such close proximity and yet feel so distant? With Nathaniel, it's the opposite. My emotions spike every time I simply make eye contact with him. Right now, my thoughts gravitate back to Nathaniel, and I realize that this isn't for me.

"You know what…I just can't do this." I pull myself away from Gavin and begin to back away.

"Hey," I hear over my shoulder, "wait."

But it's too late. I am already elbowing my way through the sea of people, frantic to find respite from these aliens whom I call my classmates. I weave and dodge, desperate to break free.

Finally, I find an opening on the dance floor and lunge forward, breathing a deep sigh of relief. I hurry over to the row of foldable wooden chairs lining the wall and plop down. Once I catch my breath, I turn to the mechanical clock hanging from the wall of the gym.

Great, one more hour of this madness, I think to myself.

I sit in my corner sulking, wondering how I got stuck in this position, and, more importantly, how I'm going to occupy myself for another whole hour. I can't go back there. And I certainly don't want to stay sitting here for the rest of the night. Maybe, the time has come to cut my losses and play Candy Crush on my phone for the remainder of the evening.

I glance up at the front of the gym, considering leaving. As I contemplate the option though, I begin to distinguish two silhouettes entering through the doorway. I recognize their outlines from afar, and a burst of relief washes over me. It's as if my prayers have been answered. Making my way straight for my targets, I wave and call out their names.

"Nathaniel! Liam!"

Considering the darkness of the gym, it takes a minute for them to recognize me.

"Scarlett." Liam smiles. "What's up?" He opens his arms and pulls me into a hug before releasing me. I turn to Nathaniel, who grins at me and follows suit.

"I wasn't sure if you'd be here. Macie said you were meeting up with some friends first."

Nathaniel nods. "We got a bit of a late start tonight, but we didn't want to miss this. Especially since it's our senior year."

Liam points his finger, motioning toward the dance floor. "Hey, I see the swim team over there. You want to come with?"

Nathaniel shifts his eyes from Liam and to me. "You know, I think I'll stick here with Scarlett for a bit. I'll meet you in a few."

I let myself absorb his words. He wants to stay here. *With me.* This night may have started on a rough note, but it's definitely taking a turn for the better.

With a nod, Liam waves and then vanishes into the crowd.

Meanwhile, Nathaniel turns back toward me. "Hey, want to see something cool?"

I lift a brow in curiosity, wondering what he could possibly want to show me. There isn't much to the gym besides bleachers and sweaty lockers.

"Come with me," Nathaniel motions for me to follow him.

I let him lead the way to an exit at the back of the gym. Nathaniel quickly glances back, making sure that none of the chaperones are watching us. Technically, we're not supposed to leave the gym due to liability issues. But we might as well try.

"Coast is clear." He places one hand on the handle.

"You sure about this?"

"No." He flashes a lopsided smile. "But you're going to have to trust me anyway."

With that, he holds the door open for me, and I slip through, bracing myself for the cool winter air. Thankfully, tonight is warmer than usual.

"This way." Nathaniel guides me forward. Our feet echo along the pavement as we walk side by side in the direction of the main building. I follow him along the path until we round the corner.

When we stop, my jaw drops. I stare awestruck at the courtyard nestled between corridors of the building. The focal point is a lion's head water fountain with a basin below. Between the stones covering the ground, overgrown pieces of moss peek out. For the occasion of Winter Formal, it's completely lit up. Strings of lights hang around the perimeter of the space.

"It's beautiful," I stammer as I absorb my surroundings, like a sponge that has just been thrown into the ocean. I've walked past this courtyard during the day before, but I've never seen it adorned with the pretty lights, the way it is tonight.

"Liam and I walked in this way. I come out here to practice my lines sometimes."

I soak in the view. "Do you usually bring other people here when you come?"

He moves closer until he's standing right in front of me. "Nope. Not usually."

I feel my cheeks grow warm.

"You know, I'm turning into a rule-breaker because of you—sneaking out of the gym and all. What am I going to do with you?"

The light of the courtyard reflects in his eyes. "Well, first, you could dance with me."

My heart begins thrumming in my chest, as if someone is repeatedly beating a drum inside of it. I'm about to respond "yes" when my voice catches in my throat. I think back to the previous situation. Casting my eyes down, I rub at a patch of moss with my shoe.

"I'm not very good at, you know, how people at our school like to dance."

When I look up again, he's got a bemused expression on his face, and his arm is outstretched. "I didn't mean that kind of dancing."

My brain feels like a radio station that's lost signal, but I nod in acceptance.

Carefully, Nathaniel reaches out his arm and gently places his right hand on my waist. He takes my left hand, lifting it to shoulder level. As we both turn to face each other, I'm surprised that I can still make out the faint sound of music blaring from inside the gym.

Our eyes meet momentarily, but the closeness causes me to flick mine away just as quickly. Instead, I focus on my feet.

"How's this?" I refer to our stance while trying to maintain a steady voice.

"You're a pro already," Nathaniel laughs. "Now, we just need to move our feet."

I realize that we're standing still, our hands interlocked, but our feet stuck to the ground, as if it's made of molasses. With care, Nathaniel begins swaying, transferring his weight from one foot to the other. As he moves, I mirror his steps, and we start to rotate in a slow and smooth motion.

"Where did you first learn how to do this, anyway?"

He chuckles. "My mom taught me when I was younger. She used to lift me onto her feet and spin me around when I was just a little kid. Told me it might come in handy someday."

I can almost picture a young Nathaniel being whisked around a room on the edge of his mom's toes. The thought makes me smile.

"You know how I said," his voice lowers, "that I liked to practice my lines out here? Well, I remember seeing you in the audience. The day I performed my monologue after we met in the costume shop. I know this is going to sound a little crazy, but you almost reminded me of the girl Dorian was describing."

I think about the passage, remembering how the physical traits of Sybil's paralleled my own. At the time, I thought that I had been the only one to notice. Yet he had been staring directly at me, as if he had known me well before he even knew my first name.

"It almost felt like the girl from my book had jumped off the page and landed right in the middle of the theater."

My head spins. *Is what I think he's saying true?*

"That day, I wasn't sure if you were paying attention to me," I cast my head down. "I thought I was just a girl in the crowd."

I keep my eyes focused on the ground. All of a sudden, I feel a thumb lift the base of my chin. Nathaniel tilts my head up, bringing my eyes up to meet his.

"You may have been just a girl in the crowd, but you couldn't have stood out more to me. Just like when I first met you."

With those simple words, I find that my supply of oxygen has been cut off, and I can feel the adrenaline coursing through my veins. As I look at Nathaniel, I catch his gaze shift to my lips and then back to my eyes. It's as if there's a force drawing the two of us toward each other. Tilting my head, I lean in with anticipation. I'm about to close my eyes.

But then, I hear it.

Footsteps approaching.

The noise grows progressively louder on the pavement. In surprise, I turn back toward the gymnasium to distinguish the source. I recognize the jet-black hair and chestnut eyes. It's my Modern European History teacher, Mrs. Walton.

"Scarlett Clarke—is that you?" Mrs. Walton calls out to me. "I barely recognize you when you're not sitting in the front row of my classroom."

"Hi, Mrs. Walton," I exhale, allowing my breathing to return to equilibrium.

"I wish I could tell you that you could stay out here—isn't the scenery wonderful?" Mrs. Walton gawks. "But as a chaperone, it's my duty to make sure all of you kiddos stay inside of the gym."

I feign a remorseful tone, "I completely understand—we didn't mean to break any rules. We just wanted to get some fresh air."

"I know where you're coming from. It's a sweatbox in there." Mrs. Walton begins fanning herself. "Anyway, the dance is just about over, so you might want to start grabbing your coats early to beat the rush."

I check my watch. We only have ten minutes left. Why does time seem to zoom by whenever I'm with Nathaniel?

Mrs. Walton nods and points in the direction of the gym. "I'll leave you two to walk back when you're ready." She spins around to make her way back toward the gym. "Enjoy the rest of your night. See you in class on Monday, Scarlett."

Her heels clack against the pavement, as she fades out of sight. When I turn back to face Nathaniel, he's staring at me with an unreadable expression. My heart sinks in my chest. Another almost-kiss interrupted.

I motion toward the gym. "I guess we should probably head back now."

He nods and gestures for me to lead.

The night is calm as we make our way back. Neither one of us speaks. My mind is still reeling from his confession. Could he possibly feel the same way I do—that this isn't all in my head? I wonder if Nathaniel is lost in his own thoughts right now, too.

As we reach the exit door we came from, Nathaniel breaks the silence. "Let's go through the locker rooms." His voice is soft. "It'll give us a few more minutes to walk."

He wants to prolong this—walking with me. I can't contain the grin that's forming. This is a good sign.

"Yes, let's do it."

We veer in the direction of the locker room entrance. As we approach, Nathaniel pulls the door open. I slide into the dimly lit hallway lined with athletic lockers, and Nathaniel follows from behind. The room smells strongly of sweat and grass stains—not the most ideal combination. But it delays us from going back, at least for a few more minutes.

Snaking our way through the zigzagging lockers and benches, we continue in the direction of the gym, each step echoing along the vinyl floor. It's funny that we're in a dingy locker room, but somehow, this moment still feels right. I've only met Nathaniel a few times now, and yet I feel comfortable in his presence. I already like spending time with him, and even more, I like the person I am when I'm with him—like I can really be myself.

I'm about to speak when, all of a sudden, I hear muffled voices from behind a set of lockers at the end of the hallway. I tilt my head to listen to the source. My body freezes. I recognize one of the voices, and something is wrong. *Very* wrong.

I start running, and Nathaniel picks up the pace behind me. The voices grow louder as we get closer until the words become discernible. It's Macie in distress.

"Stop it. I said no."

"Come on. We're just messing around."

"I mean it, Ashton. I don't want you going there," she says. "Please, don't."

"It's no big deal," the other voice coaxes. "Just relax."

After a few moments of silence, there's another cry, "I can't do this. Stop. I said stop!"

I round the corner in time to observe two people huddled on

the ground in the corner, their bodies partially interwoven. When Ashton looks up at me, he looks like a deer caught in headlights. He immediately removes his hand from beneath Macie's dress and pulls himself off the ground, dusting himself off with his hands.

"Get away from her," I demand in a voice icy enough that I barely recognize it as my own. "Right now."

Macie is sitting on the ground, shaking. Turning my attention to Ashton, I sneer between gritted teeth, "What the hell did you think you were doing?"

"It's not what it looks like." He raises his hands in the air.

My hands ball up into fists. "Oh, really? Because I think it's exactly what it looks like."

Ashton tries to push his way past Nathaniel and me. "You know what—I think I should just head back to the gym."

Before anyone can stop me, I lunge forward and grab Ashton's button-down shirt, bunching up a section of the fabric. Pulling him toward me, I maintain laser eye contact. I know it's not the most strategic move, considering he's about a foot taller than me. He could probably do more damage to me than I could ever do to him, but still, I stand my ground.

"Scarlett." I hear Nathaniel warn from behind me.

But it's too late, and I'm too angry.

"If you so much as lay a finger on Macie again, you won't be getting off this easily." My eyes narrow at him. "Is that clear?"

Ashton doesn't move a muscle.

With every fiber in my body, I muster the willpower to release him from my grasp unscathed. As much as I want to punch him square in the face, he isn't worth the energy, or a bruised hand, for that matter.

"Go right now," I snarl, "before I change my mind."

As tough as Ashton comes across, I can tell that I've shaken him.

"Don't worry," Ashton raises his hands in the air again. "I'm out of here."

In one fluid motion, he turns on his heel and walks brusquely in the other direction toward the gym.

Once he's out of sight, I turn to Macie. We spring for each other at the same time. As she reaches me, I pull her in and wrap my arms around her. She releases a jittery breath as she lowers her head to rest on my shoulder.

Nathaniel moves toward us. Meanwhile, I bring my attention back to Macie, and squeeze her tighter, providing what comfort I can.

"Macie," I pull away, "we need to tell someone. I'll go find one of the chaperones."

I'm about to spin around when Macie grips my shoulder and pulls me back. "Scarlett, please don't."

I'm caught off guard by her plea.

"It was a misunderstanding. Really, I'm okay."

Surely, she can't be serious.

"Macie, you call repeatedly saying 'no' a misunderstanding? He knew what he was doing. And it was *not* okay."

"I swear," she pauses, "this isn't who he is."

I look gravely into her eyes. "You have to trust me on this. If he's capable of doing this once, he's capable of doing this again."

"His scholarship," she murmurs.

"His what?"

"If he gets in trouble, he could lose his swim scholarship." Her eyes dart around frantically. "I can't jeopardize that for him."

I let out a frustrated breath. "You're actually making excuses for someone like Ashton? I can't believe this."

"I know it doesn't make any sense," Macie implores, "but please don't say anything more about this right now. For me?"

My jaw clenches. How can I simply ignore his actions? How can I stay silent when my best friend could have been harmed? How can I forgive myself for letting him get away so easily? At the same time, I want to respect Macie's wishes. She's the victim, not me. I let out a reluctant sigh.

"Fine," I mutter.

"Fine?" Macie beseeches.

"I won't say anything...this time."

Relief floods across her face. "Thank you, Scarlett. I'm sorry. I know I keep messing things up. But I won't let something like this happen again."

I stare at her incredulously. "Macie, this is not something you should be apologizing for. Do you understand?"

She casts her eyes down and nods, as if trying to convince herself. "Yeah, I guess you're right."

I feel like I should be telling someone for Macie's sake. And for any girl who gets involved with Ashton in the future. Yet I force myself to suppress the urge, at least for the time being.

"Hey," I speak softly, hoping to lighten a heavy situation. "Do you want to go back in there and dance for one last song? We still have another minute or two left."

She reaches for my hand and gives it a squeeze. "Yeah, let's do it." Before moving forward, she glances at Nathaniel. "You coming, too?"

He seems lost in a trance—like he's still processing what just happened. At the sound of Macie's voice, he snaps out of his daze and follows us. The dance is probably just about over by now, anyway. In silence, the three of us make our way back to the gym. As we enter, the DJ announces a final love song for the night.

How are the three of us going to dance to a slow song together? I feel guilty for dragging Macie back on the dance floor after her distressing experience. If anything, she's probably ready to get as far away from here as possible, at least for tonight.

"You know, Macie," I motion to the exit doors, "let's just grab our coats. We can get out of here."

I'm about to move forward when Macie halts me. "Scar, let me grab the coats. You two stay and finish up the last song."

Before I can object, Macie turns away from me. The next thing I know, she weaves her way into the crowd and out of sight. Here she is, the one in need, and yet she's making sure I get a last dance. What did I do to deserve her?

As I return my focus to Nathaniel, I notice the sadness in his eyes. I'm sure we both wish we could undo the past ten minutes and simply rewind to our stolen moment in the courtyard. But this seems to be all we have left.

As I'm about to reach for Nathaniel's hand, a familiar high-pitched voice calls out in our direction. I lift my head to see the auburn-haired girl from the department store, Tina. She's barreling toward us, getting closer by the second.

"Nathaniel. I've been looking for you all night," she exclaims. "You promised to save a dance for me—you know when we were at rehearsal the other day?"

He had promised her a dance? The thought bothers me more than I'd like to admit.

Nathaniel runs a hand through his hair. "Tina, I said I probably wasn't coming to the dance, anyway." I see the conflict in his expression as he looks from her to me. "And now's not a good time—I'm dancing with Scarlett."

Tina feigns surprise as she turns to me, "Oh, Scarlett. I didn't see you there."

I, on the other hand, glare in her direction. She'd probably say the same thing to a 5,000-pound elephant standing in front of her.

"Scarlett and I were actually just catching up the other week—we had quite a constructive discussion."

Oh, something like that. I narrow my eyes at her. My mind circulates back to our heated conversation in the department store.

"Scarlett," she continues, batting her eyelashes, "you don't mind if I steal Nathaniel for a dance, do you?" She poses the question in a way that sounds more like a threat than an inquiry.

I still can't get over the thought that Nathaniel had promised Tina a dance. I know that it shouldn't matter—that I'm the one standing with him now. Who cares what kind of promises he had made to her in the past?

Yet I can't shake the feeling that I'm going to end up getting hurt, like Tina had warned. What if she's right—that it's silly for me to think I might have a shot with him? My fear is that she'll snake her way into Nathaniel's life, whether I like it or not. After all, if she's this desperate for a dance, I can only imagine what lengths she'll go to in the future.

"Well, if Nathaniel promised you a dance," I hesitate, "then I guess it's okay."

With disappointment, I step backward, leaving space for Tina to step in.

I debate whether or not to rescind my invitation, but when I turn back, it's already too late. Tina is bouncing enthusiastically toward Nathaniel, taking up the space I had just occupied. The damage has been done: I've just successfully pushed myself further away from him due to my own insecurities.

I decide instead to find Macie and make our getaway. There's only so much high school drama a girl can take in one night. Who knew one mundane school dance could induce such a rollercoaster ride of emotions?

Turning on my heel, I begin zigzagging my way through the gym. I hear Nathaniel call out my name, but when I glance back, Tina has already taken over and is wrapping her arms around Nathaniel's neck affectionately. With a heavy heart, I walk in the direction of the exit. I am so focused on escaping that I almost fly past Macie, who is holding both of our coats on her arm.

"Let's get out of here." I snatch my coat from her and sling it over my shoulder.

"Scarlett, is everything okay with you and—"

"Yup." I cut her off, not wanting to discuss it more in such a public location. "Let's just leave. I'm ready to go home."

With irritation, I stomp toward my car. Macie follows quietly behind me. We reach our spot, and I swing my car door open, clambering inside and slamming it shut. Folding my arms together, I sit fuming in my seat. Meanwhile, Macie opens her door and slides into the passenger's side next to me. She swivels her body, so she's facing me straight-on.

"So," she breaks the silence, "what happened in there?"

I let out a resigned huff. I hate that I'm letting Tina get under my skin. Especially when I'm partly to blame for letting her do so in the first place. "It's stupid of me to care," I huff. "It's just," I pause, not sure how to explain why I'm upset, "Nathaniel promised Tina a dance."

Macie remains silent as she watches me from the other seat.

"I'll never be good enough for someone like Nathaniel Wilder. Honestly, she's doing me a favor by helping me realize that now rather than later."

I cast my eyes down, wallowing in my own self-pity. Once I've calmed down, I turn back to Macie to gauge her reaction. I expect compassion or sympathy, but when I look back up, she's giving me an unexpected grin.

"Macie. This isn't funny."

Shaking her head, she reaches her hand out to me. "I just thought it was funny that you could ever think you're not good enough for someone. You're Scarlett freaking Clarke. You're not good enough for Nathaniel. You're *better*."

My mouth hangs open at her words. I let out a liberating breath of air. Maybe all I need is a bit of her self-confidence.

"Macie, what would I do without you?"

"You'd probably die," she states matter-of-factly, "but thankfully, we'll never have to find out."

I'm suddenly consumed by emotion at the thought of what could have happened to her tonight. How does she stay so brave, even after what Ashton did to her? Here I am, blubbering about a stolen dance like an elementary schooler, yet Macie's the one in need. I should be focused on her emotional state tonight, not my own.

I turn toward her, nervous to reintroduce a sensitive subject. At the same time, I want her to know that she's not alone...that I'm here for her in whatever she's feeling.

"Forget about me right now," my voice falls to a whisper. "How are you? I mean, after what happened tonight."

Macie glances out in front of her, staring at the cars turning in and out of the parking lot. For a moment, she seems unreachable. I want to ask her what she's thinking, but I don't. Instead, I stay quiet, waiting for her to speak.

"I feel like it's my fault," she mumbles, continuing to stare vacantly out the window.

I can see the hurt in her eyes as she internalizes her confession. It seems as though someone more guarded has overtaken the carefree best friend that I've always known—that tonight has shaken her trusting spirit.

"Maybe I led him on too much. Or I wasn't assertive enough in saying 'no.' I should have known better."

I grab her hand. "You are not to blame for what happened to you tonight. Do you understand that? You have a right to say 'no' at any time. You did, and he didn't respect that."

Her eyes cloud as she takes a shaky breath. "I thought maybe for a minute, he actually cared about me. But when he started getting so handsy, I just felt used. Like he didn't even see me as a person. Just a means to an end."

I wish that I could say the right words to make her feel better—that I could take away her pain. Unfortunately, I don't think there are "right" words for situations like these...only genuine ones. So instead, I choose the truest words I know.

"Macie, I know you might not believe me right now, but I want you to know that I admire you. I admire you more than you know."

She shakes her head, as if she doesn't want to accept my words. I squeeze her hand tighter and lean in to look at her.

"You, Macie freaking Young, have one of the most unshakeable spirits of anyone I have ever met. No matter how anyone tries to bend you, you can't break," I whisper. "And that's why I admire you."

Before I know it, she reaches for me and pulls me in for a hug. I wrap my arms around her in return. No matter how heavy, I'll always be there to carry her burdens along with me, just as she does with mine. After all, that's what friendship is about.

"Scarlett?" She speaks my name softly.

"Yeah?" I respond.

"Don't change. Do you think you can do that for me?"

By now, my eyes are misting as I nod with certainty. "Yes, I can do that."

Chapter Seven

I stare out at the mall, which is buzzing with shoppers. After the whirlwind of emotions that was Winter Formal, it feels strange to get back into an old routine—especially when that means working a shift at Fashion Fwrd.

With our current seasonal sale, the store has been packed with customers purchasing items at steep discounts. Right now, I'm helping an older gentleman shop for a cashmere scarf for his wife.

"I'm sorry, sir. Unfortunately, we're out of stock in that scarf right now," I say to him. "Would you like me to order it for you online instead?"

With a look of irritation, he turns toward me as if he expects me to make this scarf magically appear for him out of thin air. "I'll just look in another store." Before I can suggest our bestselling perfumes for the low price of $14.99, he turns around and exits the store as swiftly as he had entered.

Another customer, in and out, with no purchase. Steering toward the front display, I pick up a discarded cable-knit sweater and begin to refold it as I wait for more customers to approach the store. I glance out halfheartedly at the surrounding mall.

Before I started working at Fashion Fwrd, the mall had been a place of respite for me. Sometimes after school, I would stroll from shop to shop, letting my mind wander. I loved the sensory experience.

Listening to the chatter of voices around me. Touching the silky clothing fabrics. Smelling the fragrances wafting from each store.

Now I feel more like a robot: pre-programmed to excel at store greetings and register transactions. My job is built for repetition—informing customers of the same promotion and performing the same motions over and over again. Working retail is no easy task, but one day when I become a designer, I hope to have my own clothing line featured throughout a store like this.

I return my attention to people passing outside Fashion Fwrd. Parents wheeling children in strollers. Couples holding hands. Cliques of teenagers laughing. As I stare aimlessly at the hustle and bustle, my eyes suddenly freeze on one particular subject. I do a double-take just to make sure my vision isn't playing tricks on me. What is Nathaniel Wilder doing outside of a store like Fashion Fwrd?

I haven't spoken with him since the other night at the dance. And honestly, I'm not sure what to say now that we do have the chance to talk again. Is he here by chance? Are he and Tina a thing now? Or maybe, just maybe, could he be here to see me?

I prepare myself mentally, because Nathaniel is approaching the entrance of the store, getting closer by the second. I'm ready to brace myself for a potentially awkward encounter. But instead, I'm surprised when Nathaniel waves at me, flashing his familiar smile.

"Scarlett, just the person I was looking for."

He's so calm. Maybe I overanalyzed Winter Formal. Regardless, I'm glad there are no hard feelings after I left him to dance with Tina.

"So this is where you work, huh?" he asks.

I blink my eyes, still processing the fact that he's standing in front of me right now. "Yup, this would be the place." As the words come out, I make a face, suddenly wondering how he figured out that I work here. "How did you know?"

He shrugs. "Macie mentioned it during class. I asked her today what

76

time your shift goes until."

He asked Macie when I get off work? I'm at a loss for how to respond.

"So, what brings you into Fashion Fwrd today?" I find myself repeating the mechanical greeting I echo to every customer who enters this store. Nathaniel is anything but a regular customer.

"First, I wanted to, you know—apologize—for the way we left things at Winter Formal. I know Tina can be a lot, and I didn't mean to let her steal the last dance like that.

"I understand how she can be," I say. "I probably shouldn't have let her pull you away so easily."

"Don't worry about it," he says. "And second, I'm glad I caught you, because there is actually something I'm looking for."

I'm intrigued by what he's about to say next.

"I'm looking for," he turns around and gestures to a hole in the back of his coat, "a new jacket. I was walking around backstage, and mine snagged on one of the props. Think you might be able to help me out?"

I smile. "I think I can help you out there."

With that, I motion for him to follow me to the back of the store. Once we arrive at the coat racks, I search for the same type of twill-hooded jacket he's wearing. As I spot a row of them in the corner, I realize that the jackets are positioned too high for me to pull down. Reaching up, I go to grab hold of the jackets. But before I can, Nathaniel stops me.

"Let me help you."

As he reaches for a jacket, his body brushes up against mine, and I get a whiff of his cologne—a rich scent that smells like sandalwood.

"There we go."

Who knew one simple action could give me such a rush? I give myself time for my breathing to return back to normal. Meanwhile, Nathaniel slides into the jacket and takes a look in the mirror next to him. As expected, it fits him exceptionally well. He takes the jacket back off and slings it over his arm approvingly. "This should do the trick."

I'm about to respond when I hear my manager, Tasha, over my headset. "Scarlett, I'm ready for you on Register Two."

I motion to my headset with a groan. "Looks like I've just been summoned for register duty."

"All good. I'll see you up at the cash register soon." Nathaniel rests his hand on my arm. "Thanks again for your help, Scarlett."

As he turns around to explore more of the store, I remain stationary. What I would do to have Nathaniel shop here more often. If that were the case, I might actually look forward to this job—maybe enough so that I'd even ask Tasha for overtime.

A girl can dream.

Brushing the thought away, I make my way over to the second register. The line has rapidly expanded, zigzagging back and forth like a snake. Customers already look impatient, standing with crossed arms and irritated expressions. Taking a deep breath, I brace myself for the onslaught of frustrated comments. I'm not sure whether it was my encounter with Nathaniel or the general claustrophobia of the store, but the temperature feels like it's risen at least twenty degrees. I fan my face with my hand before motioning to the next customer in line.

A woman with furrowed eyebrows and narrow lips makes her way toward my register. "I'm in a bit of a hurry," she informs me, dumping her merchandise onto the counter.

With a polite nod, I begin scanning the tags of her items. She clacks her long fingernails repeatedly on the counter. As I finish with the last shirt, she swipes her card, and checks her watch with a huff. Then I hand her bag to her, so she can make it to wherever she needs to hurry off to. She snatches it from me without as much as a thank you.

I'm about to motion to the next customer in line, but before I can, the woman returns.

"Is everything okay?" I ask as she slaps her bag back down on the counter.

She practically flicks her receipt in my face. "You scanned my accessories wrong. They don't have the discount on them."

I eye the receipt dubiously, because I'm sure I applied the discount. But it looks like I'd been in such a rush to scan her clothes that I had, indeed, missed it. Murmuring a quick apology, I begin computing on the cash register to add the discount.

"This is ridiculous," the woman mutters.

Out of the corner of my eye, I spot Nathaniel. He's standing two registers down, observing the entire interaction. *Great.* I look back to my own register, scrambling to apply the discount to the woman's accessories.

As I hand her back the final receipt, she sends me a glare so glacial that my body stiffens. "I can't believe they hired such an *incompetent* associate."

"I'm," I stutter, stunned by her icy words, "I'm so sorry." I can feel myself struggling to breathe.

"This is just great. Now I'm going to be late."

Tasha makes her way toward my register, and she glances from the woman to me. "Is everything all right over here?"

Before I have time to respond, the woman speaks. "You should really reconsider the employees you hire." She points her finger at me. "So stupid."

I can barely think straight as the woman shoves her receipt in her bag and stomps away, disappearing into the crowd. My turtleneck feels like it's suffocating me.

"Scarlett, what happened?" Tasha's words sound slurred.

I open my mouth to respond, but something feels off. It's as if my body has lost control of itself. Clutching the counter for support, I try to stand upright, but my head feels like a pile of bricks tugging me down. Legs weakening beneath me, I sway gradually from side to side. Black spots form in my line of vision, and I can no longer see ahead of me. The realization sinks in: I can't stand anymore. I am going down.

My knees buckle. The last sound I hear before my vision fades to black is Nathaniel's voice calling out my name.

* * *

I must be dreaming, because I swear that Nathaniel is hovering over me. Blissfully, I savor the illusion, and I blink my eyes open. I'm sure I'll be waking up from this sweet dream any second. As I prepare to return to reality, I notice a different face has replaced Nathaniel's. It's my manager, Tasha. What is she doing in my dream? I open my eyes further, attempting to make sense of my blurry surroundings.

Suddenly, reality comes crashing down. I am not in a dream. This is real life. My ears ring, and my head aches. I hear a blur of sounds. Am I on the ground right now?

"Someone, get her water," says Tasha.

Other voices become discernible.

"Is she okay?"

"I think she fainted."

"I have a water bottle," someone else calls out.

"Scarlett." Tasha leans toward me. "Can you hear me?" Her words come out in slow-motion.

I nod as I try to push myself up with my elbow, but my body feels like Jell-O. With no success, I slump back down.

Before I know it, Tasha is lifting a plastic bottle to my lips. She helps me sip water until my vision returns to normal. With care, she lifts me, assisting me into a nearby chair.

"You're going to be alright, sweetie. Just a little light-headed, was all. Not the first time this has happened in this store, unfortunately. I swear I keep telling our district manager we need to get a fan behind this register."

I smile at her weakly, appreciating her empathy.

"Sit here, and drink water for a few more minutes. Then, I'll send you home."

From the apparent surprise in my eyes, she waves a hand. "Just for today, Scarlett. I want to make sure you're well-rested before you come in for your next shift."

I nod, silently thanking her for all she's done for me. When I look back out in front of me, I notice the store has begun to return to normal, and a backup sales associate is taking over my register.

"Do you know her?" Tasha directs her question to a figure to my right.

Swiveling my head, I see Nathaniel kneeling beside me with concern in his eyes.

"Yes," Nathaniel says.

"Can you make sure she makes it back okay?" Tasha asks.

"Of course."

Nathaniel places his hand on my shoulder as he bends down toward me. "You ready to go, Scarlett?"

I blink my eyes. How did I let myself get to this point? Somehow, I manage to look back at Nathaniel and offer a weak nod. Looping his arm with mine, he lifts me from the chair and keeps me steady. Customers turn to watch as Nathaniel ushers me out of the store.

The next few minutes are a blur while Nathaniel guides me in the direction of the food court. As we reach our destination, he finds an empty table and lowers me slowly into a metal chair.

"Wait here."

I don't think I have much of a choice. I feel too drained to even question where he's running off to. My body feels like a limp noodle.

I watch Nathaniel disappear into the crowd, and then I drop my head to my hands. The past ten minutes play back on repeat: the angry customer, the fainting, and the aftermath. My cheeks burn in utter mortification. How am I ever going to recover from this? Physically, I may already be feeling better. But emotionally, I'm afraid this experience will remain imprinted in my brain for years to come. As I lift my head, I notice Nathaniel returning. He sits down in the chair across from me, bearing a gift.

"This is for you." He slides a chocolate milkshake toward me. "I really hope you're not lactose intolerant."

Gratefully, I pull the drink toward me. I take my first sip, and the iciness instantly makes me feel better.

Nathaniel's eyes are still alert, as if he thinks I might pass out again. "How are you feeling now?"

I look down in order to avoid Nathaniel's gaze. I'm humiliated enough that I fainted. But the fact that Nathaniel saw it makes me want to throw a paper bag over my head.

"Nathaniel." I have difficulty getting the words out. "I'm sorry you had to see me like that. I can't even tell you how embarrassed I feel."

"Scarlett." His voice is a warning that catches me off-guard. "Don't do that."

"Don't do what?"

"Don't apologize. Especially for something like that." He holds a finger in the air. "Number One, that customer should be banned from the store permanently."

I smile at the fact that he's trying to comfort me now.

"Number Two," he raises a second finger, "you're great at your job. I mean, you helped me find the exact type of jacket I was looking for." He lifts one last finger in the air. "And Number Three, the only thing I care about is that you're okay."

In one minute, he single-handedly transformed me from feeling lousy to feeling self-assured again. How did he do that? With a deep breath, I decide to let my shame go.

He reaches across the counter and gives my hand a reassuring squeeze. I sit motionless as he returns his hand to his lap, like it was no big deal. Meanwhile, I'm left reeling at the subtle touch. One thing's for sure—today has turned out differently than I was expecting it to. For better or for worse.

"You know, you don't have to sit here with me if you don't want to, right?"

Nathaniel laughs. "I want to. Don't worry." He looks out at the surrounding mall. "And I know what we can do while we're waiting for you to feel better."

I tilt my head in curiosity. I'm getting to the end of my milkshake, but I want to prolong this for as long as possible.

"How about we get to know each other better? I hardly know anything about you."

Sounds like a good way to kill time to me. Plus, how could I pass up the opportunity to learn more about him?

"Since we're already making lists of threes," I tap my chin, "what if we play Two Truths and a Truth? It's like Two Truths and a Lie, but instead of lying, you have to tell me three honest truths about you."

"Sounds interesting," Nathaniel says. "I'm in."

"You go first. Just tell me three things about you."

He leans back in his chair. "Okay, let's see. My first truth is that I moved here this year from Philly. My second truth is that I turned to theater after getting a serious ankle injury in football. And my third truth is that I'm colorblind. I'm glad you helped me pick out a jacket today, because, for that reason, I don't know much about fashion."

I cross my arms together. "Am I allowed to ask follow-up questions to your truths?"

"Only if I get to ask them for yours."

I take another sip of my milkshake. "Was it tough moving here your senior year? I'm sure you miss your friends and your life back in Philly."

"I do," Nathaniel admits. "But I still talk to them regularly, and I know I'll still get to see them from time to time. It's weird to uproot your life right when you're finally getting comfortable with it, though."

"I can imagine," I nod empathetically. "And with your injury—do you wish you could still play football? I mean, if the injury hadn't happened, would you choose football instead of theater?"

"I would say football was my first passion. I was devastated when I found out I couldn't play anymore. I always thought I would go to college for that. But thankfully, I found theater, and it gave me a creative outlet. My motto is that you can't always control what happens to you in life, but you can control your reaction."

His words strike me. I can't help but appreciate Nathaniel's positive outlook, even after experiencing a serious injury like that. With each question I ask, I'm uncovering more about him, and it's helping me fit the puzzle pieces together.

"And lastly, this one's very important," I pause for dramatic emphasis, "when you see a stoplight, do the red and green lights look the same color to you?"

My question makes him laugh. "I can still see the differences in color. I just can't discern them as well as people with normal vision." He uncrosses his arms. "Okay, your turn to be in the interview seat. I want to know three truths about you."

I take a deep breath. "Okay, here goes nothing: I'm an only child. I'm not lactose intolerant. And I want to be a fashion designer after I graduate college."

Nathaniel purses his lips together. "So, you don't get tired of being the only one your parents nag when something goes wrong?"

I shake my head. "No. Actually, my parents and I have a really great relationship. They've always been supportive of me and encouraged me to pursue my dreams. Sometimes, they can be over the top, but it's just because they want what's best for me. They even bought me a sewing machine this year, so I can work on my designs."

"Sewing, huh?" he responds. "You should work in the costume shop for us. I'm sure the theater department could use all the extra help it can get."

It's not like the thought hasn't crossed my mind, especially after I stumbled into the costume shop on the day I first met Nathaniel. Should I consider helping with the spring play? The idea is becoming more appealing the more I contemplate it. "I've thought about it."

"Good. You really should." Nathaniel points to my Styrofoam container. "Ah, I see you've inhaled your milkshake. Is chocolate your favorite flavor?"

"Yes," I say immediately. "Vanilla pales in comparison. Chocolate all the way."

"I'll have to remember that for next time."

Next time? I try not to dwell on the meaning behind it right now.

"And lastly, you said a fashion designer." Nathaniel shakes me from my thoughts. "Can I ask you another question? Just because I'm genuinely curious. Promise me you won't be upset."

I nod, even though I can't make that promise just yet. "What is it?"

"As I've told you, I don't really know much about fashion, but I know you do. I was just curious what people love so much about the industry. I mean, at the end of the day, I know it's important, but isn't clothing just clothing?"

This boy is easy on the eyes, but man, does he need some schooling.

I shake my head incredulously, like he just asked me why puppies are cute.

"Clothing may just be clothing," I chuckle, "but that doesn't mean what's on the outside can't make you shine, too. For me, fashion is integral to who I am. When I was younger, my mom used to dress me in these frumpy outfits, and kids used to make fun of me for it. Once I discovered the world of fashion, I was able to create my own personal style and showcase myself in the way that I wanted to be seen. It gave me an outlet to express myself." I didn't realize quite how strongly I felt about the subject until explaining it to Nathaniel just now. "I mean...is acting just acting for you?

"Touché," he grins. "I know some people like it because of the applause and admiration. But acting is freedom of expression for me, too. I used to have stage fright when I was younger, but acting helped me break out of my shell. I guess acting and fashion aren't that different then."

As I stare back at Nathaniel, I realize maybe we're not polar opposites after all. We may have different interests. And we may feel comfortable in different social settings. But at the end of the day, we're both two people who use our creative outlets to make us feel more alive. To give us purpose. To overcome adversity. And that's pretty darn cool.

I go to take another sip of my milkshake but realize that I've reached the end. I check my phone and see that another half an hour flew by just sitting and talking. Why does this always happen when I'm with him? I'm not sure how much shopping Nathaniel has left to do, and he's already sacrificed enough of his time in order to make sure I'm okay.

"Well," I sigh, "I'm beginning to feel much better now, thanks to you, and I don't want to take you away from the rest of your shopping," I scoot away from the table. "I guess I should probably start heading back to my car now."

I begin to lift myself out of the chair. But before I can stand, Nathaniel swings around the other side of the table to assist me.

"Easy there. Are you sure you're going to be okay to make it back?"

I wave my hand, wanting to appear confident. "Yes, I'm good."

Still, Nathaniel takes the opportunity to loop his arm around mine one more time. "Let me walk you back to your car. It's the least I can do."

I shrug with attempted indifference, even though it's far from what I'm feeling. With his arm linked to mine, we make our way back in the direction of the parking garage. To an onlooker, it almost appears as if we could be on a date. The thought makes me giddy.

I point in the direction of my car, "I can take it from here. Thank you again for, you know, what you've done for me today."

When I look back up, Nathaniel is staring at me with his piercing blue eyes. The intensity makes my heart race. "My pleasure," he speaks carefully. "You don't have to thank me."

I'm about to turn around when he pulls out his phone. "Hey, I know you said you were starting to feel better, but let's exchange numbers. And then you can text me when you make it home safely. You know, just so I know you're okay."

This time, my head is spinning but for a different reason. I would faint all over again just to have Nathaniel ask for my number. He hands me his phone, with the screen already open to "Add New Contact." Trying to maintain my composure, I plug my number in and type out my name. "There you go."

I watch his fingers tap the keyboard and then press a button. When he does so, my phone screen lights up with a buzz.

Hey, this is Nathaniel. So you have my number, too :)

I wave my phone in the air. "I'll let you know when I get home." Then I pull out my keys and head for my car. The moment I unlock the door, I slump into the driver's seat and let my head fall back against the headrest. I let out a deep sigh as I look over at the dashboard.

This all could have been avoided if weren't for one stupid accessories discount, but somehow, I don't regret any of it.

* * *

"You fainted?" I hear the panic in my mom's voice as I break the news.

"Yes, Mom. But don't worry. I'm okay."

She releases a breath as she paces back and forth in our kitchen. "Why didn't you call me?"

"Really, just a little dehydration was all it was," I reassure her. "Once I drank some water, I felt much better."

"And you drove home by yourself?" Her eyes grow wide at my apparent indiscretion. "Scarlett, you shouldn't have been driving in that condition. What if you had felt dizzy again on the road?"

"I didn't, and I made it back." I hadn't realized this would be such a big deal.

"Honey," her voice grows softer, "I'm worried about you now." She pauses before speaking again. "Have you been feeling okay lately? Any extra stress at school?"

I am not in the mood to field intrusive questions about my mental state right now—especially those concerned with the stressors building in my life. After all, the newest one will be recovering from my post-fainting shame.

"No, Mom. Actually, you're the one causing me stress right now," I snap.

My mother's face falls, and I realize I've hurt her with my curt reply. Suddenly, I feel guilty. She only wants what's best for me.

Sometimes, I let my teenage angst take over. It can be tempting to shut her out from my world. Yet I have to remind myself that my mom was once my age, too. I'm sure she had to grapple with much of the same high school drama.

"I'm sorry, Mom. Maybe I am just a bit overwhelmed right now."

She taps her fingers along the counter.

"You know, Scarlett, you really are going to have a lot on your plate this year. Between classes, researching colleges, taking standardized tests," she walks around the table to be closer to me, "and your job on top of all of that…I'm worried it's taking its toll."

I release a drawn-out sigh. While I don't like to admit it, the job has a way of depleting my energy. My weekends aren't always my own. It's hard to participate in school social activities. I don't have as much time to do homework after working long shifts. I know a retail job is supposed to look good on my college applications, like my dad had said, but maybe it's time for a break. After all, I've been putting my paychecks in the bank, and I still have another year to save up money before college.

Absorbing my mom's words, I nod. "You know, it is a lot right now."

"You don't have to stop your job completely. You can keep in contact with Tasha, so you can work this summer. And maybe even next school year once you finish your applications." She puts a hand on my shoulder. "I just think it would be for the best, especially after this scare."

"I'll talk to Tasha this week. We'll figure it out."

I feel a weight being lifted off of my chest. If I have more time on my hands, time that's not taken up by a job, I can work on my sketches more, or learn how to sew, or…I could volunteer to help out in the theater department for the spring play.

The more I think about it, the more sense it makes. My parents have been encouraging me to participate in theater since my youth. Macie would love it if I joined her. And even Nathaniel suggested the idea to me himself. Plus, if I'm only volunteering, I won't be overly stressed about the time commitment. It's the perfect solution.

Grabbing my laptop off of the counter, I get up from my chair. "Mom, I'm going to go upstairs for a bit."

She nods, and I wave to her before exiting the kitchen. Once I get to my room, I set my laptop down on my desk. I open the screen and type in the drama department's website. I see various tabs for contact information, past performances, and a calendar of events. Finally, I spot the section that says "Opportunities to Participate." I scan the page and see that the department is currently accepting ushers for the spring play.

In the center of the page, it says to contact Mr. Walsh for more information starting next week. I tap my pencil on my desk, thinking about my class schedule. I'll go to him first thing on Monday to sign up. With my pencil, I make a note in my planner. Speaking of things to remember, I haven't texted Nathaniel yet to let him know I made it back safely.

I pull out my phone. *Made it back safely. Thanks again for the delicious milkshake.*

A minute later, I get a response. *You're welcome. Glad you made it back in one piece.*

I smile. I can't believe we're on a texting basis now. This feels like I'm living a parallel life.

Another text lights up my screen. *Btw, are you going to be at Dotty's on Friday?*

I grin at my phone. Dotty's is our town's quintessential 1950s-inspired diner. It's located right near our high school and serves classic American cuisine, including burgers, shakes, and fries. As the weather gets warmer, students usually eat there on Friday nights after getting out of sports practices and rehearsals. Macie and I used to go when we were underclassmen, but we haven't been in a while.

I might, but I'm not sure yet. HBU? I respond.

Liam and I are going with some friends. Nathaniel texts. *You and Macie should swing by.*

Wow, I have so much to catch Macie up on after the past couple of hours. I need to call her.

I message him back. *Sweet. I'll check and let you know soon.*

Excitedly, I exit out of my text messages page and go to my contact list. I press Macie's name and hope that she answers.

She picks up on the third ring. "Hey, Scarlett. What's up?"

"I have so much to tell you," I speak hurriedly into the phone. "First, I fainted. Second, I'm quitting my job at Fashion Fwrd. Third, I'm going to sign up as an usher for the spring play. Oh, and fourth, we're going to Dotty's this Friday."

"Whoa, whoa—slow down there, Scarlett." I hear the concern in Macie's voice. "You fainted? What happened to you?"

"Long story," I say. "I'm okay. I promise. I'll tell you more about it later. Anyways, just promise me you'll come to the diner with me this Friday. Nathaniel and Liam are going to be there, too."

Macie breathes a sigh of relief into the phone. "Okay, that sounds like fun. I'll come this Friday. As long as you plan to give me a full report of what happened to you."

"You're the best. I'll talk to you soon." I hang up the phone and text Nathaniel back to confirm.

Next, I set my phone down and look back at my desk. The sewing machine I got for Christmas is still sitting in the corner. What if Mr. Walsh knows someone from costume design who can help me with my technique? Then I'd be one step closer to designing my own line of clothing. After all, who says fashion has to be my only area of interest? Maybe, there's room in my heart for theater, too. And even better, a way to combine the two. Now I'll have the opportunity to explore the best of both worlds.

Chapter Eight

C heese fries!

"Macie, we're definitely ordering these," I point out.

She grins. "Only if there are mozzarella sticks involved, too."

Looking up from my menu, I take a minute to soak in the neon lights, red vinyl booths, and checkered flooring of Dotty's Diner. Now that Friday has rolled around, the place is filling up with other students. My eyes graze over the classic posters and vintage records that hang decoratively around the restaurant. From the looks of it, Nathaniel and Liam haven't arrived yet.

"So," Macie regains my attention, "you're not going to be working at Fashion Fwrd anymore?"

I nod. "Yup. Talked to my manager right after I called you—I let her know how hectic things have been, but I asked if I could stay in the system, so I can still work over the summer."

"Yay, Scarlett," Macie claps. "Now we'll have even more time to do fun things together. And I'm so happy you're going to be a part of the play."

Owning the decision to leave my job was harder than I thought it would be. Although the work itself was grueling, I'm going to miss the sense of financial independence and adult responsibility it gave me. Plus, the discounts weren't so bad either. But thankfully, I'll still have this summer.

Closing my menu, I spot our server as he approaches—*oh no*.

Macie waves him over. "Gavin! I didn't know you work at Dotty's Diner."

Oh, yes. The memory is coming back to me now. *Gavin*.

He walks up to our booth. "Yup, it's a pretty good gig. I can't complain."

"Well," Macie laughs, "if you ever get free mozzarella sticks for working here, don't hesitate to send some my way." She turns in my direction. "By the way, I don't think the two of you have met yet. Gavin, this is my best friend, Scarlett. Scarlett, this is...."

I stare daggers at her, willing her to remember. Gavin looks uncomfortable, too.

"...Gavin." Her voice trails off. "Ah, I remember now. The two of you have met before."

Thanks for stating that out loud, Captain Obvious.

The air suddenly feels thick around me. We had done more than meet, that's for sure. He had asked me to dance at Winter Formal. And now, we're in a public restaurant, barely capable of acknowledging each other.

To make matters worse, I had turned him down that night. I remember my words from the dance coming back to bite me: *"I just can't do this."*

At the time, I had thought that he was just another face in the crowd. Someone I likely wouldn't see again. Little did I foresee that he would be standing two feet away from me at Dotty's, waiting to take my order.

I realize that Macie and Gavin are both waiting for me to respond. I keep my eyes glued to my menu. "Nice to see you." I pray my words don't sound sarcastic as I speak them. "I'll have the cheese fries, please."

"And I'll have the mozzarella sticks," Macie says.

He confirms the order and then darts away from our table. I don't blame him.

"Well, that was awkward," I whisper once I'm sure he's out of earshot.

"I forgot that I had introduced you both at Winter Formal. I guess I was a little distracted." She grits her teeth. "How did that go, by the way? I mean, after the two of you met?"

"I just kind of panicked, and I ran away after we started dancing. So considering that, not so well."

Her face falls, "Oh, Scar. I shouldn't have made you guys dance together. I just thought the two of you might hit it off. He's a sweet guy. I'd never try to pair you with a jerk intentionally."

I had assumed he was just some random dude that Macie had found for me. I didn't realize she had marked him with her personal stamp of approval.

Before I have time to think about it more, I spot Gavin ambling back toward us, balancing a tray on his arm.

"One order of cheese fries and one order of mozzarella sticks coming in hot," he places the plates in front of us. "Let me know if I can get you guys anything else."

When I look up, I notice Gavin is standing in place, staring directly at me. I flash a weak smile before breaking eye contact. As he leaves, I take a deep breath and try not to dwell on our reintroduction. Instead, I pull a gooey glob of fries to my mouth, and Macie does the same with her mozzarella sticks. After a few more bites, Macie says, "I have to use the bathroom real quick." She pushes herself up from the booth.

As she trudges off in the direction of the restroom, I turn toward the window next to me. Cars are turning in and out of the adjacent lot, their headlights reflecting along the glass. I stare out absentmindedly, watching the sun set into the distance.

When I rotate back around to see if Macie has returned, someone is standing in front of me. I tilt my head, and I'm surprised to find Gavin with two plastic containers.

"Oh," I wave my hand, "those must be for someone else. We didn't order anything to go."

He shakes his head and motions to the containers. "Macie mentioned she wanted some extras. I thought I'd box some more fries up for you, too."

He's giving me extra fries? I'm taken aback by the gesture. "Wow, Gavin, that's really thoughtful of you."

He runs a hand through his hair nervously. "Hey, I realize we may have gotten off on the wrong foot the first time we met. I don't want that to be your only impression," he finishes sheepishly, motioning to the box again.

Macie was right. This guy seems sweet, after all. I extend my hand. "My name's Scarlett. What did you say yours was again?"

I can tell Gavin is startled by my question, considering Macie just reintroduced us no less than ten minutes ago. But then, the light bulb goes off.

He gives my hand a firm shake as he realizes that I'm recreating the introduction we should have started with all along. "I'm Gavin. It's nice to meet you, Scarlett. And I hope you like cheese fries, because I've brought you enough to last you a solid week."

I giggle. "Gavin, knowing me, these fries will last two days, max."

As the words leave my mouth, I feel a familiar hand rest on my shoulder. I whip my head around at the source of the unexpected touch and see Nathaniel behind me.

"Scarlett," Nathaniel says.

"Nathaniel." My breath hitches. "Hi."

Instinctively, I move my hand away from Gavin's and tuck it back into my lap.

"Mind if I join you for a minute?" he asks. His voice is even, but his stare makes my stomach want to flip. If I didn't know better, I would think he looks jealous.

As I nod, Nathaniel slides into the booth next to me.

When I look back at Gavin, he's flashing a tight smile. "Your bills are underneath the boxes."

"Thanks," I murmur. I really had misread him the first time we met. Gavin spins around and walks back toward the kitchen.

"So," Nathaniel leans in closer to me, "how are you feeling after what happened earlier this week?"

He's still thinking about my health? I'm feeling better in general, but especially better now that he's here. I always feel better in the presence of Nathaniel Wilder.

"Clean bill of health. Nothing to worry about."

"Good. I was worried I might have to keep buying you milkshakes."

Does he mean like a date, date? Between Nathaniel's proposal to buy me milkshakes and Gavin serving me extra cheesy fries today, I think I could get used to this lifestyle.

Before I can respond, Macie slides back into the booth. "Oh, hey, Nathaniel. I see you've taken over in my absence."

"Just keeping Scarlett company for you while you were gone," he says.

When I look again, I'm somehow not surprised to see Liam scoot in next to Macie, too. "What's up, squad?"

"Wow, what a party," I exclaim.

"We won't crash for too long," Liam reassures me. "We should get back to our group." He points at a huddle of guys sitting in the corner. "Just wanted to stop by and say 'hi.' By the way, are you guys getting excited for the spring play?"

Macie points toward me. "Guess who's going to usher for it."

Liam looks back at me in surprise. "Scarlett, you're helping out, too?"

He reaches across the table to grab a fry from my plate. "You don't want to miss another one of Macie's legendary performances."

Macie elbows Liam forcefully. "Watch out. Or I'll push you out of this seat."

I laugh. There's nothing more entertaining than watching my best friend on a stage. "Well, I'm definitely looking forward to being there."

"What about Fashion Fwrd, Scarlett?" Nathaniel asks. "Are you still doing that, too?"

I appreciate his question, even though I haven't told him about my recent resignation yet. I decide to catch everyone up to speed.

"Well, actually, I'm taking a break for now. I've been looking for something to occupy my time, and I'd love to get a closer look at the costumes."

And spend some more quality time with Nathaniel, I think to myself. But I omit that part.

Nathaniel smiles. "Awesome. It would mean a lot to have you there." He clears his throat. "To Macie, of course."

I smile.

"Well," Liam interrupts my thoughts, "we better get back to our table before the guys banish us for good." Liam pops one more fry in his mouth. "You coming, Nathaniel?"

Nathaniel sighs with seeming reluctance. "Yeah. Coming."

The air feels colder as Nathaniel slides away from me. When he pushes himself up from the booth, I notice that he's wearing the new jacket I had recommended for him.

"Nice jacket, by the way," I compliment.

"I had this pretty great sales associate. Maybe you know her." He winks at me. "I'll see you later, Scarlett," he enunciates my name carefully before turning around and heading back in the direction of his table.

Meanwhile, I'm left starry-eyed. When I turn back to face Macie, she's smirking at me. "You two are into each other." She leans in, so no one else can hear her. "And you can't tell me you aren't."

She's right—I can't deny it.

"Okay. Maybe there is a little something there between Nathaniel and me. But it's minuscule, microscopic, practically non-existent."

Macie reaches for her bill. "You could argue that aliens are non-existent, too," she counters. "But we all know that they're out there floating around on other planets as we speak. Just because you won't admit to seeing something doesn't mean it doesn't exist."

I reach for another fry and pop it into my mouth. "Well, that doesn't mean it does exist either," I respond. "Like ghosts, for example."

Macie laughs at my counter-argument. "Ghosts could totally exist, you know."

"Well, if they do," I joke, "there are a lot of people I want to haunt when I become one."

Macie repositions herself in her seat. "Like Tina, for example?"

I stop mid-chew, freezing at the sound of her name. Tina's the last person I want to be reminded of right now.

"Did you ever talk to Nathaniel about her?" Macie seems to notice my sudden mood shift. "About those things she said to you in the department store?"

My heart sinks in my chest. "No, I haven't." I've been trying not to let my mind go back there.

"Well," Macie lifts a finger in the air, "at least you'll be able to keep tabs on her now."

"What do you mean?"

"Considering you'll be at the play." She places her card in the cardholder. "You can keep her in line if she tries any funny business in front of Nathaniel during the performances."

I feel my face light up. "Macie, you're a genius." I glance back over at Nathaniel from across the room before turning back around to Macie. "Yes," I say. "That's exactly what I'll do."

Chapter Nine

First thing on Monday morning, I make my way to Mr. Walsh's office to ask about ushering for the spring play. When I knock on the door and peek my head inside, he motions for me to enter. I step into his office and approach the chair in front of his desk.

"Miss Clarke." Mr. Walsh looks up, his thin rectangular glasses directed right at me. "What brings you into my office today?" His pierced ears and slicked-back hair contribute to his overall artistic edginess.

"I hear you're looking for ushers for your play." I clear my throat. "I'd love to help out if possible."

Mr. Walsh studies me in silence, tenting his fingertips. He leans one hand on the desk in front of him. "Do you know what this play is about?"

I shrink in my chair, realizing I haven't done my full research before showing up to his office. After deciding to sign up, I hadn't even considered that I'd need background knowledge, especially for a job as straightforward as ushering.

"No, sir. I'm not exactly sure what the play is about."

"Ever heard of *Our Town* before?" he asks.

"No, I don't believe so."

"Well, then," he waits a long beat before continuing, "You're in for a treat. It's one of the most performed meta-theatrical plays of the 20th

99

century. Won a Pulitzer Prize for Drama in 1938."

I let out the breath that I've been holding in. "Wow, that's really cool."

"Takes place in the fictional town of Grover's Corners, New Hampshire," Mr. Walsh continues. "It's a three-act play that depicts the complexities of humanity."

I nod intently.

"Anyways, we would love some help ushering," he concludes. "Our spring plays are always popular ones, and we're expecting a big audience."

"Excellent." My face lights up at his words. "Let me know what I can do to help, and I will be there."

"Your responsibilities will be pretty straightforward." He rests his hands on his desk. "You'll simply be escorting patrons to their seats and providing them with programs. Once everyone has been seated, you're welcome to stay and watch the rest of the performance. We'll be showcasing the play over three days. From Thursday to Saturday."

I nod. "Sounds great."

Mr. Walsh releases a lighthearted chuckle. "Good to hear, Scarlett. Your help will be appreciated."

Little does he know that I'm the appreciative one—appreciative that I'll get to help out as an usher. And also that I'll be spending extra time with a certain someone over the course of those three days.

I remember the other reason I'm here. "Mr. Walsh—I have one more question to ask you." I fidget with my hands in my lap, the nerves building. "Since I'm going to be around during the play, I was wondering if I could shadow someone in the costume shop. You see, I got a sewing machine over the holidays, and I'm not quite sure how to use it yet, but I'd love to learn more about stitching techniques. My dream is to go into clothing design, and I was thinking there's no better way to learn than from someone in the drama department."

Mr. Walsh purses his lips. "Absolutely, Scarlett. I think that's a great idea. You know, I actually took a number of theater costume design courses over the years before I went into directing. I'd be more than happy to give you a quick demo if you want to come into the shop before or after rehearsals to practice."

"You would?" I clap my hands together. "Mr. Walsh, that would be amazing. I can bring in my sewing machine and my own fabric swatches, too."

"Sounds great," he responds. "The next week or two is going to be crazy with the play coming up so soon, but shoot me an email, and we'll choose a time to give you some pointers."

I scoot out of my seat and pick up my backpack. "Thanks again, Mr. Walsh. I won't let you down with the ushering." I make my way toward the door. "And I'm looking forward to learning more about sewing."

"Excellent to hear. We'll see you soon, Scarlett." He waves at me as I turn to leave his office.

I do a little happy dance. Soon, I'll no longer be an aspiring designer. I may actually get to create some of my own designs. With the few extra minutes I have, I decide to head toward Macie's locker. It's on the way to my next class, and I'm excited to tell her that I'll officially be ushering for the performance. Not to mention, I'll be spending more time in the costume shop. She's probably just getting back from her lunch period now, so I'll have the perfect opportunity to catch her before class.

As I approach the correct hallway, I see her standing beside her locker with her back toward me.

"Macie," I say. "You'll never guess what."

I tap her on the shoulder. But her head remains cast down in the direction of her locker.

"Macie?" I try again more cautiously.

When she turns around, my stomach drops. Her eyes are puffy, and she swipes at a tear rolling down her cheek.

"Macie." My hand goes to her arm as the panic sets in. "What happened?"

Rubbing away at a mascara stain, she inhales a shaky breath. "It's nothing, Scar. It's not a big deal."

"Macie."

She sniffles before shaking her head. "It's just—"

"You can say it," I prompt her.

With a frenzied glance, she looks around the hallway and then leans in closer to me, "Ashton pulled me aside today." Her voice shakes. "I guess you could say we came to an understanding about the night of Winter Formal."

An understanding?

My fists clench. Even the sound of his name makes me want to toss a heavy object at a wall. "What kind of understanding are you talking about?"

She stares at the ground. "He promised he wouldn't bother me again as long as I promised I wouldn't say anything to anyone about that night."

My eyes narrow. "That's not an understanding, that's a threat."

"It's not like that, I swear," Macie raises her hands in defense. "I wasn't going to tell anyone, anyway. This way, at least I know he'll keep his distance."

"And what would happen if you did tell, Macie? He wouldn't keep his distance?"

My question hangs in the air. Macie looks away.

How can she let him do this to her? By keeping quiet, I feel like I'm an accomplice in Ashton's ultimatum.

"Macie, you really should say something to someone," I urge.

"Trust me, Scar, I'm okay. Really. Just promise me you won't say anything?" Her eyes search mine.

I look back at her, unsure of what to do.

"Now, what was it you wanted to tell me?" Macie changes the subject before I have time to object.

I wish she hadn't just dismissed the situation so easily, especially after how upset it's making her. How is she willing to drop the subject, just like that? I won't say anything more about it for now, but it doesn't mean I won't speak out if and when the time comes.

Looking at her warily, I sigh. My news seems trivial now, considering the context. "Just that I got the ushering position for the play. I talked to Mr. Walsh today. He's going to let me shadow in the costume shop, too."

For the first time since I've seen her today, Macie gives a weak half-smile, "Scarlett, that's awesome. You're going to be the best usher out there," she says. "And one step closer to your design dreams."

Meanwhile, the unsettling pit grows in my stomach. I may become the best usher after the play, but I don't feel like I'm being the best friend that Macie needs right now.

* * *

I've barely seen Macie since our conversation in the hallway. She's been acting distant lately. Usually, she's an open book—she tells me everything. But since we talked that day, she's hardly spoken to me. I haven't even seen her at her locker, like I normally do. I've sent her a couple of funny memes over text, but rather than responding, she's just given them a thumbs-up or pressed the heart button. It's starting to make me nervous.

I want to check in on her, and since I'm not working my job anymore, I'm thinking it would be a fun idea to surprise her during swim practice. I'm sure she'll appreciate having someone there to cheer her on, and it's been a while since I've come out to support the team.

Once the final bell rings for the day, I sling my backpack over my shoulder and make my way to the pool. As soon as I enter, the strong scent of chlorine hits me. I walk along the tiled surface beside the indoor pool, fanning myself as swimmers slice through the turquoise water. Scanning the lanes, I look for Macie, but I don't see her.

How strange.

I walk up to one of the coaches, who's wearing a white polo and a whistle around his neck. "Excuse me; have you seen Macie Young today?"

The coach looks down at his watch and then nods. "Oh, yeah. Macie called about ten minutes ago. Said she wasn't coming in today."

"Did she say why?"

"No, she didn't mention the reason."

I thank the coach for the information, but my concern grows. It's unlike Macie to skip swim practice. I know how dedicated she is to the team, and when she makes a commitment, she usually keeps it. As I walk away, I pull out my phone and go to the "Find My Friends" app. We've always shared our locations with each other in case of emergencies. When I press Macie's name, her location shows up near the football field. I zoom in to get a closer look. She's not inside the stadium, but she looks like she's near it. There's a hill near the stands where some people go to watch the games from afar. Students like to call it "the viewing hill." Could she be there?

I walk briskly in the direction of the football stadium. As I get closer, I spot someone sitting alone at the top of the hill. I squint to get a better view and recognize the familiar strawberry-blonde hair. It's her.

Macie's sitting in the center, looking out into the distance. She has her knees pulled in toward her chest, with her head resting on her elbows. She seems lost in thought—a girl at the center of an empty landscape—almost like a painting you would see at an art museum.

I raise my hand to capture her attention. "Macie. What are you doing out here all by yourself?" I break out into a light jog, climbing up the hill to reach her.

When she lifts her head in my direction, her expression is indifferent. "Not much. Just doing some thinking."

Her voice is void of its typical cheery emotion.

"What about swim practice?" I ask, the worry growing. "Aren't you supposed to be there right now?"

She shrugs. "I decided to take the day off. We get three days during the season without penalty."

"Oh, okay." Her behavior still feels odd, but I decide not to question it.

"Well then, let me join you, at least." I sit down beside her. "You know, we could go back to my house and watch an eighties movie. Or go to the mall and make fun of people's outfits who are shopping there. Or go to Dotty's and get more mozzarella sticks."

Hopefully, one of those will cheer her up.

"Thanks, Scar. But I think I'll stay here. I just need a little time to myself today."

Surely, she can't mean without me. Macie's never turned down a request to hang out before. I face her straight-on. "Hey, is everything okay? Is this about what happened the other day with Ashton?"

"Don't worry about it," she sighs. "I just was feeling overwhelmed and needed a break."

She continues to stare out at the field in front of us.

"Macie, talk to me." I plead. "You went through something traumatic, and now you're skipping swim practice. I'm just...I'm worried about you, is all. I mean, we're best friends. You can tell me anything."

"You don't have to make it something bigger than it was. Really, I'm fine."

I nod, but I'm not convinced. "Well, maybe I should at least go back and tell your coach that you're okay. You know, just in case he's worried about you, too."

"I'd rather you not."

"It might be for the best. Just to be safe. I want to make sure we're doing the right thing."

"See, this is what I'm talking about," Macie's voice becomes more clipped. "It's not your job to look after me all the time, like the night of the New Year's Eve party. You act like I'm this fragile porcelain doll that could break at any second. Yes, I've gotten drunk before. Yes, I've fooled around with a boy. Yes, I'm skipping a swim practice. I'm a teenager. You treat me like I need to be this pure, innocent person all the time."

I freeze. Her words are a punch to the gut. "You mean like me? That's what you think of me?"

"That's not what I was saying."

I shake my head incredulously. "That's how you feel though?"

Macie grows quiet. We sit in silence as the truth sinks in. "Sometimes, I just need some air to breathe, Scarlett. That's all."

I blink my eyes, still in disbelief that she could feel this way. Macie and I have always had a conflict-free relationship. How can she say she needs space from her own best friend? I want to be the one person she can turn to in her time of need. Not the one she runs away from.

"You're a swimmer," my voice shakes. "I thought breathing underwater is what you do best."

As the words come out, Macie turns her body away, so she's facing the other side of the field. The knot in my stomach twists, and I can tell I've hurt her. This isn't how I imagined our conversation playing out, and this isn't how I want her to feel about our relationship.

"Listen," I try again more gently. "I don't want to suffocate you or anything like that. I'll give you as much space as you need. I just care about you, and I want you to know that you're not alone. When you're ready to talk to someone who would love to be there for you, let me know." I get up and dust myself off. "I'll see you at rehearsals, okay?"

CHAPTER NINE

I take a deep breath and glance back at Macie one more time. She's sitting motionless with her back facing me. With difficulty, I begin making my way down the hill. It's painful for me to walk away when all I want to do is stay. But I remind myself that this isn't about me. It's about her. If time and distance is what she needs, then that's what I'll give her.

Chapter Ten

The theater department is only about a week out from the play, and the cast has been practicing like crazy. I've gotten a couple of glimpses from afar of Nathaniel, Liam, and Tina, but technically, I'm not supposed to interrupt during their practice time.

Macie hasn't reached out to me yet since our conversation. I've checked "Find My Friends" a couple of times, though, just to make sure she's okay. She's been back at swim practices, and she's been showing up for rehearsals, so I'm relieved to see that she's still participating in day-to-day activities. I've been trying not to reach out other than that, but it's hard. I want to text her just to ask her about her day, to share stupid school gossip, or to send her funny videos. My hope is that once the stress of the play is over and everything has settled, we'll talk, and things will return to normal.

In the meantime, I've made arrangements with Mr. Walsh to do our sewing demo. In my email conversation with him, he said that I could come in today, so I'm carrying my sewing machine into the costume shop from my car. When I walk inside, I find the nearest table and set it down with a thud. I check my watch and see that it's right around the time Mr. Walsh said to show up.

"Scarlett, there you are." He waltzes into the costume shop right on cue and comes toward me. "Nice sewing machine you got there. Is that the Singer Heavy Duty 4423? She's a beauty."

I'm impressed by Mr. Walsh's apparent sewing machine knowledge. I didn't realize that this model was so distinguishable.

"Creating costumes can be difficult even for the most advanced sewers, but it seems like you've got the interest and enthusiasm it takes." Mr. Walsh comes closer to the machine. "Isn't it amazing how a simple costume can transport you into a different world? It can take you to a different time period. Transform you into a whole new person. I think the world of costume design is just fascinating."

I love that we share a mutual interest in clothing design. "I couldn't agree more."

"We'll start off with the basics," he says. "We can go over the terminology, the supplies, and then do a basic tutorial."

"I'm so ready. Let's do it."

"All right. First, we'll plug the cord into the machine. Let's power this baby up."

I grin at his enthusiasm. He seems like the perfect mentor to have for this type of lesson. I do as Mr. Walsh says and plug the machine in.

"Great. Next, we're going to slide our needle into the top of the machine and screw it into place. You're going to want to grab an empty bobbin, wrap thread around it, and step your foot on the pedal to thread the machine." Mr. Walsh sits down on the stool and demonstrates for me.

I'll admit, it kind of sounds like he's speaking a foreign language, but it helps to have him point out the parts of the machine, so I can understand what he's talking about.

He motions to the table next to me. "If you're serious about learning, you may want to invest in some other supplies, too. Fabric scissors, a rotary cutter, a mat for fabric, a tape measure, a seam ripper. Helps for cutting and measuring fabric."

I grab a sticky note and begin jotting down his instructions. I'll have to go to a fabric shop and get those.

"All right, now comes the fun part. You're going to thread your needle, place your fabric, switch the stub, and then gently press on the foot pedal. You'll want to sew down to the corner, then raise the foot and turn the fabric to continue your stitch." He gestures at his expertly crafted cross-stitch. "See. Easy, right?"

I laugh, even though I'm feeling slightly overwhelmed. They say practice makes perfect, though, and I'm determined to succeed. Mr. Walsh gets up from his spot, and I sit down in his place. Ever so carefully, I press down on the foot pedal and hold the fabric in place, moving gradually in a straight line. Once I reach the corner, I raise my foot off the pedal and turn the fabric like Mr. Walsh instructed. The stitch is a little jagged, but it doesn't look half bad, if I do say so myself.

"Look at you," Mr. Walsh commends. "Bravo."

I grin. "I think I'll need some more practice before I try creating any outfits, but it's a step in the right direction."

Mr. Walsh is about to respond when his phone buzzes. He looks down to check the notification. "Listen, Scarlett, I need to get back up there for a meeting with the lighting and tech team. Looks like you're off to a great start. You have everything you need for ushering?"

I nod. Mr. Walsh had sent me an email detailing the time I would need to arrive at the theater and other instructions related to ushering. I feel confident about my responsibilities, and I'm excited to see what the class has put together for the performance. "Yup, I should be all set."

"Wonderful. You're welcome to keep practicing here, and just holler if you have any more questions. Also, feel free to come in at any point this week if you want to continue your work or observe others."

"I will. Thanks so much," I say as Mr. Walsh exits the room.

I decide to continue with another piece of fabric I brought from home. As Mr. Walsh mentioned, the more practice, the better. Soon,

I'll be able to tackle even bigger projects, like a wrap scarf or a tote bag. The thought excites me. With determination, I sew a couple of inches in the reverse direction to finish out the seam. Then I continue sewing parallel to the edge of the fabric.

I'm getting into the zone when I hear someone entering the room. I assume it's Mr. Walsh coming back to check on me. But when I look up, I notice Nathaniel is watching me from afar. I stop pressing on the foot pedal.

"Hey, you. What are you working on?" He walks over to me.

"Just practicing my sewing technique. Mr. Walsh was giving me some pointers." I sigh. "I still have a long way to go, though."

Nathaniel comes over and pulls out a stool. "Teach me." He looks at me intently. I imagine he's joking at first, but when he continues to stare, I realize he's serious.

"I thought you didn't like fashion or clothing design," I joke.

"Well, I know you like those things. I like learning more about the things that you like."

I couldn't be more excited that Nathaniel is curious about something that I'm so passionate about. "Okay, come here then."

He pulls his stool closer. Our knees touch, and I'm not mad about it. He looks at me expectantly, with a hand placed underneath his chin, waiting for me to begin.

I put my hand on the piece of fabric, but it's hard to concentrate. I'm afraid my stitch is going to come out zigzagging like a heart monitor strip, considering the way he's looking at me. I take a breath to compose myself and get the fabric ready. Then I turn to face him. "So, what we're going to do is press the foot pedal. It's kind of like a gas pedal. The harder you press on it, the faster you go."

His eyes light up. "Well then, let's pedal to the metal."

"We're not actually driving a car." I smirk. "We just need to steer the fabric in a straight line and guide it over the curves. You'll want to make sure not to force the material while it's going under the needle so the fabric doesn't stretch too thin or bunch up."

I press my palm down firmly on the fabric and begin moving it away from me. I'll demonstrate and then give Nathaniel a chance to try it out.

My attention is focused on the needle moving up and down as I push the material forward. I'm about to make sure he's following along when suddenly, my hand freezes. I feel Nathaniel rest his hand gently on top of mine, like a warm glove being stretched over my fingers. As I move the fabric forward, our hands move in unison, and the machine guides the fabric in a straight line. Any more of this, and I'm afraid I might puncture both of our hands under the needle. As we reach the corner, I take my foot off of the pedal to stop the machine. His hand is still pressed against mine. Neither one of us moves.

"How did I do, Scarlett?" Nathaniel breaks the silence.

I clear my throat. "Could use a little work, but thankfully, I think I can help you with your technique."

"You're a good teacher." He grins as he removes his hand from mine. The second he does, I wish he would keep it there. "Thank you for the tutorial."

"My pleasure," I respond.

He stands back up and pushes the stool in. "I should get back to rehearsal before they come looking for me. But I just wanted to check in and see what you were up to."

I nod as he begins to walk away. Just before he makes it out the door, he turns back to me. "Scarlett, I'm really glad you're going to be here for the play."

His words ring through my ears.

"Me too, Nathaniel." Little does he know just how much I mean it.

* * *

I came into the shop again today to work on my basic stitches. I've loved getting more exposure and observing other students in their element working on costumes, even if I haven't been able to help out with the costumes directly. It's fascinating to see the assortment of color palettes, silhouettes, and styles from other performances—and how the students are able to transform everyday swatches and bring them to life. The more time I spend here, the more I don't want to leave.

I've packed up my sewing machine for the day, and now I'm working on a new sketch. It's been a while since I've focused on my designs, but just being in this environment has helped to spark my creativity.

I put my colored pencil to paper to begin. Usually, I start by sketching out a croquis—the model-shaped figure to display my illustration on. From there, I'll go in and add the actual outfit, whether a dress, a top, or a skirt. Then I'll build out the additional details, like ruffles or buttons. The best part of the process is that I often don't know what I'm going to draw until I'm in the midst of sketching. The vision will come to me, and my fingers will work to catch up.

"Look at your cute little doodles." Someone speaks from behind. When I turn, I'm surprised to see Tina eyeing me curiously. She comes over to where I'm sitting, holding one of her costumes. "I didn't realize we were back in kindergarten."

"Funny." I try to keep my voice level.

"It's really nice of Mr. Walsh to let you work backstage in the costume shop like this. You know, since some people don't have what it takes to actually be in the play. He likes to make the crew still feel like a valuable part of the team."

"Actually," I correct her, "I was the one who reached out to him. I'm more interested in learning how to sew than performing. And as hard as it is to believe, not everyone craves the spotlight as much as you do, Tina."

"Oh, so that's what you tell yourself," Tina snickers. "That's adorable of you, though. You're like a wannabe Cinderella with your scraps. I mean your pieces of fabric."

At this point, Tina's just provoking me, and she knows it. The last thing I want is to be a doormat that she can walk over whenever she pleases. It's time to stand my ground.

"Okay, Tina. I know you're in one of the lead roles, but that doesn't give you the authority to go around treating people like they're below you. You never know. One day, I might be the one designing the clothing you wear."

Tina feigns alarm with her hand. "Oh no, I've poked the bear."

I grit my teeth. This conversation is not going anywhere. "Anything else you came here to tell me?"

"Nope," she grins. "Just that I'm looking forward to having you here for the play. So, you can watch Nathaniel and me be together on stage."

I've never wanted to shake someone so badly. Instead, I force a tight smile. "Looking forward to it. Since the stage is the only place it's ever going to happen."

She narrows her eyes. "We'll see about that." Then, she slings her costume over her shoulder and stomps out of the room as quickly as she came in.

There's no getting through to a girl like Tina. I just feel bad that Nathaniel has to endure practicing with her every day. Checking my phone, I realize it's getting late. I should probably head out, so I can make it home for dinner in time. I pack up my bag with my machine, sketches, and fabrics, and then I make my way into the hallway. A couple of theater students are filing out from practice, too. I go to brush past them when I see Macie's ringlets of curly hair out of the corner of my eye. She's looking down at a sheet of paper, which I'm assuming is her script for the play. I quicken my pace, so I can catch up to her.

"Macie!" I call out. "Hey."

She looks up from her sheet.

"How have you been? Getting nervous for the big day?" All I want is for her to talk to me like normal again.

"A little. How are you?" I notice her answer is polite but curt.

It feels strange to skirt around someone so cautiously who you're supposed to be best friends with. I don't understand why there needs to be this tension between us.

"Good. I've been learning a lot from Mr. Walsh about sewing. One step closer to becoming the next Vera Wang." I echo her words from before Winter Break. "What are you up to now? Are you heading home?"

The idea pops into my head to invite her over for dinner tonight. How could she say "no" to my mom and dad's cooking?

"Um, I'm not sure," she responds. "I think some people from the swim team are going out to get food tonight. I should probably leave soon to meet up with them."

"Oh. Gotcha." I can't help but notice she doesn't extend the invitation to me. Usually, she wouldn't hesitate to bring me along. It hurts that she's shutting me out, and there seems to be nothing I can do about it. I try to keep my tone optimistic. "Well, I'm excited to see you in the performance. Break a leg."

"Thanks, Scarlett. I appreciate it. I'll see you at the play, okay?"

I nod my head.

What I really want to say is: *I miss you. I'm here for you. Let me in.*

But instead, I keep my mouth clamped shut, and I watch her walk away. For now, I have to remind myself that this is enough.

With a heavy heart, I go to pull out my car keys when I feel a vibration in my pocket. I pull out my phone and see my mom's name on the screen, so I answer.

"Hey, hon. Are you on your way home for dinner? We finished

cooking early tonight."

"Yup, just finished up in the costume shop," I say. It occurs to me that I'll be flying solo for dinner with my mom and dad tonight after all.

"We're so excited to come to the opening night. How wonderful is it that Mr. Walsh is helping you learn how to sew? Seems like theater is having a positive impact on you."

I smile weakly. "Yup, just like you and dad wanted for me. It's been a win-win."

"Okay, well, hurry home. We want to hear all about what you've been learning."

"See you soon." I end the call and make my way toward my car. As I open the door, I let out a deep breath. I just hope that there's no more drama this week besides the kind happening onstage.

Chapter Eleven

The first night of the play has arrived, and I'm looking forward to seeing Mr. Walsh's vision come together. Now that I'm an usher, I have permission to wait around the theater before the audience gets here. I'm stationed out near the back entrance, hoping to catch a glimpse of the cast before the performance begins. I poke my head in to see if I can spot anyone, particularly Nathaniel or Macie. At first, I can't find either of them in the group. But then my eyes land on Nathaniel. To my chagrin, I see that Tina is following along closely by his side.

"Nathaniel." She bats her eyes flirtatiously at him. "I just wanted to let you know that I sure hope you break a leg out there tonight."

"Oh, thanks, Tina. You too." Nathaniel says indifferently.

"Speaking of things breaking, I have to take my car in tomorrow. The radiator is leaking." She shrugs. "Do you think you might be able to help a girl out and give me a ride back home tomorrow night?"

He scratches his head. "Uh, sure, I think that should be fine."

Tina claps. "Ah, thank you so much. I just don't know what I would have done otherwise."

Take an Uber. Ask a friend. Walk.

Sighing, I walk away from the back entrance. That girl would do just about anything for attention, especially when it comes to Nathaniel. I've listened to as much as I can handle for now.

With a deep breath, I take up my post at the double doors of the theater. It's just about time to assume my ushering responsibilities, and I'm excited to greet everyone coming to watch the play. As the minutes pass, I spot early attendees filtering into the foyer. One by one, they make their way to where I'm standing. With a smile, I greet each person, hand over a theater program, and guide them in the direction of their seats.

I continue passing out programs until I spot my parents. They wave as they approach me.

"Honey, look at you!" My mom claps. "Our very own usher. We're so proud."

I laugh. "Mom, I'm just handing out programs to people. It's not rocket science."

"Still, you're doing a fantastic job. Let me get a picture." She scoots back with her camera.

I groan, but I hold up my stack of programs to humor her. Once she captures the shot, she nods in confirmation. "Perfect. We'll see you later."

They enter the theater just as the lights in the lobby dim, signaling that the play is about to begin. Glancing left and right, I search for any stragglers. Then I open the door and step inside to watch the play. As I make my way into the darkness, I spot a seat near the aisle a few rows down. The air is abuzz with chatter as I take my seat. Finally, as the curtain rises, conversation around me ceases.

When I look at the stage, I see the set is bare—no props, except for two wooden chairs placed in the center. The costumes are modest and traditional, reflecting the historical tone of the narrative. The actors wear a mix of knit skirts, wool hats, and plaid fabrics—representative of New England small-town life. From the left side, footsteps echo across the floor as Liam makes his way to the front of the stage. He greets the audience and sets the scene by explaining the history of the town. It's then that Nathaniel strolls on stage as George Gibbs, accompanied by Tina who's playing Emily Webb.

As I watch the play unfold, I become more swept up in the plot, seeing the cast bring the story to life. The characters, George and Emily, announce their decision to wed in the second act. Nathaniel and Tina speak about plans for the future and make preparations for the big day. To distract myself from my envy of their onstage chemistry, I concentrate on watching Macie as one of the townswomen. She doesn't have many speaking lines, but I'm still proud of her for acting convincingly, considering this class is an elective and not a career path.

By the time the third act rolls around, nine years have passed, and the townspeople are gathered around a nearby cemetery. It becomes evident that a number of town members have passed away. My jaw drops as I realize that Emily is one of them, having died in childbirth. Tina may have mentioned playing the romantic lead with Nathaniel, but she sure omitted the part about her character's "passing."

Devastated, George kneels at Emily's grave, mourning the loss of his young wife. As the townspeople disperse, Emily reappears as a ghost. She questions whether anyone fully understands the value of life while living it. Finally, Liam returns to the stage and wishes the audience a good night, concluding the performance.

As the curtain descends, the audience sits in silence. When the curtain rises again on the now-fully-alive cast, the theater breaks into a resounding round of applause. I follow suit, cheering for my friends as they bow and motion to Mr. Walsh. After bowing one final time, the cast filters off of the stage, and audience members shuffle out of their seats toward the exit doors.

I make my way down the rows one by one, picking up discarded programs. I'm about to pick up a stray water bottle on the ground when I hear a sound from the right wing of the stage. I glance over and notice Nathaniel is standing next to the curtain, rummaging for something behind the stage. He grabs his coat from a table near the wall and slings it over his shoulder.

Meanwhile, I grab hold of the railing and climb up onto the stage.

"That was some performance there." My voice reverberates through the theater.

He whips his head around, startled to find someone in the audience. His expression transforms to one of amusement as his eyes lock with mine.

"You give me too much credit," he says. "It was Thornton Wilder's play. I just helped it come to life."

"Between you and the playwright," I respond, "I'm kind of starting to like the last name Wilder."

Wow. I think a second too late. *Did I really just say that out loud?*

Wincing, I prepare for Nathaniel to turn away from me and leave. What I don't expect is for him to take a step closer.

He joins me in the center of the stage. "And I'm kind of starting to like the fact that you'll still be here tomorrow and Saturday, too." He leans in closer. "Speaking of tomorrow, I was hoping maybe we could meet up after the performance."

My stomach drops.

After the performance? What does that mean?

I don't even need to think about it. I nod before my brain has time to catch up. "Yeah," I stammer. "I mean, for sure."

"Great," Nathaniel flashes a glowing smile. "Let's plan to meet by the stairwell tomorrow—say around fifteen minutes after the show ends?" He motions to the side door connected to the theater entrance.

"Okay," I manage. "Side stairwell. Tomorrow after the show."

"I have to get going," he says. "I should get back to the backstage classroom now. We're supposed to listen to Mr. Walsh's critiques of the performance. See you tomorrow night, though?"

"Yes," I nod, "I'll be there."

He smiles one more time before walking off the stage. I hear his footsteps fade into the distance as he opens the door and disappears behind it. Once he's out of sight, I let out a deep breath I hadn't realized I'd been holding in.

What is this life?

* * *

The next night, here I am, pacing back and forth in the stairwell we'd agreed upon. I check the time on my phone again. Just about fifteen minutes have passed since the end of the performance. He should be here any second.

To say that I've been anticipating this all day would be an understatement. In fact, this moment is all I've been able to think about for the past twenty-four hours. Mrs. Walton had to repeat my name twice today during Modern Euro when she called on me, just because I had been so distracted.

With my nerves running wild, I force myself to sit down on the stairwell. I take a deep breath and tuck my hands into my lap to prevent my nervous fidgeting. Time feels like it's ticking by at a snail's pace.

I listen for the sound of a door opening or footsteps approaching, but I hear nothing. For some reason, all of my senses feel amplified right now. Even the softest noise makes me want to jump in my spot.

After what feels like an eternity, I check the time again.

It's now ten minutes past our planned meeting time.

Could he be running late?

Did he forget?

Am I facing the worst-case scenario, and he's standing me up?

The doubts begin to creep into my mind. Pushing myself up, I decide I should check to see what's going on. I grab the railing and climb the stairs two at a time to get to the top.

Reaching for the handle, I go to open the door. Instead, I'm caught off-guard when the door swings forward by itself, causing me to lurch back in my spot. When I glance in that direction again, I'm met with a familiar set of blue eyes. Standing in the doorframe, clutching the handle, is Nathaniel.

He rakes a hand through his hair. "I'm sorry I kept you waiting. Mr. Walsh's notes ran a bit longer than expected."

My body fills with relief. He's here, after all. "I know those things tend to run over."

"Want to sit down with me?" He motions to the ground. "I've been standing for the past two hours, and my legs are about to cave."

I laugh. "Yes, let's sit."

Releasing an exaggerated sigh, he bends his knees and drops down onto the first stair. "Ah, that's much better."

I follow his lead, lowering myself down next to him until our bodies are practically touching. We turn to face each other, and I realize just how close we're sitting.

Bless this stairwell and its narrow architecture.

"Thanks for meeting me here," Nathaniel says softly. He motions in the direction of the door. "It can get overwhelming out there sometimes. With all of the people and noise and commotion. It's nice to, you know, have a place to escape."

I look at him doubtfully. "Really? Someone like you needs a place to escape?" I let out a mocking laugh. "I'm sure it's just exhausting being the star of the show—having all those people cheering for you."

"You wouldn't think so," he grins, "but the pressure can actually be a lot up there with people watching your every move. Especially right now for me."

It's hard to believe that such a natural performer could become overwhelmed by the pressure. I guess I've always assumed that his confidence was unwavering.

"You said the pressure is a lot right now for you. Why, especially now?"

"Well," he fiddles with his hands in his lap, "I've been waiting to hear back from my dream school. It's been hard to think about much else this month."

College.

My chest tightens at the thought of Nathaniel leaving me behind once he goes off to school in the fall. I look away from him, hiding the disappointment on my face.

"So, what's your dream school?" I ask.

He turns until he's directly facing me. "NYU. Well, the Tisch School of the Arts, to be more specific. I can't imagine a better place to study acting. My goal is to get a BFA in Drama."

I can't help but think about how my dream school is FIT, which is also based in New York City. There's no better place than the Big Apple, and the thought of us both studying there one day gives me hope.

"Wow, it sounds like you have your career all figured out, don't you?"

He chuckles dryly. "Well, if things fall into place. As much as I'd like to wish, I also have to be realistic with myself."

"Realistic with yourself?"

He sighs, "Scarlett, the chances of me getting into a school like that are slim to none. I want to be optimistic, but it's better that I keep my options open."

"Nathaniel," I say slowly, "if anyone can get into that school, it's you. They'd be crazy not to admit you. I mean, did you see yourself up there tonight?"

I reach for his hand to give it a reassuring squeeze. I can't believe he could ever doubt his greatest talent. Once my fingers interlace with his, I prepare to pull away, but Nathaniel squeezes even tighter. There's a pulsing electricity between the two of us. It reminds me of the other day when we were sewing. I can tell Nathaniel feels it, too, because his eyes remained fixed on our interlocked hands.

My heart beats faster in my chest. I sit immobile, afraid to move and afraid not to. Afraid to do anything that could ruin this deciding moment.

"You know how I told you before when we were playing foosball," Nathaniel's voice is soft, "that I could read body language?"

He can never know how many times I've replayed the New Year's Eve party in my head. I nod.

His fingers move farther up my arm. "Do you think you might be able to read mine, too?"

I feel as if I might explode. I know where this is going, but I won't be the first to say it. Instead, I shake my head slowly.

A hint of a smile appears on his face as he moves his hand to my cheek. The side of my face goes numb at his touch. "How about now?" he teases.

I purse my lips together to hide the grin forming on my face. I shake my head, playing into his game.

"Tell me," I whisper.

Tilting his head to one side, Nathaniel leans in closer to me until his face is only inches from mine. "How about you let me show you."

With those words, I suddenly become incapable of breathing. I have to remind myself to inhale.

Ever so carefully, Nathaniel hooks his fingers around the nape of my neck and gently pulls my face toward his. His eyes meet mine, searching for consensus.

For once, I don't hesitate or shy away. I'm not letting distractions get in the way this time. The anticipation builds as we both linger on the cusp for a moment longer. We've reached the precipice; it's time to jump over the edge. I lean into him, ready to close the distance between us.

Our lips touch for the first time.

And I.

Die.

I swear, I have been whisked off of the ground and transported to another world. In school, they warn you about the dangers of substance abuse, like cocaine or heroin. But holy hell. They never warned me about the addictive properties of a kiss. Nathaniel's is a drug. And I am hooked.

When we pull away for breath, my eyelids flutter open, and I'm left reeling. We're both breathing slowly, unable to look away from each other. Before I know what's happening, my body moves into autopilot. I move for him at the same time that he reaches for me. Pulling him to me, I wrap my arms around the base of his neck and press my lips to his. He responds by bringing his hands to my waist as he draws me even closer to him.

When I hear the sound of a door opening, a chill ripples through me. I feel Nathaniel freeze at the same time I do. Breaking away simultaneously, we whirl our heads around in the direction of the noise. At my level of vision, there are two feet in the doorway. In slow motion, my eyes travel upward, from legs, to waist, to neck, to head. Until I am looking into the cold, hardened eyes of Tina.

"Tina?" Nathaniel manages hoarsely. "What are you doing here?"

She snickers, but her face is void of emotion. "Looking for you, as a matter of fact." She bats her eyes. "Don't you remember? You're driving me home tonight."

As I turn back to Nathaniel, I watch the realization register on his face. He sighs heavily and places a hand on the railing. "Shoot. You told me your car was in the shop. I wasn't even thinking."

"No biggie, Nate." She chuckles a little too cheerily. "I'm just glad I found you."

Nate? Did she really have to call him that? And is her car even in a shop?

Nathaniel lets out a deep breath, "I'll be right there, Tina. If you could just give me a minute to—"

"Oh, sure thing." She cuts him off with an artificially bubbly voice. "I hope I wasn't interrupting anything."

We wait for her to close the door, but she doesn't.

Nathaniel clears his throat uncomfortably, "Alone, please?"

"Fine." Her eyes narrow. "Find me when you're ready."

We both watch as she turns and then loudly shuts the door behind us. I flinch as the door closes with a thud. The sound echoes against the walls.

A few seconds of silence pass before Nathaniel tips his head back and groans, "Nothing like an interruption from Tina."

It's a relief to think that maybe, just maybe, he finds her as unbearable as I do.

Slowly, Nathaniel pushes himself up from the stairwell and reaches for my hand. I place mine in his, allowing him to pull me to his level. Once we're upright, I turn to face him. We both stand next to the stairs, frozen in place.

What happens now?

Nathaniel shakes me from my haze, "I should probably get going." His voice is low, with a hint of reluctance.

I smile weakly, casting my eyes away from him. "I understand."

Folding my arms together, I create a shield for my body. For some reason, I feel too exposed now, like Nathaniel can see directly through me.

Seeming to notice my change in posture, Nathaniel takes a step closer. He extends his hand and touches his fingers to my cheek. Once again, I find that my supply of oxygen has been cut off.

"I'll see you tomorrow," he whispers, "for the last performance."

I tilt my face into his touch. "I'll be here."

Before I know it, he leans in and kisses me again, cradling my face in his hands. When he lets go, my head is spinning.

Trying to maintain a sense of composure, I clear my throat. "Goodnight, Nathaniel."

He flashes his boyish grin. "Goodnight, Scarlett."

The next thing I know, Nathaniel turns around and slides through the door, disappearing out of sight.

Once the door shuts completely, I lower myself back down on the stairs and attempt to catch my breath. I can still feel the fireworks booming in my chest. In the span of one night, my world has shifted from black and white to Technicolor, and I'm more alive than I've ever been before.

My biggest fear now is simply taking the leap. I'm afraid if I let my heart fall further, there's a chance Nathaniel could split it in two.

I'm ready to go all in. I just hope that falling is worth the risk.

Chapter Twelve

Two hands cover my eyes, obstructing my vision. Before I can speak, a smooth voice whispers in my ear, "Guess who…."

With those two words, everything in my body freezes. If this is my kidnapper, then call me a willing victim.

"Your voice sure sounds familiar," I murmur.

"I would hope so," he says. "Maybe this will trigger your memory."

The not-so-mysterious figure releases me and spins me around, pressing his lips to mine in one swift motion. As we break away from the kiss, my head falls back against the wall behind me.

I attempt to remain calm, but I feel like a fish out of water. I never believed this could be happening to me, Scarlett Clarke.

"I hope I'm not distracting you from ushering."

"I could use a little distraction," I respond, "and you're a pretty good type of distraction."

"Well, in that case," he tucks a strand of my hair behind my ear, "I'm happy to oblige."

Right now, Nathaniel and I are standing in a corridor behind the theater. It's hard to believe that tonight is the final performance of *Our Town*. To kill time before ushering, I'd been admiring a bulletin board of past theater production pictures. Nathaniel must have seen me passing by their classroom and come up to surprise me.

"So tonight, after the show ends, I was thinking," Nathaniel shakes me from my thoughts, "you and I could go out for milkshakes to celebrate? Chocolate ones, of course."

I beam at him.

"Hm, let me think about it. I'm going to go with: Yes."

Nathaniel grins back at me, "It's a date, then."

I try to prevent myself from smiling too widely. I can barely contain my excitement.

Before he can object, I stealthily duck under his arm and sidestep away from him. Once I'm free, I turn in the direction of the main entrance, glancing over my shoulder one more time.

"Promise me that you'll look for me in the audience tonight."

When I turn back around, I hear his voice from behind.

"You know I will."

* * *

Until now, I didn't know time travel was possible. Yet here I am in the theater, watching Nathaniel's performance again as if it were the first time. He commands the stage, captivating the audience with his words.

As the cast takes their final bow, Nathaniel scans the crowd until his eyes find mine. Despite the distracting cheers from the audience, his gaze remains on me and nothing else. Months ago, when he had spotted me in the audience during his monologue, I had assumed Nathaniel was searching for a different person. This time, I know that I'm the one he's looking for.

When the curtain call ends, the cast members exit the stage for the last time, and the curtain falls. Getting up from my seat, I watch as people begin to leave the theater. I scan the aisles one more time and then head in the direction of the lobby.

Friends and family of the cast are dispersed throughout the room, congratulating the theater students. I decide to head back in the direction of the dressing rooms and look for Macie. It's been too long since we've talked, and I want to congratulate her. Now that the stress of the play is over, hopefully, she'll be ready to open up to me, and we'll finally be able to get back to normal.

As I approach her dressing room, the door is slightly ajar.

I halt when I hear voices. In my line of sight, standing across from Macie with his arms crossed, is Ashton. I want to barrel into the room and interrupt, but my sensible side wins out. Instead, I round the corner of the hallway until I'm obstructed from view.

While I feel guilty for eavesdropping, I also want to be at the ready in case Macie needs me. After all, Ashton's not even in the production. Did he come here just to talk to her? Why is he here in the first place?

I continue to listen as the voices become more distinct.

"Ashton, I still don't understand what you're doing here," Macie speaks in a hushed tone. "I thought we had an agreement."

"Well, I also thought we had an agreement that you'd keep your mouth shut, but you had no trouble breaking that one."

"I promised you I wouldn't. I didn't say anything, if that's what you're thinking."

"Really? Because this note appeared in my locker the other day." The edge in his voice is unmistakable.

My heart pounds at his accusatory words. I can't believe Ashton would keep targeting Macie like this.

I hear him uncrumple a loose leaf of paper. The room goes silent as Macie reads it and gasps. "Who wrote this?"

"Don't act surprised. I know you had something to do with it."

"Ashton," Macie speaks slowly, "I swear. I have no idea where this note came from. I never said anything."

"I don't think you understand." His voice sounds crazed—almost manic. "My swim scholarship is everything to me. If someone reports me, I'm done."

"Ashton, calm down," Macie whispers, as if she's a mother trying to pacify an upset child. "Everything's okay. You're just overreacting."

"You'd better hope so. If they try to take this away from me, someone's going to pay."

I almost miss footsteps approaching from the other end of the hallway. Thankfully, I'm still obstructed from view. The dressing room door opens with a swoosh, and I hear Nathaniel interrupt the conversation.

"Ashton, what's going on here?"

"Back off, Wilder," Ashton scoffs. "This isn't your place."

"I don't like the idea of you threatening one of my friends," Nathaniel says. "I think it'd be wise of you to leave before you do something you regret, Ashton."

"What's happening, Nathaniel?"

I'm caught off-guard as another familiar voice becomes discernible. I realize the high-pitched chirp must be Tina's. I swear—the girl deserves to win an award for being in the wrong place at the right time.

"Tina, this isn't the time," Nathaniel warns.

"Both of you," Ashton raises his voice, "leave the two of us alone. Macie and I need to talk in private."

"Ashton, stop," Macie continues.

"Fine. If they're not going to leave, just admit it, Macie. Admit what you did."

"I didn't do anything, Ashton."

I can't listen to this any longer. I need to act, and I need to act quickly.

"That's a load of bull, Macie. If you're not going to tell the truth, then how about I tell you the truth? You were asking for it that night. You're such an effing tease."

My vision becomes tinged with red. I feel the steam within me building as if I'm about to explode.

131

I round the corner and barge into the dressing room. The group turns toward me in surprise, but my tunnel vision is focused on Ashton, and Ashton alone. With brutal force, I grab Ashton's shoulders and knee him hard between the legs.

As if in slow motion, Ashton hunches over, releasing a desperate huff of air. His face contorts in agony as he wilts in pain. His hands cover his crotch as he doubles over.

"You better savor that feeling," I speak slowly, barely recognizing the fury in my own voice, "because it's the most action you're ever going to get down there."

My hand unclenches, and I point a shaky finger at him.

"You deserve every punishment you get after what you almost did to Macie." I stop to collect my breath. "And I hope that you do lose your scholarship."

I keep my eyes trained on Ashton, who is still hunched over in pain. "C'mon, Macie. Let's hope I left permanent damage."

With that, I turn around to face Macie, who's rooted in her spot, blinking at me with wide eyes. I don't wait for a response. I don't even glance back to see the reactions from Nathaniel or Tina. I simply link arms with Macie and pull her toward the exit.

Leading her to the lobby, I want to get as far away from the dressing room as possible. We round the corner and find a pocket of empty space. Finally, I let go of her hand and look down at the ground, absorbing the impact of the last few minutes. The adrenaline is still coursing through my body, like I'm a balloon over-pumped with helium. I'm desperate to let the air out, or I am going to burst.

Inhale. Hold. Exhale.

I repeat the meditation to myself as I release deep breaths, allowing myself to cool down. My chest deflates, and I can feel the air circulating once again. Finally, I lift my head up to Macie, ready to explain myself. My eyes meet hers, but my heart stops. She's standing still as a statue, with an expression that's void of any emotion at all. It's as if a switch has been turned off, causing the life within it to be extinguished, too.

Where is my best friend?

I open my mouth and speak carefully. "Macie?"

No response.

She doesn't move a muscle. It's as if I'm invisible to her, like I'm a hologram that she's gazing straight through.

"It was you," she mumbles, looking at me like she's never seen me before.

"Me?" I ask. "I mean, I know it was *me* who kicked him in the crotch. But you know he deserved it. What else was I supposed to do? Just stand there?"

She takes a step back, as if I'm a contagious disease that could infect her, "That's not what I meant."

"What are you talking about then, Macie? You're starting to scare me."

She shakes her head. "I trusted you. You promised me you wouldn't tell anyone about that night, but you must have."

The lightbulb finally goes off. I realize what she's referring to.

"I didn't—what makes you think I would do that?"

"You're the one," her voice grows louder, "who kept pushing me to say something."

"Macie, you have to believe me. What Ashton did was awful. But it wasn't me."

"I want to, Scarlett." She drops a crumpled piece of paper into my hand. "But I can't."

I feel like I've just received a direct punch to the gut. With shaky fingers, I unfold it and read the words scribbled hastily across the page.

I know what you did to Macie. Next time, there will be consequences.

My mind goes blank as I flounder for answers. This must be the note that Ashton had handed to Macie in the dressing room. The one that he had found in his locker. The reason he had confronted her just now. *Who wrote this?*

"I just didn't think my best friend would go behind my back like that." Macie shakes her head. When she looks down, her phone lights up with a message. "My ride's here," Macie says, turning abruptly and walking away in the direction of the car. I listen as her footsteps fade into the distance, until I can no longer hear them anymore. Macie disappears out of sight, leaving me alone in the corner, dumbfounded.

How could our relationship spiral out of control like this? Up until these past few weeks, our friendship had been the one source of solace that I could depend on at all costs. Yet now, our solid foundation feels shaken.

I suck in another deep breath and remind myself to keep breathing.

Everything's going to be okay, I reason. It's been an eventful night, to say the least, and I'm sure she craves space. By Monday morning, she'll realize I would never do anything to hurt her intentionally. We'll make up and go on the same way we have for all these years.

Yes, I repeat. *Everything's going to be okay.*

Speaking of okay, my mind returns to Nathaniel. My next priority is to check in on him, especially after his heated confrontation with Ashton. I head back toward the dressing room, hoping to find comfort in the one thing going right in my life right now.

Just as I round the corner, I stop in my tracks. Tina is making her way in my direction.

Prepared to excuse myself, I open my mouth to speak. But she puts a cautionary hand in the air before I have the chance.

"Who knew Scarlett Clarke had such an aggressive side? I'm not sure Nathaniel's safe around you anymore," she snickers.

What a bee-otch. She doesn't know about what happened to Macie that night. If she did, she wouldn't be saying something so callous.

"If you'll excuse me," I go to brush past her, "I need to talk to Nathaniel."

Tina turns away with a wave of her hand, "I hope you tell him 'hi' for me."

Whatever games she's playing, I'm far from in the mood. I shake myself out of my funk and prepare to face Nathaniel. After all, I agreed to go out with him tonight after the show, and I want to at least try to focus on enjoying our date instead of my own unrest right now.

Once I've collected myself, I turn the door knob and slip inside the room. When I spot Nathaniel in the corner by himself, my body relaxes. He's sitting at a dressing table, lost in thought, with his back toward me. I walk forward, and his eyes dart up to meet mine through the mirror's reflection. Keeping my eyes fixed on his, I make my way across the room. When I finally reach him, I gently wrap my arms around him from behind and rest my chin on his shoulder.

"What a night." I sigh, squeezing my eyes shut and leaning against him. "Ready for those milkshakes? I feel like we could both use them right now."

I look at Nathaniel in the mirror.

"Scarlett."

There's a hint of resignation in his tone that sends a ripple down my spine.

"What's wrong?" I attempt to suppress the unsteady waver of my voice. I've already had one person I care about turn on me tonight. I don't think I can handle another.

"It's been a long day." I feel his body grow tense. "And it's getting late."

We're still physically touching, but mentally, he feels light-years away. His mind seems consumed by something he's not telling me.

"I promise there's nothing a milkshake can't fix."

"I think," he shakes his head slightly, "that we should just call it a night."

"Oh." I try not to show my disappointment. I'm not sure what's causing his sudden shift in spirits, but it feels as if he's purposefully avoiding me.

Slowly, I pull my arms away from him. "You sure everything's okay? Want to talk about it?"

Today's been a whirlwind—that's for sure—but he has to know that he can confide in me.

Nathaniel tears his gaze away from mine in the vanity mirror, unable to look me directly in the eyes.

"Yup, everything's okay."

I wait for him to elaborate, but he doesn't.

That's it.

That's all he gives me. He doesn't try to explain further or reassure me. He just sits motionless, not even wasting the energy to turn around and face me.

"Okay then," I stutter, disconcerted.

What do you say to someone who won't throw you a line? I'm about to probe further, but I decide against it. My brain is a mixture of confusion and hurt at the same time, so I fight to maintain my composure.

"Look. I understand," I reassure him. "You're tired. You just finished up your last performance. It's been a crazy couple of hours. You should go home and get some rest. We can talk on Monday."

He nods, but doesn't say anything else. I take the opportunity to lean in and plant a quick peck on his cheek. At least the gesture will let him know that I'm here for him. My lips brush against his face, but as they do, I'm met with an unexpected reaction. Nathaniel flinches—as if he doesn't even recognize me. A lump rises in my throat, and I get a bitter taste in my mouth. I can feel my heart sinking so low in my chest that it might hit the bottom. I back away, speechless.

A thick silence fills the air. Nathaniel remains stationary at the dressing table with his head cast down. I don't wait for a reaction, and I don't look back. Instead, I slip through the door, hoping he doesn't get a glimpse of the tear rolling down my cheek.

Chapter Thirteen

I am in paradise. Sunbeams dance across my face, and a warm breeze sweeps over my skin. From afar, I can hear the faint sound of ocean waves crashing against the shore. The sand is soft in between my toes.

All of a sudden, a buzz startles me, and I am falling, falling, falling. I jolt forward. The world is dark, and my head throbs. I attempt to make sense of my surroundings.

I am in my room. Turning to my alarm clock, which is still chiming relentlessly, I hit the "off" button and slump back down, closing my eyes again. All the events of the play rush back to me in a blur. I groan and turn over on my side.

Usually, getting up in the morning for school is a sluggish process. Today, it seems nearly impossible. Every morning, I have the urge to fall back asleep, but today, I have the urge to crawl under the covers and hide rather than face the realities of the world. Everything feels off. Everyone in my life feels unreachable. It's as if I'm on an island with nothing but ocean for miles. I don't know if I can get up, much less go about the day like a functioning human being.

The drive to school is hazy. I feel like a human zombie, going through the motions, but lacking a conscious direction. The emptiness within me grows as I open my locker to grab my books. Before our argument, Macie would swing by around this time to ask how my weekend was.

Now, she is nowhere to be found.

I float down the hallway like a ghost, watching other students amble to class. The sick feeling in my gut is unbearable. I need to get to the source of this problem, with both Macie and Nathaniel, whatever it takes. It's the only way I'll feel whole again—the only way my life can begin to return to the way it was.

I know what I need to do.

The question is, do I have the courage to do it?

* * *

Study period ends, and I bolt for the theater. Class is just beginning to file out, so I stay against the wall, looking for my targets. I scan for Macie, but I don't see her. Instead, Nathaniel emerges from the door, clutching his binder to his chest. It looks like he's seen better days himself. His hair is unkempt; his eyes appear sunken with bags underneath them. Maybe I'm not the only one who's been suffering. The thought gives me a faint sliver of reassurance.

As he walks in my direction, I muster up the courage to call out his name.

His eyes meet mine, piercing me with just one glance. I'm afraid he might walk by without acknowledgment, simply ignoring my presence. Instead, he swivels away from the rest of the class and makes his way toward me. Pointing in the opposite direction, he motions for me to follow him around the corner. As I trail behind him, he darts his eyes around the hallway anxiously, as if he's afraid someone might see us together.

Is he embarrassed to be seen in public with me?

Once we're successfully obscured, he turns toward me with a worried expression. His voice is a hushed whisper. "What's wrong, Scarlett? Are you okay?"

My jaw drops.

Is he really doing this to me?

I let out an incredulous laugh, reeling from the fact that he could be this obtuse. "Seriously? You're asking me if I'm okay?"

"Scarlett, this isn't the best time for us to have this conversation."

"Well, I'm sorry if talking to me is such an inconvenience to you now. It didn't used to be." I tap my foot, waiting for an explanation, a response, anything. Instead, Nathaniel remains silent, barely able to look me in the eyes. "Is this about what I did? To Ashton?" My voice is quiet. I look down at my feet, afraid to go further. "Are you afraid of me?"

This is the only rationale that I can think of for Nathaniel's with-drawal. Did I frighten him with my outburst? I search his eyes earnestly, hoping he'll tell me the truth.

A look of empathy flits across his face. "No, of course not."

"I swear, I'm not normally a violent person. I didn't mean to lose control like that."

A ghost of a smile forms on his face. "That is the farthest thing from what I think of you."

"Then why are you acting this way?" I implore. "Why can't you talk to me?"

For a moment, I swear I can see pain on Nathaniel's face. Then Nathaniel looks up, and his expression immediately goes blank. As I turn in the direction he's glancing, I notice Tina coming from the opposite end of the hallway.

"Scarlett," his voice rushed, "I should get going now." He looks back at me remorsefully. "Tina's waiting for me."

"Tina? That's what this is about?"

Nathaniel shakes his head. "I swear, it's not like that." He pauses with a conflicted face. "Scarlett, I'm sorry. I need to go."

As quickly as he had come over to talk with me, he left me standing alone in the hallway, gaping at him. I now feel even more perplexed than before our conversation.

Doesn't he realize that pulling away from me hurts me more than anything he could possibly tell me? If he's going to end whatever this is between us, can't he at least have the decency to say so?

I shake my head. If only I could leverage Macie's guidance during a time like this. It's too bad that she's been avoiding me, the same way Nathaniel has.

Wow.

Two of the most important people in my life, abandoning me when I need them most. Where do I turn? Who can I talk to about this when it feels like I am alone? Like I have no one? I glance up at the hallway to see other students walking to their next classes. Among the sea of faces, I recognize one in the crowd.

Liam.

One person who isn't completely against me right now—at least, I hope not.

"Hey, Liam." I wave.

When he sees me, he smiles. It's only a smile, but I'm grateful for the simple gesture. Boy, could I use one today.

"Hey, Scarlett," Liam greets me. "What's up?"

I'm reassured by the fact that Liam seems to be acting normally around me. Whatever mood Macie and Nathaniel are in, I'm at least glad it hasn't rubbed off on him, too.

"Not much. Just heading to lunch." I shrug, even though I've never felt more off-kilter. At least I have someone to talk to, even when the rest of the world seems to be shutting me out.

"I never got a chance to tell you," I turn to Liam, "but you did a great job in the show. You killed it as stage manager."

He chuckles at my compliment, "Thanks, Scarlett. I appreciate it." He looks back at me. "Did you have fun ushering this weekend?"

I flash a weak smile.

"It's just," I sigh reluctantly, "Macie and I are going through a bit of a rough patch right now. Kind of put a damper on the weekend."

Liam's face softens. "I'm sorry, Scarlett. I'm sure whatever you two are going through, you'll work through it. You guys are practically inseparable."

I smile back at him feebly. "Thanks, Liam. I hope so."

Liam suddenly turns back to me with a glimmer in his eyes. "You know, I'm sure I can see what's up. I can talk to her at our open swim period tomorrow if you want me to."

"You'd do that for me? I knew I liked you for a reason, Liam."

For the first time today, I feel more reassured.

"Happy to help," Liam says. Then he puts a finger in the air. "Well, actually, there is one thing you could help me with, too."

Why didn't I see that one coming?

"What did you have in mind?"

He leans in to whisper into my ear.

I nod with excitement. "Deal."

Chapter Fourteen

When I get to the pool the next day during free period, I see Liam waiting along the row of metal bleachers. He's wrapped in a towel, surrounded by a few of his friends. As he sees me approach him, he removes his swim cap, motioning for me to come over.

"Good, you're here. I was getting nervous."

I laugh. "You have the sign ready to go?"

"Yup, it's all set." He points next to him and then gestures to a couple of guys sitting around him. "A few of my buddies are going to help out with the execution."

I nod at the guys. "Perfect."

"You sure this is going to work?"

It's amusing to see Liam's confidence shaken for the first time. "I'm positive. You're going to be great."

He cracks his knuckles anxiously. "She should be coming out from the locker rooms any minute."

The door swings open.

"She's here," I hiss.

I give his shoulder a quick squeeze and then round the corner, so that I'm out of sight. Macie comes closer, making her way toward the bleachers. Retreating behind a wall, I wait for the cue from Liam. Finally, he calls out her name, drawing her attention to him and giving me the opportunity to peek around the corner.

"Liam, what's going on?" I see the surprise in Macie's expression from my vantage point.

Instead of answering her question, Liam signals to the swim guys who are sitting around him.

"Now!" he exclaims, his voice echoing through the indoor pool.

At his command, the group of guys who had been sitting next to Liam on the bleachers suddenly stands. Liam's friends swing four yellow kickboards over their heads. The letters P, R, O, and M are written distinctively on the front of each one. At the same time, Liam whips out the neon poster he had been hiding behind his seat. The brightly-colored piece of paper displays the words:

Forget fly, back, breast, and free. Will you go to prom with me?

As Macie absorbs the sign's message, her mouth drops open. She gapes at Liam in astonishment.

"Oh my gosh," she stammers.

With hesitation, Liam looks up at her and then shrugs. "What do you say, Macie? I promise it will go *swimmingly….*"

Swimmers doing laps in the pool have stopped to watch. All eyes are on Macie. The room is silent as everyone awaits Macie's response.

She taps her finger to her chin. After what feels like a lifetime, she turns back to Liam, rolling her eyes. "Duh, you goofball."

At those few words, relief washes over Liam's face. The swimmers in the water start clapping. Meanwhile, Liam wipes his forehead as Macie rushes to him and knocks him back with a hug.

Liam shakes his head at her. "I'm not sure if it was my nerves or the humidity of this pool, but you sure had me sweating."

I smile. Regardless of where Macie and I stand right now, her happiness with Liam is infectious. I silently rejoice. My best friend is going to prom!

As the commotion dies down and the swimmers return to their laps,

Macie looks at Liam, her eyes wide with disbelief. "I can't believe you did this! How, of all people, did you manage to pull this off? I mean, no offense, but you can't even manage to wear matching socks to school."

Liam flashes a devious grin. He takes the opportunity to extend his hand and motion to me. "Well, I didn't do it all alone."

By this point, I've already stepped into view. Macie's eyes lock with mine, and I feel a sudden frog in my throat.

We haven't spoken since our argument on Saturday night. Though I've been wanting to text her, to call her, to reach out in any form, I haven't. Instead, I've willed myself to give her the space she's asked for, as difficult as it's been. I realize I've been making her distance about me and our friendship together, when it's really been about her needing time to heal instead. I clung to her when she wanted room to breathe. I swooped in to save her, but I ended up making the situation worse.

All I want is for Macie to have faith in me again. I hope that standing in front of her now will prove just how much I care, because I don't know if I can go any longer without her.

Macie's expression remains unreadable as she stares back at me.

"Scar, did you help out with all of this?"

I scramble to find words. Thankfully, Liam must sense my hesitation, because he interjects, "Helping would be an understatement. She didn't just help. She practically planned it all. Went with me during lunch yesterday to get the supplies and make the poster." He winks at me, bringing his point home. "I don't know, Macie. I think you're pretty lucky to have a friend like her."

Nothing like a shameless plug from Liam.

When Macie turns back to me, her eyes search mine.

"Is that true, Scarlett?"

I know if I speak right now, my voice will come out shaky. All I can do is nod.

Closing my eyes, I prepare for the worst. But when I open them again, Macie is standing in front of me with arms outstretched. She motions for me to come forward. "Scarlett, I'm going to need you to get over here right now, because I really need to squeeze you."

By the time the words reach my ears, I am already moving toward her. Macie pulls me in close, crushing me in her embrace. Meanwhile, I throw my arms around her, hugging her back as tightly as I can.

"I'm sorry," she whispers in my ear. She pulls back to look at me. "For doubting you. For the way I treated you. For jeopardizing our friendship. I don't know who wrote that stupid note, but it wasn't even your handwriting."

I shake my head, my resolve crumbling. "I promise, it wasn't. And you didn't jeopardize our friendship, Macie. I'm sorry that I've been so clingy and protective of you recently. I don't want to hold you back from living your life and trying new experiences. It's just everything in high school's constantly changing, and you're the one constant in my life. I just don't want to lose you."

"You're not going to." Her voice is soft. "Before the play, I was in a rough place, and I think I just needed an outlet. I took my anger out on you, and that was really unfair of me," she says. "But Scarlett, you've been there for me through it all. New Year's, Winter Formal, the show. You came to bat and stood up for me at a time when I needed it most. And for that, I'm so grateful." Her eyes search mine. "So, thank you. Thank you for being your fiercely loyal self, Scarlett. That's all I could ever want."

This is the Macie I've missed so dearly. After what we've been through together, she's finally come back. "Good, because you're not getting rid of me that easily."

Macie takes the opportunity to pull me in once more for a hug. We're so preoccupied with our reunion that I barely hear Liam as he calls out behind us.

"Aw, cute. Now get a room, you two."

We laugh as we pull away from each other.

"You know how I said 'yes' before?" Macie hollers to him. "I'm thinking about changing my mind. Speaking of prom," Macie looks from Liam back to me, "do you think that Nathaniel is going to ask Scarlett?"

Nathaniel. At the mention of his name, my heart constricts. The one person my mind keeps circulating back to.

I don't think I can bear to hear the answer. Since our conversation in the hallway the other day, it's been nothing but radio silence on his end. At this point, it's time to cut my losses, not only for my pride, but also for my sanity's sake. I've decided to assume he's just not interested in me anymore, as much as the thought kills me. I keep replaying that night in my head, attempting to pinpoint exactly what I did—what I said—that could have gone so irreparably wrong.

Macie is still beaming as she jumps up and down. "Wouldn't it be so much fun if the four of us all went together?"

Liam's face falls as he turns to Macie, then shifts his eyes uncomfortably back to me. It seems as if he's about to confirm what I already know.

"You haven't heard? Nathaniel's going to take Tina to prom."

If liquid was in my mouth, I'd do a spit take. Macie gasps in horror. "Tina?"

Liam looks apologetic. "I know, I know. I don't know what's gotten into him recently."

My mind goes blank. As agonizing as it is, I can understand him not wanting to take me. But Tina? Anyone is more deserving than her.

"I can't believe he would ask her," Macie shakes her head in a daze.

"Me neither," Liam responds. "Just between us, I think Scarlett's the obvious choice."

I offer a weak smile. "Thanks, Liam."

"Nathaniel was pretty vague about it when I asked him. He said it was just 'something he needed to do.'" Liam makes air quotes for emphasis.

Something he needed to do?

"He's been acting weird lately," Liam continues. "Wouldn't even stand in the doorway with me after lunch the other day, like we used to do."

I have to get to the bottom of this. For closure, if nothing else. I need Nathaniel to personally tell me he's moved on. It's the only way I'll ever be able to.

"Hey, Liam," I ask, "do you know what his next class is after lunch?"

He shrugs. "It should be Stats with Mr. Erickson." Liam tilts his head in my direction. "Do you want Macie and me to come with you?"

"It's okay," I say. "I should do this by myself."

I need to have a last word with Nathaniel.

And I'm planning on doing it as soon as possible.

* * *

I find myself waiting outside of Mr. Erickson's classroom for Nathaniel to show up. I need to understand what's going on, and this seems to be the quickest way. After all, what do I have to lose? This might be the last time I speak to him.

I'm about to question whether I'm even standing by the right classroom or not when Nathaniel comes into view from around the corner. I suck in a deep breath, wishing I had thought this plan out more thoroughly first.

When he sees me, he stops. I half expect him to brush past me, but to my surprise, he scans the hallway and then walks toward me. As he gets closer, my lungs constrict.

"Nathaniel," I blurt out, attempting to exude a confident air, even though I feel anything but. "We need to talk."

He nods slowly. "I've been thinking the same thing."

I don't even attempt to hide my surprise at his agreement. But now that I have him, I'm not sure where to even begin. I think of the most pressing matter at hand and decide to go with that. "So, is it true that you're taking Tina to prom?"

He tenses at my question.

I'm hoping, more than anything, that he has a reason. Tina's dog died, and he feels bad. That she paid him $1,000 dollars to take her. Or better yet, that this is all one big gag, and he's planning on asking me any minute.

But his silence speaks louder than any defense he could give.

"Obviously," I continue, the lump rising in my throat, "you should be able to take anyone you want, and I know it's not my place to say, but this just doesn't seem like you."

He looks back at me with melancholy eyes, unable to give me the reassurance I need. "Scarlett, I wish it didn't have to be this way," he inhales, "but this is just something I have to do."

Something he has to do?

He's repeating back to me the same excuse that he threw at Liam. My hands ball up into fists at my side.

"You're a coward, you know that?" The anger comes out of me, like water spewing from a broken dam. "I understand that you're not interested in me anymore. You've made that clear, considering the way you've been acting. But couldn't you have at least told me first? You can't just go around messing with people's feelings for the sake of it and then avoiding all responsibility for the damage that you cause."

I am out of breath as I finish. I had no idea how much pent-up resentment had been building inside of me until this point. I can feel the tension leaving me as my anger is released. Now that it's out in the open, the oxygen begins to circulate again.

Nathaniel's face is ghostly pale. After several seconds, he manages to compose himself, but he still looks wounded.

"Scarlett, you have every right to be angry with me. This isn't easy for me either." He leans in closer, until his face is inches from mine, "I wish I could tell you everything, and I swear I will soon, but I just can't yet. If you can just wait for me. Just for a little while."

Is this some kind of joke?

"Wait for you?" I ask, still at a loss. "Until next week? Until you take Tina to prom? Until you graduate and move away to college forever?" I point an accusatory finger at him. "What am I even waiting for?"

The realization hits me like a splash of ice water. What we had during the play was an illusion, a staged act, just like the performance itself. Now that the show is over and the lights are back on, it's time to return to reality and see each other as we really are: two different people who want different things.

I've got to get out of here. The longer I stand in front of Nathaniel, the more pain I feel. Casting my head down, I go to walk past him, but he grabs my arm.

"Scarlett, wait."

I shake my head. "I'm tired of the cryptic excuses you've been giving me."

I'm about to wriggle out of his grasp, but he keeps a steady grip on my arm, holding me in place.

"Scarlett, just hear me out. Please."

I wish my arm weren't being held captive right now, so I could throw it up in aggravation. I settle for narrowing my eyes. "You know what, Nathaniel? I can't believe I ever let myself have actual feelings for you."

I'm on a roll at this point, so I decide to continue, letting Nathaniel take all the harsh words I can throw at him. "Remember what you said in your monologue, about how you can fall for the fantasy of someone rather than the reality? Well, that's exactly what I did. I fell for the fantasy," I shake my head, "because the reality is not what I expected."

I scoff. "You know what? Maybe, you'd be better off in a painting, just like Dorian Gray."

Nathaniel's face twists, and he shakes his head, "You don't mean that, Scarlett. I know you don't."

I let out an exasperated sigh. He's right: I didn't mean what I said literally. I'm tired of feeling powerless.

Meanwhile, he loosens his grip on my arm but doesn't let me go completely. Instead, Nathaniel leans in closer to me, so that I have no choice but to look at him. His voice is soft as he whispers, "You said you have feelings for me?"

Of course, that would be his takeaway from all of this.

"Had," I correct him. "But not anymore."

Who knows if my clarification will even make a difference, but at least it's worth a shot.

"I still have feelings for you," he says.

The sentence comes out of Nathaniel's mouth so quietly that, at first, I think it's a figment of my imagination. *What?*

As if his words weren't enough to shock me, he grabs my hand, interlacing his fingers with mine and giving me a quick squeeze.

Feeling the warmth of his palm against my own, I stare back in shock.

"If there's any possibility that you might still feel the same way, please trust me. I know I have no right to ask you that right now, but I'll tell you everything soon."

I'm about to respond when the bell rings.

"Just think about it, Scarlett. Don't give up on me yet." His eyes are hopeful as he slowly releases my hand from his and begins walking backward.

As quickly as Nathaniel had appeared in front of me, he disappears into his classroom. Once again, I'm left standing in the hallway, utterly baffled and with less clarity than before.

Don't give up on him yet? What else is there to do? I feel like I've been spun on a merry-go-round one hundred times at lightning speed. It's hard to know which way is which anymore.

Can I let myself wait for him, when the end might never be in sight? Can I just sit by the sidelines while he takes another girl to his senior prom? Can I trust him blindly, when he's given me no reason to, and on top of that, nothing to trust? I think about it for a minute before making up my mind.

Hell and no.

Chapter Fifteen

"I'm not going to the prom," I say flatly to Macie when I find her at her locker after class gets out. I'm slowly cooling down, but I've been worked up all day since my confrontation with Nathaniel.

"Nonsense," she responds. "Of course, you're going. You're not letting some foolish teenage boy make that decision for you. You're going, and you're going to have fun whether you like it or not."

"Thanks, Macie, but I just don't see the point," I groan. "I don't want to see Nathaniel and Tina together. I'd rather stay home than subject myself to that."

"C'mon, Scar. We can find you another date who's even better. I'm sure Liam has other friends he could ask. Then, you won't even notice the two of them are there."

"It's not about having someone else to go with," I sigh. "It's that the one person I want to go with doesn't want to go with me. And I don't think there's anything that could change that."

"Scarlett, don't say that. Anyone would be lucky to have you as their date." Macie shakes her head, "What about our plan from when we were younger? To go to prom in matching dresses with matching corsages and then fool people, so they can't tell the two of us apart."

I laugh. "Macie, we look very different from each other. I think it would be obvious."

She pouts. "Scarlett, you can't abandon me. Plus, you're the one with the best fashion sense. Who's going to help me pick out the perfect dress?"

"Don't worry, Macie. I'll still help you pick out your dress—" I pause mid-sentence. How silly am I being? I stop in my tracks. "Wait, I'm not going to help you pick out your dress."

Macie looks at me with a puzzled expression. At this point, I can tell that I've lost her completely.

"You want me to wear my birthday suit?" she laughs in confusion.

"No, Macie. I have an even better idea. You don't have swim practice after school today, right?"

She shakes her head. "No, I was just planning on going home."

"We're not going dress shopping," I grin, "because I had something else in mind. I was thinking we could go fabric shopping instead." I pull out my keys and dangle them in front of her. "You said you wanted me to make you a dress when I become a famous designer. Well, I'm not there yet, but I'm working toward it. I'd need to do some research, but I could try to make you whatever kind of dress you wanted—even Lorraine's 50s dress from *Back to the Future*. Now that I have a better grasp on my sewing technique, I think I could pull it off. That would be so much better than anything you could buy at a store, don't you think?"

"Scarlett, are you sure? I mean, that would be unbelievable. I'd love for you to sew my own custom-made dress. But that's also a big time and energy commitment. I could never ask that of you."

"Macie, I want to," I reassure her. "Please, let me do this for you. You've been through so much this year, and you deserve to have the night of your life. Plus, once it's finished, I can take pictures to add to my design portfolio, so I can showcase my work in the future. It would be good for both of us. What do you say?"

Macie puts a finger to her chin.

"I say," she taps in deliberation. Then, she puts her hands together and squeals. "Yes. One hundred times *yes*. I don't know what I did to deserve you, but I'm not about to question it now."

"Yay," I cheer. "Now, what are we waiting for? Let's go fabric shopping."

With that, Macie and I run to my car. When we arrive at the local fabric store, we make our way inside and begin to roam down the aisles to grab the necessary supplies. Macie helps me pick out the tools that Mr. Walsh had recommended to me, like a rotary cutter and a seam ripper. Then we head to the fabric section. I pull out various shades of cotton material necessary for the bodice and skirt, and I grab a lace overlay to add as an outer layer. Once we have everything we came for, we head to the registers to check out.

"When do I get to see it?" Macie squeals.

I can already envision how beautiful she'll look in these colors and fabrics. I just hope I can live up to her expectations and execute the design the way she envisions it.

"You're not allowed to see it until it's finished, okay? And if it's not what you hoped for, then I promise we can go actual dress shopping."

"It's going to be perfect, Scarlett. There'll be no need for another dress. I can barely wait to see it."

I take a deep breath. I wish I could have as much confidence in myself as Macie does in me. I want her first prom to be special for her.

Once the cashier has scanned the items, she hands me the bag and receipt.

It's time to get to work.

* * *

The next two weeks pass by quickly. Between making progress on Macie's dress, studying for my SATs, and doing class assignments, I've hardly had time to think about Nathaniel. Instead, I've poured myself into my sewing project and my studies, focusing solely on my grades and my goals.

One thing's for sure. A broken heart is painful, but it certainly makes a person more productive. I still have a subtle aching in my chest, but using school and sewing as a distraction has helped me cope. I'm hoping once I finish stitching the dress together, I'll be one step closer to stitching the pieces of my heart back together, too.

Currently, I'm hunched over my sewing machine, working on the layers needed for the bodice. It's past my usual bedtime, but I want to finish one more layer before calling it a night. I'm on a tight deadline, and I want to make sure I can finish in time. I go to pin one of the finished sections to the mannequin next to my desk when I hear a knock at my bedroom door.

"Who is it?" I call out.

"It's Dad." His voice is muffled from behind the doorway. "Can I come in?"

"Yup, come on in."

I don't turn around, but I can hear my dad enter my room. Removing my foot from the pedal, I take a pause from my sewing. Then, I swivel in my chair as my dad comes over and sits on the edge of the bed next to me.

"I saw the light in your bedroom was still on. How are you doing, kiddo? Still have a long night ahead?"

It makes me smile when my dad still calls me kiddo. I have a feeling his nickname won't change, no matter how old I am. I nod. "Finished all of my work for Biology and American Lit. I have a test and a quiz this week, but I feel good about them. Now, I'm just working on the dress I'm designing for Macie. I want to make sure I get it just right."

He grins. "Sounds like a lot on your plate. You know, your mom and I think what you're doing is really admirable—designing a dress for Macie like that. You should be proud of yourself."

I shrug. "Thanks, Dad."

He repositions himself on the edge of my bed. "Also, Scarlett, I feel like I owe you a bit of an apology."

His words startle me. I furrow my brow. "Apologize to me? I'm the teenager in this house," I say. "Aren't I supposed to be the one apologizing to you at this stage of life? You know, for all the rebellious stuff I'm supposed to be doing at this age?"

My dad laughs. "Yeah, I guess so. But then again, you're not like most teenagers."

I pout. I can't even fool my dad into thinking I'm a rebel.

My dad folds his arms together and continues, "I know I told you that I wanted you to keep your eyes on the prize and have laser focus this year. That I wanted you to put all of your effort into your studies and your job at Fashion Fwrd."

I think back to our conversation during Winter Break before I quit my job. "Yeah, I remember that." I cast my head down, realizing I didn't exactly live up to those expectations. "Are you disappointed in me? That I stopped working at Fashion Fwrd and ushered for the play instead? That I took my eyes off the prize?"

He's quiet for a minute.

"No, Scarlett. I'm not disappointed in you." He shakes his head. "See, the thing is: I think I got so caught up in my aspirations for you—about getting into FIT and moving to New York—that I gave you the wrong advice. Of course, I want you to get into a good college and choose a meaningful career one day, but I know your work ethic, and I already know you're going to accomplish big things. You're a smart cookie. No matter where you go or what you major in, you're going to be successful."

"Okay, what's the issue then?" I'm trying to understand where my dad is going with this. It's rare that he opens up to me in this way.

His expression is warm. "I failed to remind you of the one thing that matters most to me."

"And what's that?" I ask.

He looks me right in the eyes. "Seeing you working on this dress for your friend and watching you use your talents to help others—it reminded me of what I care about most. And that's that you're a good person, Scarlett. You have a big heart, kiddo. You're a good daughter and a good friend. You care about other people. I just don't want you to lose sight of those qualities. So, scratch what I said before, and keep doing what you're doing."

Wow, I wasn't expecting my dad to get sentimental like that. Especially when he's usually the more stoic one. It makes me smile.

"If you're a good person," he continues, "good things will fall into place. Just wait and see."

My dad's encouragement brings up bittersweet feelings. I can't help but think of Nathaniel and where the two of us stand. I wish I could believe his motivational words, but right now, things seem bleak. "I appreciate that, Dad. How do you know for sure that things will fall into place, though?

"Well, no one can know for sure. But I believe everything will work out when it's supposed to. If not, maybe it's not the right time yet."

I absorb his words and nod, feeling slightly better. For now, that's what I need to tell myself to make it through until prom. "Wow, thanks, Dad. I think this tops the list as one of your best pep talks yet."

He grins. "I have my moments." With that, he gets up from my bed and smooths out my duvet cover. "I'll leave you to it." He walks back to the other side of my room.

Once he reaches the door, he turns his head back. "And Scarlett? One more thing."

"Yeah, Dad?"

"Don't go to bed too late. Lights off soon?"

I nod with a grin.

"Goodnight, pal," he waves before slipping through the door and closing it quietly.

I return to the dress, and I smile as I reflect on my dad's words. I've made my fair share of mistakes over the course of this year, and I'm far from anyone's definition of perfect. But maybe, just maybe, I'm doing something right.

Chapter Sixteen

"Okay, you have to keep your eyes closed." I force Macie to keep my sleep mask over her eyes as I lead her up the carpeted steps to my bedroom. "No peeking."

"Scarlett, you have no idea how much I've been dying to see it." She grips my arms as I help her up another step. "I can't believe today's the day."

After meticulous planning, measuring, and sewing, I've finally completed Macie's prom dress, and I couldn't be more excited for the big reveal. The process was grueling, to say the least—with three different layers for the bodice, an interlining layer, and the lace overlay on the outside of the skirt. I even stayed up late again last night to add the finishing touches to the collar and the belt.

But after spending hours studying techniques and slogging away at my creation, I'm proud to present this labor of love to her. Today is officially the morning of prom, and although I am cutting it right down to the wire, I wanted to make sure every measurement was as close as it could be. This will be the first time she's ever seen it, so she has no idea what to expect.

"Like I said before, you're allowed to hate it." I preface. "If it's not for you or it doesn't fit the right way, then we'll go to the closest gown boutique. I can handle the truth."

"I'm going to wear it no matter if it's the ugliest thing I've ever seen," she grins.

"Watch what you say," I joke as I open the door to my bedroom and pull her forward. She may live to regret this.

Once we've made it to the other side, I take her shoulders and position her in front of the mannequin.

"All right. Go easy on me," I plead.

I can feel my heart beating faster in my chest as I carefully lift the blindfold from her face and take a step back. I close my eyes and clench my teeth in anticipation. It's time for the moment of truth.

Wringing my hands together nervously, I wait for her reaction. "What do you think?"

The room goes silent. She stands frozen in place.

"Scarlett," her voice wavers as she walks closer to the mannequin. She puts her hands over her mouth. "This is…this is absolutely *beautiful*."

Macie examines the dress further. "The details, the stitching, the lining. It's everything and more." She shakes her head. "I have no idea how you managed to pull this off, but you've made my dream come true. You're like my very own fairy godmother."

"Well, you're going to be the belle of the ball."

"And what about you?" Macie scoffs. "You can't just make this gorgeous dress for me and then not come. It's simply not allowed."

"Fairy godmothers don't go to balls," I laugh. "They've got magic to do. Pumpkin carriages to transform and all that. I've already made up my mind," I say. "But there is something you could do for me. I was hoping I could at least get some pictures of you first." I point to my digital camera. "For the portfolio."

"Of course. As many as you need." Macie claps her hands together. "I'll take pictures for you all day long."

I pull the dress off of the mannequin and hand it to her. "Try it on, and make sure it fits."

"Let me go to the bathroom and change. I'll be right back," she says.

A couple of minutes later, she comes out of the bathroom. The soft peach color complements her skin tone, and the style of the dress gives her a vintage Hollywood glam appearance. She does a full 360-degree twirl in the dress. I can't believe it, but it fits her like a glove. The bodice hugs her in all the right places, and the A-line skirt flares out, adding a flattering and flirty dimension. I could practically cry—all of my hard work paid off. I designed and sewed a dress entirely by myself!

I guide Macie to the window where the lighting is strong and line her up next to the window frame. Then, I give her directions on how to pose as I position the camera in front of her. Looking into the lens, I snap picture after picture of her from different angles. I make her spin and capture one last shot.

"Look at you," I say. "Picture perfect."

"All thanks to you," Macie responds. "I owe you big time."

"There." I take one more picture. "Now, you're making my dream come true, too. I can't wait to add these photos to my applications in the fall."

Macie does one more spin with the dress. She shakes her head. "Nathaniel's crazy, you know that? He had the whole package in his hands, and he's letting you slip away. I can't understand how he could be so foolish."

"Neither do I," I sigh.

"Liam and I will give him trouble if we see him tonight."

I smile softly. "I appreciate that. But let's not think about that right now. You've got a prom to attend. Let's pack up the dress for you, so you can start getting ready for tonight."

"Scarlett, it's really not going to be the same without you," she whines.

"I know. But it's still going to be special. Don't you worry."

I feel a pang in my chest, but I shake the feeling away for now. After all, I still have another year to go, so missing junior prom isn't the end of the world. No matter how tempting it might seem, I'll have to live vicariously through Macie. Because I'm standing firm in my decision: There is no way I'm going to show up at prom.

* * *

Sometimes, I feel like an outsider looking in—especially in moments when the world around me seems beyond my reach. I'll envision that I'm at an aquarium, peering in from outside of the glass.

Right now, though, I'm not an outsider looking in; I am an insider looking out.

It's the night of prom, and I can see half the neighborhood from the window in my room. I watch enviously as girls file out of cars, strolling up my neighbor's driveway, arm-in-arm with their dates. I feel like I've landed a front-row seat on the red carpet, seeing celebrities promenade extravagantly.

I turn away from the window of my bedroom to avoid additional self-inflicted torment. Why should I care about missing out on this tradition? No one really enjoys prom, anyway.

But who am I kidding? I would kill to be out there, flaunting a beautiful dress, wearing a dapper date on my arm. I belly flop onto my mattress and let out a muffled groan.

I've tried to tune out the prom buzz by focusing on my sewing of Macie's dress. But now that it's here, I know tonight will be the most difficult considering what a big event it is. The truth is, I could have swallowed my pride and bought a ticket to the dance. But I don't have a date, and worse, my preferred date is taking another girl.

The buzz of my phone startles me, and I scramble to fish it out of my pocket. Macie's name flashes on the screen. She's probably meeting up with Liam and her group right now to take pictures, too. I press the answer button to pick up the call.

"Hello?"

"Scarlett," Macie exclaims into the phone, "People have been giving me so many compliments on this dress. I've been telling them it's a Scarlett original. You're going to be the talk of the town after tonight. You sure you don't want to come in our group? It's not too late."

I let out a sigh. I should stop feeling sorry for myself and go to prom with Macie's swim group. It could be that simple. But I don't even have a prom ticket to get in. Plus, I feel more like wallowing in self-pity with my two favorite men, Ben and Jerry.

"It's okay," I exhale. "I still have next year to go." I try to fake an optimistic tone. "But you guys will have so much fun. I can't wait to hear all about it. Plus, if you need anything at all, I'm only a text or call away."

"That's so sweet, Scar. It won't be nearly as much fun without you, though. Are you sure?"

"Yeah," I take a deep breath. "I'm sure. Thanks for checking in."

"Okay. I'll tell you all about it tomorrow. Love you."

"Love you, too."

I hang up and close my eyes, but the images won't stop flashing through my head. A picture surfaces in my mind of how impeccable Nathaniel must look in a tuxedo, with his tousled hair and dazzling smile. Tina probably looks stunning.

The perfect couple, I scoff.

As I lie on my bed, I ruminate over Macie's offer. A part of me is kicking myself for caring so much. I should be having fun with my friends, not worrying about what some boy thinks of me. If I sit here stewing in my own misery, does that mean I'm "waiting" for him, just like he wants me to be?

A light tap on the door surprises me, shaking me from my thoughts.

"Honey, it's such a nice night out tonight," my mom calls from behind the door. "Want to go for a walk?"

A walk.

A nice, relaxing walk could be enough to cure the toxic thoughts clouding my head right now. After all, my mother is the woman who raised me, the person who knows me best. Maybe, this will be the perfect opportunity to confide in her with my ultimate dilemma. I push myself up from my bed, smoothing the wrinkles from my comforter.

"Let me just grab my jacket."

Once I've bundled up, I trudge downstairs to meet up with my mom. She smiles at me and pushes the front door open. As we step outside, I can't help but notice how beautiful the sunset is tonight. The sky is a radiant canvas of swirly purples, pinks, and blues. A breathtaking view.

After feeling more calmed by the scenery, I glance over at my mom, whose steps have fallen into synchronization with mine. When I was younger, she was always my rock, my sounding board, my confidant. As I've grown older, I've become more private about my personal life. But right now, I have the urge to confide in her, to divulge how I'm feeling, and have her tell me that everything's going to be okay.

I plan to do just that, but before I can open my mouth, an unsettling thought pops into my head. Tonight's prom, and I'm currently walking around my neighborhood with my mom.

What if the kids from school see me?

They'll think I wasn't cool enough to have anyone ask me. And even worse, they'll think my idea of a fun Saturday night is to stroll around the neighborhood with my mother at my side. I hadn't even considered the fact that other groups would obviously be out and about around this time. As much as I love my mom, the last thing I want is to be seen with her in this situation.

Hoping she doesn't sense my ulterior motive, I clear my throat to gain my mom's attention. "Mom, how about we cross the street and go to the next neighborhood over? I'm feeling like a change of pace today." At least, if we're in a different neighborhood, there's less of a chance that I'll be recognized by someone I know.

She nods in confirmation. "Sounds good, Scar."

We cross the street, and my mom sets the pace, striding energetically. Ironically, I'm the one who usually has to worry about keeping up with her.

"So," she turns to me, "I'm sure Macie is going to look gorgeous in her dress. You truly are the best friend for making that dress for her. You said she's going with Liam, right?"

I know she's only trying to make me feel better, but right now, the pit in my stomach grows.

"Yeah," I confirm, "she and Liam are going together." My mind traces back to Liam's clever prom-posal.

"Aw," my mom muses, "it would have been fun for the two of you to go together, huh?"

I turn my attention to the other side of the street, so I won't have to look at her directly. She doesn't know the half of it.

"There wasn't anyone," she continues, unaware of my discomfort, "that you wanted to go with this year, was there?"

My eyes widen.

My mom has always been one to fish for information, but I wasn't expecting that straightforward question. I've talked a lot to Macie about Nathaniel over the past months, but I haven't brought him up directly yet with my mom and dad. They can be helicopter parents, and I'm afraid once I bring it up, I won't hear the end of it.

Plus, where would I even begin to answer her? She'd probably think I was crazy if I told her the truth: "Yes, Mom. I wanted to go with Nathaniel Wilder, a guy who claims to have feelings for me, but he's taking another girl to prom. Oh, and he also says I should 'wait' for him."

I shrug, hoping she can't sense my dishonesty.

"Nope." I pause. "No one this year." Just to hit the point home, I go further, "I'm actually glad I'm not going. This way, it'll be even more special when I go to prom for the first time as a senior."

For a second, I almost believe my own words. Too bad I know I'm bluffing.

At least my mom seems to buy them. "It's such a special night." She places a hand on her heart. "You have so much to look forward to."

Her words are a punch to the gut.

Why did I agree to go on this walk again? With each minute, I feel like I'm simply rubbing more salt into a painful wound. I can't bear this conversation any longer. I need to distract myself because I'm this close to losing it in front of my mom. To calm myself down, I decide to focus on the scenery instead. I turn my attention to the well-manicured lawns and colonial-style houses lined neatly in a row. As we walk by, I study them one by one, keeping my eyes focused on the details, so my mind won't wander to another place. My attention shifts to a sign planted in the ground of the house we're walking past.

My body freezes.

I can't move.

I do a double-take, just to make sure I'm reading the sign correctly. My eyes want to pop out of their sockets. My vision must be failing me.

It can't be.

There is no way.

This is impossible. Right?

I reread the sign on the lawn, just to make sure I'm not slowly losing my grip on reality.

CONGRATULATIONS, NATHANIEL!
NEW YORK UNIVERSITY

Oh. My. Gosh.

There may be a few Nathaniels in this town, in this neighborhood even, but I know without a doubt that there is only one Nathaniel who could possibly be attending NYU next year.

And right now, his name is displayed on a graduation banner in the middle of the lawn directly across the street from me.

What does this mean?

Could Nathaniel's house actually be right in front of my eyes? Is it true that he's lived a mere neighborhood over from me this whole time, and I've never known?

And most importantly, does this mean he's been accepted to NYU, like he's always dreamed of? Even though I'm still angry with him for the way he's left things between us, I can't help but feel proud of him for this achievement.

A shiver runs down my spine. Is there a chance that this could be some kind of sign? Well, besides the fact that it is, in fact, *a sign.*

What is the likelihood of my mom and me walking by this neighborhood in this place at this exact time? Could this be the world telling me that I should wait for Nathaniel, like he said I should?

I glance at the house one more time as it begins to fade from view. I hadn't even realized that we were still walking.

"Oh honey, I forgot to mention."

I zone back into the conversation with my mom, who is currently chattering away about plans for tomorrow, unsuspecting of my mind-numbing revelation.

"Tomorrow night is Book Club Night." She turns to me. "Dad also has a late meeting, so you're going to be on your own for dinner. We should have an extra frozen meal in the freezer that you can heat up."

In a daze, I nod, barely able to process the words flowing from my mom's mouth. Right now, I feel too overwhelmed to function, much less absorb conversation. I need an escape.

An unexpected thought pops into my mind.

"Hey, Mom?" I suddenly interject. "Can we head back? I might actually go out tonight for a bit, after all."

My mom stops in her tracks, startled by my abrupt change in mood. "You sure, honey? It's already getting dark out."

"Just for a little bit," I reason. "I'll text you if I'm going to be out too late."

After a moment, she nods. "Okay, sweetie. Just keep me updated."

I breathe a sigh of relief. I need to get away from here. And I know exactly where I'm going to go.

Chapter Seventeen

"**M**ake it a double. I really need something strong tonight."
The waitress across the counter from me looks over with a puzzled expression.

"Sure, hon. You want chocolate, vanilla, or strawberry?"

"Chocolate."

I'm sitting at the wraparound counter of Dotty's, swiveling back and forth on one of the rotating stools. The place is empty tonight, considering that any student who frequents this diner is probably at prom. I place my head in my hands and massage my temples, attempting to alleviate the throbbing headache that's developed.

"Having a rough night there, Scarlett?"

In surprise, I jerk my head up, moving my hands away from my face. Staring from across the counter with bemused curiosity is none other than Gavin. He's smirking at me, as if watching my life unravel before him is a form of entertainment. Too bad I'm not in the best mood for social interaction.

"Yeah," I respond bluntly. "It's not my finest, that's for sure."

At those words, Gavin rests an arm on the counter and leans in closer, looking at me right in the eyes.

"It's a slow night tonight." He smiles softly. "And I'm not waiting on any tables right now. Sounds like maybe you could use a listening ear?"

"Trust me," I mope, "you probably have better things to be doing with your time right now."

He lifts his arm and motions around the room at the ghost town of a diner. "Nope," he counters. "I'd say there's pretty much nothing better in this restaurant for me to do with my time right now."

I smirk. He's got a point.

"Lay it on me," he urges. "People tell me that I'm a good listener."

He won't let this go so easily, will he? I sigh, still ruminating on the sign I had walked by only half an hour ago. Before I can stop myself, the question that's been weighing on my mind comes out.

"Gavin, do you believe in signs?"

"Signs?" Gavin tilts his head toward me, caught off-guard by the randomness of my question. "What kind of signs are we talking about here?"

I scramble to piece together a coherent response. "I don't know," I say. "Maybe that there are signs telling people that they should be together?"

I expect him to scoff at the absurdity of what I'm asking. What kind of person starts off a conversation with a weirdly existential question like I did? I'm about to tell Gavin to forget I said anything. But when I turn to him, I notice his face has grown pensive, his brow furrowed, and his lips forming a hard line.

"For me, personally, I'd say no." He looks off into the distance. "I mean, I think there are certain people we come into contact with by coincidence. And certain people we're more compatible with than others, for sure, but I don't believe there's some hidden indication that we're supposed to be with a certain person."

Wow, he is a good listener. This is not the small talk I was expecting to have during a typical Saturday night at Dotty's.

"I feel silly for asking you about that now."

"Hey," his tone is soft, "that doesn't mean it can't exist for you, if you believe in it."

"I wish I knew what to believe anymore. I'm just so confused."

"Well, I'm no expert," he responds, "but I'm guessing your question wasn't asked just for the sake of asking it. What's this really about?"

"You could say I saw a sign today. A literal sign. It just felt too coincidental."

"Did it have anything to do with the guy who sat down next to you the last time you were here?"

I feel like he just opened a direct window into my brain. "Was it that obvious?"

He chuckles. "Yes."

I grit my teeth.

"That's a tough one, Scarlett. I think you'll ultimately have to decide for yourself whether you want your sign to be one or not. You're the only one who gets to choose if it has importance."

I stare back at him, impressed by his insight. "Are you sure you're only in high school? Because you seem to have the wisdom of an adult trapped inside of a high schooler's body."

He smirks at me. "I'll take that."

I'm about to respond when the waitress returns with my chocolate milkshake. Eagerly, I stick my straw into the icy mixture and take a sip. It's refreshing and just what I needed to subdue my headache. When I glance back up, Gavin is still standing there, studying me.

"Hey, Gavin?" I take a break from my milkshake.

"Yeah, Scarlett?"

"I actually feel better tonight because of you. I just wanted to say thank you for that."

He rests a hand on the counter. "Waiter by day, problem-solver by night. It's what I do."

A few minutes ago, I came into this diner feeling like no one could understand what I was going through. But thanks to Gavin and his encouraging words, I feel like my feelings are actually validated.

Suddenly, an idea pops into my head.

"Gavin." I turn toward him abruptly. "When do you get off work tonight?"

He tilts his head. "My shift ends in fifteen. Coincidence or a sign, you decide."

* * *

"Whoa—easy there, Scarlett."

I turn toward Gavin, who's tightly gripping the sides of his seat.

"Sorry," I mutter, easing up on the gas. At the moment, we're barreling down the highway, cruising at a speed much higher than we should be. With the adrenaline pumping through my veins, it's hard to slow down. "Just want to make sure we get there. Not much time left."

As the destination comes into view, I turn the wheel and make a sharp right. The parking lot is practically full, but I spot an open space a few rows away. I drive over and pull into it. Removing the keys from the ignition, I look over at Gavin, who still appears shaken from the ride.

"See?" I motion to the car in reassurance. "We made it all in one piece."

Gavin lets out an elongated breath. "Barely."

As I look down at my own outfit, I shake my head to myself. I'm still wearing the blouse and skirt that I've been in all day. Gavin is dressed in the same t-shirt and jeans that he wore for his shift. This isn't exactly how I envisioned my first prom experience. Still, we made it this far. What do we have to lose?

"You know, Gavin," the thought dawns on me, "you could have gone to prom this year. Why'd you decide not to?"

He shrugs. "I don't know. I was working."

"You could have asked for tonight off."

He tries to avert his eyes, but I keep mine fixed on him, waiting for an answer.

Finally, he exhales. "I guess I just didn't have anyone I really wanted to take."

All this time, I had been feeling bad for myself. It had never occurred to me that Gavin might be in a similar predicament.

"Well, you know what? I'm glad I ran into you tonight. Because I think we make pretty killer prom dates."

"Yeah." Gavin looks down as if he's digesting my words. Then he turns back to me. "Yeah, we do."

I reach for the door handle, but Gavin surprises me by putting a hand on my arm. "Wait there."

Before I know what's happening, Gavin hops out of the car, shutting his own door behind him. The next thing I know, my door pops open, and his hand is outstretched toward me.

"What are you doing?" I laugh.

He keeps his arm extended. "What kind of person would I be if I didn't escort my date to prom?"

I reach my hand out and allow Gavin to pull me up from my seat. He loops his arm with mine and then pushes the door shut behind me.

Arm-in-arm, Gavin and I walk across the parking lot to make our spontaneous and last-minute entrance into prom. At this point, I pray that none of the teachers are manning the doors, considering we don't have tickets.

As we approach the front door, I motion for Gavin to wait while I peer through the glass. Thankfully, the lobby is scattered with groups of students taking a break from the dance, so I give him the confirmatory thumbs up.

He pulls the door open with a swoosh, and we're hit with a warm gust of air as we enter the lobby. Capturing my attention, Gavin points to a hallway next to a sign that says "Ballroom Entrance."

Here goes nothing.

With my arm still linked to his, I let him guide me in the direction of the double doors. I push the door forward, ready to make my grand entrance into the main event. I'm about to cross the threshold when, out of nowhere, someone making a getaway shoves me backward. The abrupt contact causes Gavin and me to wobble.

"Sorry," the person mutters hastily.

My body freezes. I recognize the voice immediately. Turning back around, I confirm the identity, which I already know.

Nathaniel.

As we make eye contact, Nathaniel screeches to a halt in his tracks.

"Scarlett?" He stares back at me with wide eyes, as if I'm an alien from outer space. "What are you doing here?"

"I'm going to prom," I state matter-of-factly.

Nathaniel looks down at the ground, deflecting my gaze. "I didn't see you tonight," he speaks quietly. "I thought maybe you weren't coming."

He wishes I hadn't shown up, I'm sure.

Unfortunately, I'm no longer the girl who caters to his wishes at the expense of my own.

"It shouldn't really matter to you either way, right? I mean, after all, you did choose someone else to take."

The muscles in Nathaniel's jaw tighten. "And I see you have your own date, too."

His response irks me further. Why is he acting as if he cares? He could have chosen me all along, but instead, he deliberately picked Tina, and now he has to live with that choice. This conversation is getting to me, not to mention it's probably making Gavin uncomfortable. I need to free myself before I let Nathaniel play with my emotions any longer.

"Well, if you'll excuse us," I dismiss him, "we should start heading in now."

Nathaniel motions for us to proceed. "Go ahead," he mutters humorlessly. "I was actually just leaving."

Before I have a chance to probe further, he spins and walks away.

What just happened?

Taking a deep breath, I try to compose myself. After all, I came here to enjoy my night, not to stew over Nathaniel's infuriating behavior. I was already doing that at home.

With some effort, I redirect my attention back to Gavin. I push thoughts of Nathaniel out of my mind. What catches me off-guard, though, is Gavin's expression. He's looking back at me, stifling a smirk.

I shake my head in disbelief. "You should know, I'm not in the mood to deal with jerks tonight," I warn, "so you better not be making fun of me."

Gavin puts his hands up in defense. "No, not that. I was just thinking," he pauses, "that you sure know how to make a guy jealous; that's all."

The word rings in my ears, and I stare at him in surprise. Jealous? I let out a doubtful huff. "Thanks for trying to make me feel better, but the last thing Nathaniel could be is jealous."

"I don't know," Gavin shrugs, "I feel like I can spot another dude's jealousy when I see it. And that looked like some next-level jealousy to me."

A small piece of me can't help but smile at Gavin's comparison. As much as I hate to admit it, the idea brings me a hint of satisfaction.

Gavin's about to speak, but before he has the chance to, I grab his hand and tug him toward the door. I don't let go until we're in the ballroom. When I finally release Gavin, his eyes are wide in surprise. We turn our heads to the space in front of us and take in the view.

With wonder, I take in the ornate details of the ballroom—from the expansive dance floor to the elegant chandeliers hanging overhead, to the lively crowd of students. I almost feel like Dorothy in *The Wizard of Oz*, observing life in color after entering the Land of Oz. Never have I seen such a plethora of brightly colored fabrics in one place. I watch as girls with elaborate updos and sparkling jewels twirl in beautiful floor-length dresses.

Motioning to Gavin, I point in the direction of the dance floor. My next task is to look for Macie; she'll lose it when she realizes I'm here. Leading the way, I weave through the congestion, hoping to get closer to the front stage. As my eyes scan the room, moving from person to person, I'm met with a familiar face.

But it's not Macie's.

The first person I recognize is the last person I want to see. And it doesn't help that, right now, she looks like she jumped off of the page of a freaking Sherri Hill catalog.

Tina.

She's wearing an emerald off-the-shoulder dress that trails behind her dramatically. The vibrant green is a stark contrast to her fiery red hair and fair skin. As her eyes land on me, her face twists in shock.

"Scarlett?" she blinks.

I shrug. "Decided to make a last-minute appearance."

I'm expecting a sarcastic reaction from Tina, but instead, her eyes dart around the room with an uncharacteristic frenzy. "Do you know where Nathaniel went? I can't find him anywhere."

My eyes widen, surprised that Nathaniel hadn't mentioned the reason for his sudden departure to his own date. I turn to Gavin, and he seems equally confused.

"We just saw him leaving. He didn't tell you?"

For a moment, I think Tina is about to cry. Her eyes are large and vacant, as if her mind is somewhere miles away from the dance.

When she snaps back to reality, she mutters under her breath. "Not a word."

I can tell from her tone that Tina's angry, but strangely she doesn't seem surprised. It's as if she were expecting Nathaniel to ditch her tonight.

While I admit I've always found Tina to be rude and off-putting, part of me empathizes with her in this situation. No one, not even Tina, deserves to be abandoned at prom.

I place a gentle hand on her arm. "Tina, I'm sorry." I search her eyes with sincerity. "I really am."

She sighs and shakes her head. "Scarlett, you don't have to be sorry for me."

As much as I want to hate her, my heart actually hurts for Tina at this moment. It's like she's incapable of accepting empathy, as if the only way she can preserve her steely demeanor is by deflecting it from others. Maybe that's the reason she's been cold to me this whole time: She doesn't know how to appreciate kindness when others show it to her.

"C'mon Tina," I reason. "I know we've had our differences, but no one deserves being left like that."

Tina casts her head down, unwilling to look me in the eyes. "Scarlett, there's something I need to tell you," she begins, "but I know that after I tell you this, you're going to think even worse of me."

My heart beats faster in my chest. I glance at Gavin and then back to Tina with caution. Could this finally be the clarity I've been searching for?

Tina opens her mouth to speak, but then she clamps it shut just as quickly. With a shake of her head, she begins to back away. "I should get going." Her voice is hushed. "We'll talk sometime at school, Scarlett."

Sometime at school?

She's going to leave me hanging, just like that? I'm about to object, but before I can, Tina turns around and vanishes into the crowd, leaving me almost as confused as Nathaniel had.

First Nathaniel running off, and then Tina, too? I wish I could simply crack the code and solve this perplexing mystery.

As I stand frozen, too bewildered to speak, I feel two arms snake their way around me from behind. Taken aback, I whirl around until I am face-to-face with Macie.

"Scarlett, what are you doing here?"

Her reaction is picture-worthy. I take a step back to admire her. She looks radiant in her peach-colored dress and vintage curly hairstyle, like a movie star from the 50s.

"You were pretty convincing over the phone," I say. "I decided I had to come and see it for myself after all."

"Seriously? Of course, you would decide to come when the dance is almost over." She scans my outfit slowly, pulling at my skirt. "And wearing this." Macie laughs. "You really are one-of-a-kind, Scar."

Before I can answer, she tugs my hand, pulling me in the direction of the dance floor. "We don't have much time left. Come dance with Liam and me."

I'm about to follow her lead when I realize Gavin is still standing behind me. I motion for him to follow along.

As I do, Macie leans into my ear. "You came with Gavin?" She shakes her head. "The last time I checked, you two barely spoke to each other."

I chuckle as Gavin joins us, and we make our way to Liam. He's in the middle of the dancefloor, grooving along to the Cha Cha Slide. When he sees the three of us, he does a double-take.

"Scarlett?" he calls out, doing one hop and stomping with his right foot. "I thought you weren't coming."

I watch him execute the choreography. "Had a last-minute change of heart," I shout over the music.

Motioning with his hand, Liam waves us over. "C'mon, you guys. Only a couple minutes left to get funky."

We crack up as we make our way over to Liam. I jump in, matching the rhythm by sliding to the left and then to the right. Macie and Gavin follow along next to me. We're laughing and clapping along to the music like no one else is watching. As I look around at the three of them, I'm suddenly overcome with emotion. I've been so focused on my own unhappiness that I've been blind to the good fortune in my life.

Here are three people who make me feel better. Who care about me. Who uplift me. No more wasting my energy on someone who doesn't appreciate it. Instead, I'll start focusing more on the people who matter.

It's time to live in the moment and let go of what I can't change. It's time to close my chapter with Nathaniel once and for all.

Chapter Eighteen

As I open my locker for the first time on Monday morning, an unusual scrap of notebook paper catches my attention. It's perched on the floor of my locker, folded over in half. With curiosity, I pick it up. When I unfold the scrap, I notice the slanted handwriting:

Meet me in the theater during lunch today.
~Nathaniel

I read the note one more time, trying to subdue the rising lump in my throat. I glance anxiously down the hallway, contemplating my next move.

Do I dare go to meet him, and more importantly, do I even want to? After all, this past weekend with my friends at prom had helped me to move on. Is there anything Nathaniel could say that would make me forgive him? I can barely stand the thought of being face-to-face with him again, especially after the way he's hurt me.

Then again, maybe I owe it to myself. Our meeting could finally give me the peace of mind I've been searching for. I guess there's only one way to find out, and it's written in slanted handwriting on the back of this note. I fold the piece of paper back in half and tuck it into my pocket. It's time to get some answers.

* * *

Faint lights guide me through my dim surroundings as I enter the theater. I look around for any signs of movement, but the theater appears to be empty. My footsteps echo on the steps as I climb up the stairs until I've made my way to the center of the stage.

Turning to face the auditorium, I squint into the darkness. For a second, I envision a live audience sitting in front of me. I pretend that every seat in the theater is filled with spectators gazing up at me in unanimous admiration. For dramatic effect, I bend over with a sweep of my hand, bowing gracefully for the crowd. Just as I do, I hear a shuffling sound from behind the stage.

"I see someone's enjoying the spotlight."

I notice Nathaniel emerging from the curtain, strolling onto the stage from the right wing.

"You scared me." I put a hand over my heart.

Nathaniel joins me at the front of the stage. His tense demeanor from the night of prom seems to have disappeared, the corners of his mouth curving into the hint of a smile. "I didn't want to interrupt an actress in her element."

With a gulp, I twirl my hair with my finger. All morning, I'd felt prepared to handle this encounter—like nothing Nathaniel could say or do would faze me. But now that I'm standing in this position, a mere foot from Nathaniel on stage, I am not so sure. My palms are sweaty, and my legs feel shaky beneath me.

"I got your note." I break the silence.

"I'm glad you came."

I fight to maintain my resolve, but I can feel it crumbling. Why is standing here making me second-guess myself? I want to be mad at Nathaniel right now. Between his blowing me off for prom, his refusal to share what's going on, and the strife he's put me through, I'm more than validated in my frustration. Yet despite my wanting to stay mad at him, just seeing him makes it difficult.

"So, you're actually ready to talk to me now?" I ask.

"It will all make sense." He raises his hand, as if swearing an oath. "I promise."

Staring at Nathaniel, I find myself caught up in his spell once again—transported back to that night on the stairwell when we shared our first kiss. The sweet moment plays over in my head, making me want to forget the past couple of weeks.

But first, I have to hear the full story. I'm not about to let Nathaniel into my life again so easily after he tore it apart. If I've learned anything from this, it's that my self-esteem is not derived from how someone else feels about me. My worth is determined by how I feel about myself and myself alone.

"You have until the bell rings."

He sits on the stage and pats the ground next to him in invitation. "Deal."

I fold my arms together, as if shielding myself from what might come next. Then with a sigh, I follow his lead, making my way over to him and sitting next to him at the front of the stage. My legs dangle in a similar fashion to his. When I turn to Nathaniel, he's staring out vacantly at the auditorium, deep in thought. I can sense his explanation coming, so I brace myself.

"The night of the last performance," he begins, his voice cutting through the stillness of the theater, "the night that Ashton had the nerve to show up unannounced, I was heading to the dressing rooms to change after the show. When I walked by, I heard Ashton's voice from inside. As soon as I overheard Ashton threatening Macie, I knew that I had to intervene."

I nod, remembering the relief that had flooded through me when Nathaniel swooped in to defend Macie.

"I was this close to putting him in his place. But before I had the chance," Nathaniel goes on, "someone else stepped in to do the honors for me. Maybe you know her? I'd never seen justice served like that before. Coming in and knocking him square in the balls like she did."

I smile. Looking back now on the situation, I know I should feel a pang of guilt for causing someone so much pain. But then again, I feel less remorse knowing the person I harmed was Ashton. If anyone deserves that type of pain, it's him.

"After that happened," I continue where Nathaniel left off, "I grabbed Macie to bring her upstairs." The blur of events flashes before me. "I just wanted to get her as far away from that room as possible. As far away from him as possible. I made sure she was okay, and then I went back down to find you."

My eyes scan his, searching for clarity.

"While you were upstairs taking care of Macie...something else happened." He shifts in his spot. "First, I told Ashton that if he didn't get the hell out of there, I was going to pull another Scarlett-level kick on him. You should have seen the look on his face," Nathaniel grins. "I watched Ashton limp out the door in defeat. That part was pretty damn gratifying, I'll admit."

Nathaniel's face grows more serious. "Then I turned toward Tina, because I had almost forgotten that she was even there. But before I knew what was happening, she pulled her phone out. And started playing a video. The video was of," Nathaniel clenches his teeth, "it was a video of *you*."

My eyes widen again, and my head starts to spin.

"A video of me?" I gape. "But why would she do that? What would she even want a video of me for?"

That night, my vision had been laser-focused on Ashton, to the point where I hadn't even noticed my peripheral surroundings.

"Scarlett, I'm not sure how she managed to capture that video of you kicking Ashton. But once she had it, she used it," his jaw tightens, "to blackmail me."

The word "blackmail" rings in my ears like the chime of a loud bell. I've seen the extent of Tina's jealousy before, but I never would have pegged her as the type of person capable of blackmail.

In denial, I shake my head. "But Nathaniel, how could she use that to threaten you? You didn't do anything wrong. There was nothing that she could hold against you in the first place."

"Nothing she could hold against me; you're right." Nathaniel's words come out carefully. "But there was something she could hold against you."

He looks down at his dangling feet. "She told me that if she sent the video to the principal, it could have the potential to tarnish your permanent high school record. That according to the Student Code of Conduct, physical violence to another student, regardless of the reason, is punishable by suspension—that it could even affect your applications to colleges next fall."

My mind goes blank. At that moment, kicking Ashton had felt like a defense mechanism. But I had never considered the full consequences of my actions. How could Tina do this to Nathaniel?

Nathaniel's voice shakes me from my internal panic. "I couldn't let that happen to you, Scarlett. You know I couldn't."

I feel as if the ground is caving beneath me. The idea that Tina would devise such a twisted scheme just to get closer to Nathaniel is shocking.

My voice barely a whisper, I ask, "So what did you do?"

"Well," Nathaniel continues, "Tina told me that I wasn't allowed to speak to you anymore. And even further," he sucks in a deep breath, "that I had to take her to prom. She said that if I did those two things, she wouldn't release the video. She also made it clear that I wasn't allowed to mention any of this to you, and if you even had the slightest hunch she was behind this, she would leak the video. I was dying to tell you, but I was worried that if I told you the truth, you might try to confront her. I couldn't take the chance, Scarlett."

The past few weeks are all beginning to make sense now, like a blurry picture finally coming into focus: the reason Nathaniel took Tina to prom, the reason he ignored me in the hallway, the reason he would barely speak to me when I confronted him. It was all because of Tina. He was protecting me from her this whole time, and I never knew.

Suddenly, an unsettling thought comes to mind. "You're with me right now, and you just told me about the video." I cast my head down, unsure if I can even finish the rest of my train of thought. "Is she going to release it?"

At my words, Nathaniel brings his hand to my shoulder, urging me to look him in the eyes. "That video is gone," he says with certainty. "Permanently."

I tilt my head in confusion. *How is he so sure?*

"I haven't gotten to the best part of the story yet." Nathaniel grins, answering my unspoken question.

There's more?

"You didn't think I'd go down without a fight, did you?" He smiles. "I couldn't just sit by the sidelines and let Tina get away with what she was doing. So, I came up with a plan."

I'm almost on the verge of hyperventilation. "What was the plan?"

"Well, as you know," he glances at me regretfully, "I appeased Tina by taking her to prom. I played the role as best as I could: matched her outfit, arrived on time, posed for pictures."

My envy grows. The last thing I want is to be reminded of Nathaniel and Tina's night together. I grip the side of the stage, because my hands need a surface to clench right now.

Nathaniel must sense my jealousy, because he shoots me a mischievous glance. "Just wait," he prefaces. "So, we arrived at the venue for dinner and found a place to sit. Once Tina was distracted, talking to other people at our table, I asked to see her phone. I told her I just wanted to send the pictures to myself."

The realization hits me.

"And that's when I was able to go in and delete the video," he continues. "I even checked her texts to make sure she hadn't sent it to anyone else."

"Nathaniel," I say, "that's brilliant."

He smiles at my praise. "After that," he goes on, "I got up to leave. Decided I didn't want to be there at all if it wasn't with you."

My voice catches in my throat. He had gone through all of this with me in mind. This whole time, I thought he was being heartless when actually his heart was in the right place.

"I guess that means," I cast my eyes down, "when I walked into prom with Gavin, I caught you right as you were leaving."

"Yeah," he nods slowly. "I knew there was the possibility of you going with someone else, but for selfish reasons, I really hoped that you weren't. I didn't know if I could handle seeing you with another date."

I shake my head in a daze. I can't believe he's speaking these actual words to my face. I want to bottle them up and keep them in a jar.

"When I saw you at the dance," I admit softly, "I was angry at first. I wanted to make you feel the way I thought you were trying to make me feel. Little did I know about all of this."

"You had a right to be angry with me," he sighs. "I hate the way I let myself treat you."

We sit there, staring at each other, as if truly seeing each other for the first time. I let myself absorb the revelations from this afternoon.

"Nathaniel, I have to ask." I break the silence. "Why did you do all of this for me in the first place? I could have faced the consequences for what I did. You didn't have to protect me like that."

He smiles and then shrugs. "Maybe because I care about you, Scarlett.

Sometimes, you make sacrifices for the people you care about. This one was worth it for me."

I suck in a deep breath. If a heart were capable of breaking out of a chest, I think mine would be lying on the floor.

His light-hearted expression shifts to one of regret. "There's something else." He tilts his head back and exhales, like he's hesitant to continue. "I also feel partially responsible that all of this happened in the first place."

I look at him with confusion.

"It's my fault," he clarifies, "that Ashton came to harass Macie that night." His eyes shift away from me as if he's afraid of my reaction. "I'm the one who left the note in Ashton's locker."

His admission hits me like a brick.

It all makes sense now.

Nathaniel had been in the locker room the night of Winter Formal. He had witnessed the way Ashton had treated Macie.

I think back to the note in my locker today. The slanted handwriting closely matched the note that Macie had shoved at me the night of the performance.

Blinking my eyes at him, I shake my head as I connect the dots. "But why?"

"I didn't think I would at first," he admits quietly, fiddling with his hands in his lap. "I thought I could just let it slide." His expression grows grim. "But then, I was walking by on the day that Ashton pulled Macie aside. The day he had told her to keep quiet about that night."

I remember Macie's tear-stricken face at her locker: the day she had confided in me about her and Ashton's "arrangement."

"I didn't report Ashton," Nathaniel interrupts my thoughts, "but it gave me an idea. I thought maybe if I could just shake him a little—at least throw him off-balance—then I could make him understand the implications of his actions. I wanted him to know that someone else was watching out for Macie. I had no idea it would lead to him showing up in the dressing room that night." Nathaniel casts his head down, placing his hands on his temples. "It was my fault that Ashton was there. That you were involved." He shakes his head, as if internalizing the confession. "That Tina was able to capture that video."

I'm suddenly overcome with a swell of emotions. Thinking back to last November, I remember watching Nathaniel on this very stage for the first time as he recited his monologue. Back then, I had been enamored with the illusion of him I had created in my head—like a two-dimensional slide being projected on a wall. This time, though, I find myself moved by the real flesh-and-blood person that he is. For exposing his fears and shortcomings, his insecurities and imperfections. But most importantly, for the heart he's demonstrated to me just now.

My fingertips brush against his cheek. The movement causes him to swivel his head toward me so that we're staring directly at each other.

"Nathaniel, I just want to say…thank you."

He tilts his head toward me. "So you're not upset with me? After putting you through all I did?"

I lean into him until I'm resting my head on his shoulder. "Upset with you? After what you did for me? For Macie? No. I think appreciation is more like it."

At the sound of those words, Nathaniel exhales. He laces his fingers with mine and gives them a reassuring squeeze.

When I look up, I notice a smile flit across his face. "So, you don't think I'd be better off in a photo like Dorian Gray?"

I laugh at the absurdity of the insult I had thrown at him the other week. Looking back now, I can't believe I would compare him to such a narcissistic character.

"I'm sorry for saying that. And no. I think I kind of like you just the way you are."

His eyes glimmer. "Right back at you."

All of a sudden, I think back to the NYU sign I had seen in his lawn the night of prom. He must be over the moon about his acceptance. I'm tempted to bring it up, but I also want to sit here and enjoy this moment a little longer. I'm about to congratulate him, but before I can, the bell rings.

"I guess that's our cue," I murmur.

Nathaniel nods with reluctance. Pushing himself up from the stage, he holds out a hand to assist me. I allow him to lift me from the floor until I'm standing upright next to him. We both grab our backpacks.

"Can I walk you to your next class?" Nathaniel asks.

Looking back at him, I roll my eyes—the answer's already obvious. There's nothing I would prefer more.

As we begin to make our way out of the mini-theater side-by-side, I reflect on how far we've come in such a short period of time. Seeing the lengths that Nathaniel would go for me—knowing that he cares—gives me a renewed sense of hope. Maybe there is a chance for the two of us after all. I smile to myself as I relish the feeling of optimism, and I hope that this time it's here to stay.

We round the corner of the hallway, which is now filling with students heading to class.

"Scarlett?"

All of a sudden, I hear my name being called from behind me. As I turn around, I notice Mr. Walsh standing with his arms crossed, leaning against his office door.

"May I speak to you in my office for a moment, please?"

I nod. "I'll see you later," I mutter under my breath to Nathaniel.

"Scarlett, wait—"

But before Nathaniel can finish, I make my way toward Mr. Walsh's office.

"If you could close the door behind you." Mr. Walsh's expression is unreadable as I enter.

The panic within me grows. I think about the possibilities of what information he might have. What if Tina sent him the video? Does he know what happened with Ashton? Were all of Nathaniel's efforts to protect me and Macie in vain?

Quietly, I shut the door and make my way to the empty seat in front of his desk. With sweating palms, I lower myself into it. I watch Mr. Walsh as he fiddles with the pen on his desk, seemingly unwilling to look me in the eyes.

"So, Scarlett," Mr. Walsh clears his throat and places his hands together, "I recently found out a surprising piece of information I wanted to discuss. It has to do with Macie. And *you.*"

That's it. It's all over. I'm going to get suspended. Macie's privacy has probably been thrown out the window. Tina will get away with her scheme.

"Mr. Walsh, I can explain—" I begin. But before I can go any further, he wags a finger in the air.

"Now, be honest with me. I need to hear this straight from the source." Mr. Walsh says.

I can barely breathe.

"I found out that you," he pauses, "that you…." He waits for an excruciatingly long beat. "That you made Macie's dress at prom. From scratch?" He shakes his head incredulously. "She showed me the pictures during class today, and I thought it was magnificent. The craftsmanship, the detailing. For someone who just learned how to use a sewing machine not too long ago, I'm very impressed. You have quite a gift."

The air returns to my lungs, and I breathe a sigh of relief. This conversation is taking a different direction from what I had envisioned, and I'm so much happier with the outcome.

"Yes," I say. "That's all true. Took me a couple of weeks to do. A lot of research, late nights, and trial and error, but I finally finished it."

"Scarlett, the other reason I brought you in here, on top of telling you that," Mr. Walsh says, "is that I'd like to offer you a design internship with the costume shop this summer. We usually reserve our internships for those who have worked with the theater department in the past, but I was impressed with your initiative and enthusiasm over the course of the play. Plus, after seeing the dress you made for Macie, I think you would be an asset to the team. It's a great opportunity to learn more about design, and it will help you stand out on your high school transcript. When I was thinking about who would be a good fit, you came to mind."

"M-m-mister Walsh," I stammer, "I don't know what to say. I would love to work for the costume shop this summer." I can barely contain my excitement.

"Great," he smiles. "I'll send you the application. You can just fill it out and send it back my way. We'll make sure you're compensated with credit hours this summer, too."

"That would be awesome. Thank you for the opportunity." I grin from ear to ear. Then I pause when I think about my job with Fashion Fwrd. "Mr. Walsh, would it still be okay if I work my retail job this summer, too? I was hoping to save up some extra money for college."

He nods. "Of course, Scarlett. The internship hours are manageable, so I don't see why you can't do both."

Finally, I'll get to fuse my love of retail fashion with my new-found passion for theater. With graduation on the horizon, I'm now looking forward to this summer even more.

"Oh, and one more thing," Mr. Walsh says. "I've offered Macie an internship to help direct the junior musical this summer. I know she wants to go into teaching, and I thought it would be great exposure for her to try out directing the kids."

Macie is going to be there, too? I feel like jumping for joy.

"Yes, which means you two will be working closely together this summer. Buckle up. You both are in for a ride."

Hearing that Macie and I will be working together is the cherry on top. Who would have thought that things would turn out this way? I recall my dad's words about how in the end, good things happen to good people, and I smile.

"Mr. Walsh, I can't thank you enough." I get up from my seat and collect my backpack. "I'm really grateful to you for helping me learn how to sew."

"Hey, I just gave you the tools for success. You pieced all the material together, so to speak. You have a promising career ahead of you, Scarlett. I'm excited to see what you achieve."

I beam at Mr. Walsh as I wave to him and exit his office. Hurrying toward my next class, I pull out my phone.

Mr. Walsh broke the news to me. Can't believe we both have internships now. Excited to take on the junior musical together this summer! #DreamTeam

I watch the three dots appear on my screen. Macie responds back. *Double the trouble. Those kids don't know what's coming between your design skills and my directing. ;)*

I laugh at the screen and then exit out of my chat with Macie. When I type in Nathaniel's name, I see a new message from him has popped up.

Scarlett, are you okay? What did Mr. Walsh have to say?

False alarm. I text. *No issues with Mr. Walsh. He wanted to talk to me about working as a design intern in the costume shop this summer.*

Nathaniel texts back almost right away. *Phew—that's awesome! The drama department is lucky to have a designer like you. Maybe you can design another dress like the red one you were wearing the day we first met.*

My cheeks flush at the memory.

Another text from Nathaniel lights up my screen.

Want to go to the senior cookout this week?

My face lights up. Our school's senior cookout is a tradition hosted each year to celebrate the achievements of the senior class. It's an additional opportunity for the underclassmen to spend time with the seniors before graduation.

I type back. *Bring on the burgers and hotdogs. I can't wait.*

Chapter Nineteen

Y ou have an eyelash." Nathaniel reaches across the picnic
blanket to capture it. "Don't move."

Gently, he grazes my cheek with his thumb. I squeeze my eyes shut and remain motionless.

When I open my eyes again, Nathaniel has his thumb in front of my face with the single eyelash. "Make a wish." His face is gentle and expectant.

I look up at him and shake my head. "I don't need to. I've got what I want right here."

After all, what could be better than this? Sunshine, cookouts, and Nathaniel.

His face lights up as he pulls me closer. Leaning against him, I stare out at the courtyard in front of us. Students are sprawled out on blankets, lounging in the sun, and listening to music coming from the adjacent speaker system.

Speaking of seniors, I turn back to Nathaniel, who looks perfectly content in his baseball cap and sunglasses, lounging on the blanket next to me. A pang of sadness hits me when I think about his imminent graduation, but I push the thought away for now. I know we'll have to discuss it at some point. Right now, I just want to enjoy this time together.

Lifting myself off of the blanket, I brush the grass off my pants. "I'm gonna grab some soda. You want anything?"

"Nah, I'm good." He pats the ground next to him. "I'll guard your spot for you while you're gone."

With my empty can in hand, I trudge across the lawn, making my way over to the table lined with coolers. Unfortunately, it seems as if every other student had the idea at the same time that I did. I walk toward the back of the line and take my place at the end.

As I stand there listening to the chatter around me, I feel a sudden tap on my back. The unexpected gesture startles me, and I turn around. Standing behind me is Tina, of all people.

"Scarlett," she speaks, her voice guarded, "can we talk for a sec?"
Talk, huh?

After finding out what she did, I was hoping I'd never have to look at her, much less engage in a full-length conversation with her, again. Unluckily for me, she seems to have me cornered. Considering the mile-long line, it doesn't leave much of a choice.

Narrowing my eyes at her, I keep my mouth sealed. After all, silence is probably better than the bitter words I'm thinking of saying right now.

"Look," she breathes a defeated sigh, "I'm not here to pick a fight. I just wanted to say that," she swallows, like she's having trouble getting the words out, "I'm sorry."
Sorry? It's a little late for apologies now...isn't it?

I sneer. "Listen, Tina, I'll stand here and listen to your apology, if that's what it takes for you to leave me alone, but I need you to know that I will never forget what you did. To Nathaniel. Or to me."

"I know there's nothing I can say or do to excuse what I did. But if you just let me explain it from my perspective, then maybe you can understand where I was coming from."

"Go ahead," I scoff. "But no matter what you say, you can't make up for the fact that you blackmailed Nathaniel, sabotaged our relationship, and almost got me suspended from school."

"You're right. I know how awful it was, and how much I could have ruined your life, but I swear that wasn't my intention," she murmurs. "I think I just got so carried away that I didn't care who I hurt, as long as I got what I wanted."

I'm not sure what she's trying to accomplish with this conversation, but it doesn't seem like she's getting very far.

"Please, just hear me out," she pleads. "The last night of the performance, I started recording, because I thought that a fight might break out between Nathaniel and Ashton. I didn't know what was going on. But then, when you came into the room and kicked Ashton, it was such a golden opportunity. I was about to delete the video, but that's when the idea popped into my head."

"The idea to blackmail him, you mean?"

"Yes, and I regret it." She casts her head down. "You have to understand, Scarlett, when I first started in theater as a freshman, I was a nobody. I'd be lucky to even get cast in a supporting role. But this year, when Nathaniel moved here, I asked if he could give me some pointers. Not only did he do that, but he even spent some time helping me with my technique."

Nathaniel had helped Tina with her acting?

"It took determination," Tina admits, "but Mr. Walsh started noticing my improvement. You probably wouldn't believe it, but *Our Town* was actually my first lead role. I couldn't wait to act opposite Nathaniel for the first time. He had seen the potential in me, and I was ready to show him that I deserved to be standing up there next to him."

I'll admit—Tina's confession piques my interest. Up until this point, I never would have guessed that this was her first lead role with the drama department. She seemed so boastful the day of the department store run-in. I had simply assumed acting ran in her blood.

Tina brings her eyes back up to mine, "And that's one of the reasons

I think I snapped. I had a crush on Nathaniel, but he never showed the same type of interest in me." She releases a sigh. "But then you came along and somehow captured his interest in one night at that New Year's Party."

I feel my gut clench at Tina's retelling. All this time, I thought Tina was the threat to my relationship with Nathaniel. But I was the one posing a threat to her.

"The more I watched you two together, the more jealous I grew," she recalls. "I had hoped that if I spent enough time practicing with him for *Our Town*, he'd begin to see me in a different light. But by that point, he already seemed to be so set on you. The way his face lit up when you entered the room. The way he'd talk about you when you were nearby. I wondered if you had never come into his life, if I might have still had a chance."

Tina's admission makes my heart constrict. I didn't know how affected she was by Nathaniel, or my relationship with him, for that matter.

"Flash forward to the night I got the video footage of you," Tina resumes her train of thought. "It was at that moment I realized I could hold the video against Nathaniel, because it was of you. He would be willing to agree to my terms, because he would do whatever it took to protect you. I thought if I could just snap him out of his interest, he'd eventually move on. And that if we went to prom together, I could finally admit how I really felt.

"But I could tell Nathaniel wasn't being himself anymore. I knew what I had done was wrong, but I didn't know how to fix it. When I wasn't paying attention at prom, he deleted the video and then left right after. At that point, I realized that there was no changing his mind about you. No matter what I said, or how much I intervened, I couldn't force him to like me. And I couldn't force him to not like you." She casts her eyes down. "So, long story short, I guess that's why I did it."

A lump rises in my throat. What Tina did was inexcusable, no matter the rationale. Yet, I do feel an inkling of sympathy for Tina. Her hardened exterior isn't a charade. It's a shield built to conceal her deeper insecurities. This whole time, I felt intimidated by her when in actuality, we were both intimidated by each other.

"Tina, if I've learned anything from this past year, it's that feelings are inexplicable. Complicated. Messy. And because of that, you don't have to worry about trying so hard. When the right person comes along, you won't need to convince that person to be with you. You know why? Because they'll already know all of the reasons."

Tina looks back at me with big eyes, like she's finally seeing me for the first time. "It's not fair, Scarlett. You're so confident in yourself, and you make it sound easy. How do you do it?"

Does she really think that I have my life together? Here I am, second-guessing myself and overanalyzing every move I make. Yet, Tina thinks that I'm the one with worldly wisdom?

I shake my head. "Maybe I somehow hide it, but I can assure you: I can be a mess, just like everyone else at this school."

"Huh," she snickers. "It just seems like you always have it figured out. Like it comes naturally to you."

"Look who's talking," I shake my head. "You're the one who makes it look easy."

For the first time, the hint of an authentic smile forms on Tina's face. "Scarlett?" she asks. "You're really not as bad as I thought, are you?"

If that's her form of a compliment, I'll take it. "Thanks."

Actual, genuine praise from Tina.

I take a deep breath. Maybe it's time to let my resentment toward Tina go. I could spend the rest of this year harboring a grudge, but I know that it would only be weighing me down. After all, I want to be free, and accepting the olive branch seems like the best way to do that.

I may never be able to forget what she did, but I can at least forgive.

"You too, Tina." I smile. "Well, just minus the insults and blackmailing."

Tina blinks back at me. Her expression is indecipherable.

And then...

She *laughs*.

A real, hearty laugh.

As if this weren't enough to surprise me, Tina steps forward. Before I know what's happening, she reaches out her arms and pulls me into an unexpected hug. "Thanks, Scarlett." She squeezes me tightly.

After what feels like an eternity, Tina releases me and points in front of us. Turning around, I realize that she's motioning to the drinks table that we've finally reached. I step up and grab another soda, discarding my old can in the trash can next to me.

"Well," I turn back to her, clutching my soda can with one hand, "enjoy the rest of the cookout, Tina."

She smiles. "You, too."

With that, she turns and disappears into the crowd.

As I make my way back toward the blanket, I notice that Macie and Liam have joined Nathaniel. The two of them are sprawled out next to him, basking in the sun's warm glow.

"There you are!" Macie exclaims as she spots me. "I was worried you got lost in the drink line." She tilts her sunglasses down, giving me a direct look. "Also, was my mind playing tricks on me, or did I just see Tina give you a big hug?"

I laugh. "I'm glad I at least have a witness now. I almost didn't believe it myself."

Macie gapes, "Later, you are telling me everything."

"I promise," I nod, "I won't skip a detail."

Sinking down next to Nathaniel on the blanket, I open my soda can.

"Tina, huh?" He turns in my direction, furrowing a brow. "Should I be concerned?"

I take a swig. "Maybe about the fact that she's capable of an actual apology," I chuckle, "but that's about it."

Leaning into him, I rest my head on his shoulder. I close my eyes, savoring the carefree moment. There's nowhere I'd rather be than right here, right now.

Chapter Twenty

I glance down at my old middle school bike as I pedal. It's a pastel yellow color, with a woven basket and a bell on the handlebar. I'll admit: it's not the coolest mode of transportation, but it'll do the trick for a short ride. I've decided I'm going to surprise Nathaniel. I have yet to tell him how close we live to each other, so I thought I would swing by and see what he's up to. I steer my bike smoothly onto his road and slow down as I approach my desired destination: Nathaniel's house.

I still recognize the details, as if I had just walked past them. The winding walkway. The planted daffodils lining the exterior. The wrought iron gate leading to the backyard.

My heart beats faster. I debate turning the bike around and heading back. But instead, I muster up the courage to look in the direction of the lawn.

My eyes search out the graduation sign.

And...

It's still there.

I chuckle at my unnecessary doubt. What did I expect—for the sign to have disappeared magically overnight? For this not to be Nathaniel's house, after all? I shake my head to myself when another object catches my attention. My eyes meet another sign—but not a congratulatory graduation one. This sign is a new addition to the lawn.

It's attached to a wooden stake planted into the ground. The red background and bold letters are unmistakable. There is no denying what type of sign it is. The words "For Sale" are featured distinctively.

I blink my eyes, trying to talk myself out of seeing what I'm seeing. *My mind must be playing tricks on me.*

I shake my head, unwilling to accept the words in front of me.

It's not true, I think. *It can't be true that Nathaniel is...moving?!*

In my mind, I had envisioned the two of us having so much time. Finishing school together. Spending the whole summer together. Even once he leaves for college, I assumed he would come back regularly and visit. But if his family sells the house, then there would be no reason for him to come back, and nothing for him to come back to.

My bike continues to coast a couple more feet when a voice startles me from behind. But not just any voice—one that I could pinpoint from miles away. I turn around and see the silhouette of my simultaneous best dream and worst nightmare: *Nathaniel.*

He's making his way down toward the mailbox, eyes wide with surprise. Meanwhile, I'm frozen to my bicycle, gliding farther away.

Still in motion, I realize that my bike is no longer moving in the direction I had meant to steer it. In vain, I attempt to overcorrect for my mistake, but it's no use. The bike swerves unsteadily, veering one way and then the other. Suddenly, the trunk of a tree comes into sight, growing larger by the second. I slam on the brakes with full force, but it's too late. There's nothing left for me to do except brace myself for impact.

I watch with horror as the front of my bike slams into the tree. With no choice left, I tumble down to the ground along with my bike. My right arm breaks the fall as I hit the grass with a thud.

"Scarlett!" Nathaniel's voice grows louder.

Remaining motionless, I lie on the ground, listening to his footsteps grow closer. Silently, I plead for the superpower to disappear into a puff of smoke—how I wish I could transport myself anywhere that's not here.

As Nathaniel's face comes into view, my chest tightens. He just caught me spot on in another embarrassing moment—this time, falling off of my bicycle.

His face is etched with concern as he kneels down to inspect me. With care, he lifts the arm that I had landed on. "Does it hurt?" His voice is laced with worry. "Are you bleeding?"

Extending my elbow back and forth, I test whether it still functions properly. I may have a couple of bruises after this, but thankfully, my arm still feels operational. Since the damage has already been done, I can at least make light of the situation.

"Not my arm," I murmur. "I think my pride is pretty wounded, though."

With his gaze trained on me, Nathaniel lowers my arm back down. "You just about gave me a heart attack." His face floods with relief. We both look at each other quietly as I sit, recovering from my scare.

"You want to know something funny?" he asks.

I nod in curiosity. "Always."

"It seems like you somehow prefer being horizontal to vertical, doesn't it?"

My interest piqued, I cradle my injured arm near my chest. "What do you mean?"

"Well," he laughs, "first fainting at work, and now falling off of your bike." He reaches his hand out to me. "I think your body is trying to tell you it likes the ground."

I stick my tongue out at him. "The ground is better for circulation," I scoff playfully. With his hand, he pulls me up so I'm back on my feet. After helping me dust myself off, he flashes a grin. "Okay." He grabs my bike from the ground, which thankfully doesn't seem to have any damage. "Come with me."

Before I can interrogate, Nathaniel wheels my bike forward, leaving me no choice but to trail along next to him.

I realize that he's leading me in the direction of a park across the street from his house. As we approach, Nathaniel props my bike against the fence. He motions for me to follow him, walking over to an open spot of grass. I watch as he lowers himself to the ground until he's lying completely flat on his back.

"You're right. The circulation is better down here."

"Very funny." I fall to my knees until I'm lying down next to him.

"So," he muses, "you were riding by my house just now?"

Bringing my hands to my face, I'm thankful that I can't see my own cheeks right now. If I could, I imagine that they'd be the color of two freshly picked tomatoes.

With a laugh, Nathaniel inches forward until he places his hands on top of mine. Carefully, he pries my fingers back from my face, so he can get a clear view of me.

"Okay…" I begin. After releasing a deep breath, I decide to finally spill my confession, like ripping off a Band-Aid. "Yeah, I actually live just over there," I point in the direction of my street.

Nathaniel's eyes dart back and forth, as if he's wrapping his brain around the realization. "Have you known we're neighbors the whole time we've known each other?"

"No," I shake my head. "I found out just on prom night. When I saw the NYU sign in your lawn, I just knew this was your house."

As I look over at him again, I brace myself for the worst. But to my surprise, Nathaniel grins unexpectedly and then places his head in his hands. "I begged my mom not to buy a graduation banner, but of course, she did anyway. How embarrassing is that?"

His displeasure at the sign makes me smile. "The sign's hilarious." I turn toward him. "And it's a huge accomplishment getting into NYU. She must be so proud."

"Thanks," he exhales. "She is. And it's a relief that all the hard work finally paid off."

We continue to lie there in the grass, looking up at the sky. I feel the sun's warmth beating down on my skin as a gentle breeze sweeps over me. When I prop myself up to look at Nathaniel again, I notice his expression is pensive, as if his mind is miles away.

"We could have had so much more time together."

I interlace my fingers with his. "Maybe, the world dislikes the idea of the two of us together."

Nathaniel nods. The next thing I know, he moves until he's hovering above me, his face only a few inches from mine. His fingertips caress my cheek.

"Well then, it stinks for the world," he says, "because I kind of like the two of us together."

My heart constricts. "I kind of like the two of us together, too."

"And you want to know another thing that I like?"

"What would that be?"

"I kind of like you right now," he whispers, "in this horizontal position."

Is there a reason that my body feels like it's suddenly about to burst into flames? Before I can respond, Nathaniel moves in closer, until his lips are practically brushing up against mine. "Makes it a little easier to do this."

As my mouth pops open in surprise, Nathaniel moves his lips to mine, absorbing the shock. He places one hand at the nape of my neck, tilting my head forward as his other hand snakes around my waist. I'm grinning against him as I pull him closer, bringing my hands to his shirt. The butterflies beat in my chest as Nathaniel takes my breath away with his kiss. In my mind, I take a mental snapshot. No interruptions, no obstacles, no world "undermining" us. Just him and me in one picture-perfect moment. I wish it could always be like this.

As Nathaniel pulls away, I give my breathing time to catch up, considering he just knocked the wind out of me. I look back up at him, but the good humor I saw only seconds ago is fading, replaced with a hint of melancholy.

"What is it?" I ask cautiously, bringing my hand to his face.

"I'm guessing you saw the other sign, too."

"Yes," my voice catches in my throat as I prepare to ask the difficult question. "When are you moving?"

He looks away. It feels as if my world is crumbling all over again—like the ground is physically splitting in two beneath me. When he turns back, his eyes fill with remorse. "I just found out." He exhales. "My dad's a financial advisor, and he got a relocation offer in New York City that he can't pass up. With me leaving for NYU so soon, and my parents wanting to be closer to me, it makes the most sense for our family."

Nathaniel looks at me warily, like he's afraid to answer me. "After graduation. Right after graduation."

Right after graduation?

That's way too soon.

My eyes sting as I blink back the tears forming in them. "When were you going to tell me? Why didn't you say something earlier?"

"I'm sorry, Scarlett," he pleads. "I should have told you right after I found out." He pauses. "I guess I was afraid."

"Afraid of what?" I beseech, scooting myself away from him. I need some distance, because right now, I can barely look him in the eyes.

"I was afraid," he continues in a low tone, "that you might not want to be with me at all if you knew I was leaving so soon. I thought if I waited a couple days, then maybe we could just enjoy the time we have without anything hanging over our heads. Just for a little while."

I shake my head in disbelief. "So, you were just going to pretend like everything was okay, and then drop the bomb right before graduation?

You were going to blindside me like that?"

"Scarlett," he implores, "I know how it sounds. And I know I should have told you sooner. I was just waiting for the right time. Is it so bad, though, that all I wanted was to have as much time with you as possible before the move?"

My eyes glisten as I take a deep breath. "I think you might be right."

He tilts his head. "About us making the most of the time we have together?"

With a heavy pit in my stomach, I shake my head. My hands tremble as I prepare to speak the unspeakable. "That maybe we shouldn't be seeing each other with you moving away so soon."

"No," he says immediately.

"Think about it, Nathaniel," I whisper. "The more time we spend together, the harder it's going to be to say goodbye. I can barely handle the thought now." The lump in my throat rises.

He shakes his head. "What are you saying?"

"I'm saying," I take another deep breath, barely able to speak, "that maybe we should just end whatever this is now. It will hurt, but it can't hurt nearly as much as it will when you move."

"Scarlett," Nathaniel laughs humorlessly, "you can't expect me to agree with you on that. Knowing we still have time left after we've already lost so much of it." He motions with his hand. "I don't want to give up the time we have left."

"The thought is killing me on the inside, too. But it'll make it easier for both of us."

"Scarlett, you don't get to decide what's best for me."

I ignore the swell of tears rising to the surface. "But I can decide what's best for me."

With those words, I push myself up from the ground, brushing off the blades of grass still sticking to my shirt and pants. Once I've removed the last pieces, I begin to make my way across the park without looking back. Fighting back tears, I take my bicycle from along the fence.

Before I can mount my bike, Nathaniel runs toward me and grabs hold of my shoulders, spinning me around in one sweeping motion. "Scarlett, what are you doing? We have other options. We can talk about long-distance. We could visit each other regularly."

I want all of those things so badly, but I'm torn and confused right now. I don't know what this summer is going to look like, much less next year. What happens when he starts college in the fall? How often would we be able to see each other? What if he meets someone new?

"I need you to listen to me," I speak with determination. Placing my hands at his jaw, I tilt his head up so he's looking me straight in the eyes. "I've come to some important realizations in the last couple of weeks," I pause. "And after a lot of thought, I've come to the conclusion that I don't believe in fate. I don't believe that two people are meant to be together. And I definitely don't believe that there are signs leading us in the right direction." I shake my head. "But I swear, even though I know that those things are made-up and that the world is unfair sometimes," my voice catches in my throat, "you make me wish that, maybe, just maybe, I believed in them."

Nathaniel opens his mouth to speak, but before he can, I mount my bicycle and begin pedaling. All I know is that I need to let go right now. I want him to remember me just like this, with those words immortalized in his head. I hear him calling out my name, but I don't look back. I can't look back.

The only way to go is forward, and by setting him free, I'm helping us both move in that direction. With graduation on the horizon, this is the way it needs to be.

Chapter Twenty-One

I 'm swiveling back and forth at the counter of Dotty's Diner, watching Gavin chew on a cheese fry. Though we're technically not allowed to leave school during lunch, I convinced him to sneak off with me today, emphasizing that the matter was particularly urgent. I'll admit that may have been a slight embellishment, but the truth is that I needed a listening ear, and I could use his advice.

I grab one of the cheese fries from his plate and pop it in my mouth.

"I'm sorry that you have to see me in a rough mood," I sigh. "It just feels like the world is playing games with me right now. I appreciate you being here with me."

"No problem, Scarlett. Happy to be a listening ear," Gavin muses. "And I get it. I know things can be tough sometimes, but they'll work themselves out. The bad and good, they go hand-in-hand."

I smile weakly. "Thanks, Gavin. That means a lot. It's just so hard, you know?"

"I understand how you feel, Scarlett," he swivels his stool back, grabbing another fry from his plate. "Things seem tough at first, but they'll get better." His expression is soft. "Sometimes, we just have to make the most of the cards we're dealt."

He shrugs casually and then goes back to eating his fries. Meanwhile, I'm left contemplating his advice.

As Gavin's words ring in my head, another ring startles me from the counter. I turn to see Macie's name flash across the screen of my phone. I pick it up and swipe to answer the call.

"Hello?"

"Scarlett!" Macie practically shouts into her phone. I hold mine back from my ear, so as not to damage my hearing. "Where are you? It's almost time for the Senior Clap-Out."

"I know," I reassure her. "I'll be back soon."

"What?" she gasps. "You left campus?"

I'm amused by Macie's shock at my defiance of the typical school rules, especially since I'm not usually the rule-breaker. "Relax," I laugh. "I'm with Gavin."

"Why didn't you tell me? I'd have come with."

"Macie, you're in class right now."

She sighs, "I know, I know." There's a pause on the line. "I just want to be here for you today, Scar. I know you're reluctant to be there for the walk." I hear her voice drop to a whisper, "Considering...." She trails off without finishing her sentence.

I know what she's referring to without her having to finish saying it.

After I'd gotten home from my emotionally-fueled encounter with Nathaniel, I had called her and forced her to come over. Between heavy breaths, I'd confided in her about biking by his house, discovering the sign, and the difficult decision I made. Regardless of the reason, she hadn't held it against me or made objections. Instead, she'd wrapped her arms around me and held me, rocking me back and forth until the tears began to subside. She'd been exactly what I needed in that moment: the perfect shoulder to cry on.

And this is why she knows how challenging today will be for me, considering the Senior Clap-Out. Another ritual at our school, the clap-out, is held every year during the last week of classes. All of the graduating seniors march through the hallways while their biggest supporters—parents, teachers, and other students—gather around, clapping for the seniors exiting the building. In past years, I've always looked forward to this commemoratory sendoff—for the opportunity to congratulate my classmates on their important milestone.

It's too bad that today, for the first time, I'd rather be anywhere but.

Since our last encounter, I've done a successful job of avoiding Nathaniel. I purposefully changed my route in the hallway so there'd be no possibility of running into him. I slipped into classes early, so he wouldn't be able to wait outside for me. I even ignored the paper notes that he left in my locker, asking for me to meet with him. I knew if I saw him again, my resolve would crumble.

Instead, I've been fighting to return to a regular routine...to adjust to a world that doesn't include Nathaniel Wilder...for that matter, that doesn't have Nathaniel Wilder in it at all. This is what my life will be like next year, and the only way to embrace it is to practice living it—every painful, difficult moment of it.

But now, as much as I want to play hooky and skip the rest of the day, I know I can't miss the clap-out. It's supposed to be a special occasion. I shouldn't deny myself the opportunity to take part in it, simply because I'm afraid to see Nathaniel again. After all, he'll be so swept up by the excitement of the crowd; he probably won't even notice me.

Realizing that Macie is still waiting for me to respond, I try my best to sound cheery. "I'll be okay," I assure her. "I'll be there."

"Okay, Scar," she responds gently. "I'll see you soon."

I end the call and look back at Gavin, thinking about his advice.

Shaking my head, I sigh. Maybe he's got a point. What I really need to do is change my perspective. Why am I sitting around sulking when I'm the one contributing to my own unhappiness? Here I am grieving the loss of a short-lived relationship with Nathaniel, when in fact, maybe I should be doing the opposite, like reveling in the rarity of it.

How unique is it for two people to come together the way we did?

Can't we still savor the moments we have left, appreciate the time we have while we still have it?

The realization hits me. If I want something, I need to change my mindset rather than allow myself to remain a victim of circumstance. I don't need some stupid sign to tell me what to do—it's time I take matters into my own hands.

"Gavin," I shake my head. "You're right. I can't just sit here feeling helpless. If I want something, then I should make the most of the cards I've been dealt and go fight for it."

He slips one more fry from his plate before nodding in approval. "That's the spirit."

Before getting up from the counter, I swivel toward him again, "Can we do lunch again sometime soon?"

After his reassurance today, I want to work on making Gavin a more constant person in my life. He's been a good friend, and I'm getting used to having him to talk to. Plus, he deserves to have someone who will be there for him, the same way he's been there for me.

Grinning, Gavin nods. "You bet."

* * *

The stomping of feet reverberates throughout the corridor as I hear the seniors approaching. I watch them shake hands with teachers, high-five their friends, and wave to parents as they march by. Taking a deep breath, I think about my own future clap-out. A shiver surges through me as I imagine myself in their shoes. In exactly one year from now, that will be me.

Macie, who's cheering loudly beside me, points her finger at the crowd.

"There's Liam!" she claps enthusiastically, calling him over. Liam makes his way toward us, pushing through the swarm of students.

When he finally gets to us, he reaches out and engulfs Macie in a massive hug.

"Wow," Macie sniffles, "I told myself I wasn't going to cry."

Liam laughs as she wipes a tear from her face. "I told you that you would. Who wouldn't cry saying goodbye to me?"

"The last thing you need is an ego boost." Macie squeezes him harder.

Liam reacts with a mocking grimace. "Wow, has anyone ever told you that you have a tight grip?"

"Shut up," Macie snaps, finally releasing him. "You love my public displays of affection."

He winks at her as he spins back around toward the crowd. "You know I do," he calls before being swept away by the other students.

As I stare back out at the herd of moving seniors, a sudden pit forms in my stomach. If Liam just walked by, then I can't deny the sense that another person I know cannot be far behind. Taking a deep breath, I move my eyes back to the general crowd.

And that's when I spot him.

As if we have telepathic powers, his eyes meet mine at the same second. My first instinct is to look away, but I don't. Instead, I keep my eyes on him, like I'm being hypnotized.

I had told myself that I was doing the right thing by ending things when I did—that I was protecting both him and myself from further heartache. Yet, here in this moment, watching him make his final strides through the school, my justification disappears. Every feeling I've felt for him comes flooding back, engulfing me.

What was I thinking before? He was right; we still had time. Why was I not focused on enjoying it before it was gone? I should be cherishing the moments we have left, not running from them. I know he had waited to tell me about the move, but his intentions weren't to hurt me. They were to spend as much time with me as possible, trying to make up the time that had been taken from us.

Before I'm aware of my actions, I begin shoving my way through the unrelenting crowd, like a fish swimming upstream. I hear Macie call out my name, but I barely notice. The only person in my line of vision is Nathaniel. And all I know is that I need to get to him.

Pushing through the sea of moving bodies, I reach him before he is halfway down the hall. We both stand stationary, unable to move. Neither one of us looks away, and neither one of us speaks.

Exhaling sharply, I take a shaky breath. "Nathaniel."

Before I know what is happening, Nathaniel grabs my arms and pulls me to him. He presses me against his chest in one swift motion, wrapping his arms tightly around my shoulders and resting the base of his chin on my head. Hugging him back, I melt into the warmth and familiarity of his embrace. Once again, I find myself consumed to the point where our surroundings don't even matter. I cling to him like I don't want to let go.

As we both pull back slowly, untangling ourselves from each other, my heart aches.

"I thought I could do it before, but I just can't say goodbye." My voice wavers.

"Then don't." He stares back at me with intensity. "I'm sure I'm not ready to say goodbye to you."

I nod in a daze. "So just to be clear, this interaction is not a goodbye."

"Nope." He raises his hand in the air for effect. "No goodbyes being said here."

"Good." I nod with more conviction this time. "I'm sorry about what I said before. I take it all back. I know you're leaving soon, and we don't have much time, but I want to be with you. Whatever time we have left before the move, I want it to be with you."

He wraps his arms around me and crushes me in his embrace one more time. "It feels so good to hear you say that."

Lifting my head from his chest, I notice the flood of students jostling us on both sides. With remorse, I pull away from him. "I should let you go now," I whisper.

His eyes widen as if I just shot him directly in the heart. At the same time, I realize the misinterpretation of my words. I give him a knowing smile. "Let you keep walking, I mean."

"My grad party is next weekend, right after graduation. Promise me you'll be there?"

I nod immediately. "Of course," I assure him. "Of course, I'll be there."

"It's at 6:00 p.m. that Saturday," he says hurriedly as the crowd begins sweeping him away. "At my house."

With that, he fades into the distance, leaving me breathless in the middle of the hallway.

Chapter Twenty-Two

Over a week has passed since the clap-out, and today is officially the day of Nathaniel's grad party. I've spent the last week hanging out with him, Macie, and Liam, maximizing our time together before the move.

It's hard to believe that today was officially graduation. I would have gone to the actual ceremony itself, but it turns out that tickets were restricted to only a few guests per graduate. As much as I wish I could've been there cheering Nathaniel on, it makes sense that his immediate family and relatives would take priority. Because of this, the graduation party will be the first time I'm seeing him on the flip side: officially a graduate. The thought both excites and terrifies me.

Right now, Macie and I are making our way up the sloping path leading to Nathaniel's house. I'm purposefully going at a slower pace, just to delay the inevitable.

"I don't know if I can do this," I groan. "Maybe, we should just turn back now."

Gazing at the sky, I inhale a deep breath and then turn to Macie.

"Scarlett," she says matter-of-factly, "you're not missing Nathaniel's graduation party. Even if I have to pick you up and drag you straight through that door."

I release a defeated huff. "But it doesn't make it any easier to know he's leaving."

Macie's face is soft with sympathy, "I know, Scar. I know." She places a reassuring hand on my shoulder. "It doesn't have to be easy. But it has to be done."

I hate that she's right.

We walk up the steps to the front door, stopping directly on the porch. Nervously, I reach out for the brass door handle. I'm about to turn the knob, but then I stop myself.

"Macie." I'm suddenly unable to go any further. "How do I even say goodbye?"

Macie's expression turns to a mixture of amusement and compassion. "C'mon, Scar. It's not goodbye forever. Just a goodbye for now."

I soak in her words. "Just a goodbye for now," I repeat. "I might be able to do that."

"Now, what are we waiting for?" Macie asks. "I want to play some cornhole and take advantage of free food." She reaches for the handle and swings the door open in one quick motion. "Let's get in there."

I take another deep breath and then follow her inside. As I step into the entryway, the first sound I hear is the chatter of voices drifting from the kitchen. Looking around, I notice how bare the foyer is, nothing but white walls and empty floors. The only objects in the adjacent dining room appear to be a number of cardboard boxes stacked around the perimeter.

Macie nudges my shoulder, shaking me from my trance. "You comin' slowpoke? I'm getting old here."

Mustering up as much of a smile as I can, I bump her back. Following Macie down a narrow hallway, we enter the kitchen. Groups of people linger around the room: theater kids, neighbors, extended family members. In the center of the kitchen, I spot a marble island countertop occupied by a spread of catered food. Macie and I grab plastic graduation-themed plates and help ourselves.

Once we've filled our plates, we make our way over to the decorative side tables filled with mementos. I glance at the keepsakes of Nathaniel's school days: an old signed football, theater award trophies, and a picture of him with his car after getting his driver's license. On the other side of the table, his diploma and graduation cap are featured proudly. My eyes land on a senior portrait of Nathaniel, sitting on the stoop of his house, smiling. As I stare, I can't help but smile to myself. He made it.

Holding up her plate of potato salad, Macie points toward the bay window overlooking the backyard. We walk over and stop once we reach the windowsill. In the middle of the backyard is an outdoor canopy tent with circular tables and wooden chairs beneath it. I look out at the cluster of partygoers until I suddenly spot Nathaniel. He's preoccupied, talking to a young couple with two children in tow. I watch as he bends down to give the youngest one a high-five.

Macie turns to me, pointing to the backyard again. "What do you say? You ready?"

"I don't know if I'll ever be ready," I sigh, "but I guess we have to go out there at some point."

Macie shepherds me forward. "Let's go."

We descend the steps of the back patio, and Macie nudges me, pointing to where Nathaniel's standing.

I should be accustomed to the rush I get from seeing him by now. After all, he's seen me at some of my most embarrassing moments, so it's not like I have anything to feel particularly shy about. Yet, I still can't seem to shake the butterflies I get whenever I see him. I guess it's just one of the pesky side effects of liking someone this much.

Sensing my reluctance, Macie takes the initiative, calling out Nathaniel's name. He spins toward the source of the noise, and thankfully, the look on his face puts my mind at ease. His expression lights up with a glowing energy.

"Scarlett, Macie, you made it." He traverses the lawn, extending his arms out in front of him.

"Congratulations to the grad." I put my game face on and flash a bright smile as I walk toward him. When we meet in the middle, he encompasses me in a tight hug and then greets Macie in the same fashion. I love how joyful he seems, as if he doesn't have a care in the world. I can feel myself grinning right along with him.

"So, what do you think?" He motions to himself. "Do I look like a different guy to you now that I've walked across the stage?"

"Definitely a little older and a little wiser," I chuckle. "But still the same you."

"I'm glad you think s—"

Just as he's about to finish his sentence, I hear a woman's voice behind me.

"Sweetheart, Grandma just got here. You should go and say 'hi.'"

As I spin around, I'm met with a head of dark hair and a pair of blue eyes identical to Nathaniel's. The wrinkles around the woman's face deepen as she flashes a glimmering smile. Without the need for an introduction, I already know exactly who she must be.

"Mom," Nathaniel confirms my hypothesis, motioning to me, "I don't think you've had the pleasure of meeting Scarlett yet."

"No, I don't think I have." She extends a slender arm. Though she's petite in stature, her grip is firm enough that I'm left feeling numb afterward. "It's very nice to meet you, Scarlett."

"Nice to meet you, Mrs. Wilder." I return her warm smile.

"Make yourself at home. You'll have to excuse us for the clutter in our house right now though. Especially with the big move in progress."

The pit in my chest expands. I clear my throat, attempting to answer her. "We're all really sad to be saying goodbye."

"Even more reason to come back and visit soon. Right, Mom?" Nathaniel pushes.

Mrs. Wilder laughs. "He's been especially insistent about coming back. We've lived in a lot of places, but he's taken a particular liking to this town. I'm sure we'll be back at some point." She pats Nathaniel on the back. "Now, like I said before, go say 'hi' to Grandma."

As his mom turns away, Nathaniel places his hand on the small of my back and leans in closer. "Be right back."

"Go do your thing."

Nathaniel walks away to greet his other family members while I make my way back over to Macie.

"Meeting the family already, huh?" She folds her arms together. "Things must be getting pretty serious."

I elbow her jokingly. "Let's not get ahead of ourselves."

"Watch out," Macie continues. "You could be her future daughter-in-law someday."

I place my hand over her mouth to shush her. She squirms in my grasp and then pulls away from me, giggling. "On another note, you'll never guess what Liam's doing over there."

"Oh no. I'm afraid to ask."

Grabbing my hand, Macie whisks me across the lawn until we've reached another decorative table near the tent. In the center is a glass jar with pieces of blank paper scattered around it.

"It's an inspiration jar," Macie explains. "You can leave inspirational messages for the graduate."

I look at Liam, who is hunched over the table, scribbling rapidly on a piece of paper. After finishing his note, he glances up at us. "Or you can leave *anti*-inspirational messages."

I lift a brow in confusion. "Anti-inspirational messages? What are those, Liam?"

His face twists into a mischievous grin. "You could say they're your cliché inspirational quotes, but with a darker twist."

I laugh out loud. "Liam, why?"

"You have to keep life interesting somehow." He smirks. "Plus, I don't want Nathaniel to get a big head now that he's a hotshot NYU student."

I lean over the table and tilt my head toward the scrap of paper he'd been working on.

If at first you don't succeed, you weren't good enough to succeed the first time.

"Ouch, that's brutal." I shake my head. "But an interesting interpretation, I guess?"

Nodding, Liam turns toward me. "Nathaniel doesn't have time for mushy, motivational words. They've got to be tough and character-building. Just like the world."

I reach out for another note he wrote underneath the original one.

Follow your dreams. They probably won't become a reality, anyway. That's why they're dreams.

Macie and I both laugh.

"Where do you come up with this stuff?" I grab one more piece that he scribbled on.

Believe in yourself. You're the only one who can when no one else does.

I set the piece of paper back down on the table. "What if Nathaniel actually takes these to heart?"

Stretching across the table, Liam grabs one last note and hands it to me. "Read this."

Just a few anti-inspirational messages to keep your ego in check. Love you, man. You've got big things ahead of you. ~ Liam

"Just in case." With that, he compiles the four notes together, rolls them up, and drops them into the jar.

"Aw," Macie gushes. "Who knew Liam had a sappy side after all?"

"If you tell anyone, I'll have to kill you." He shuts the lid on the jar and places the pen back on the table.

Macie winks. "Your secret's safe with me."

* * *

Liam, Macie, and I spend the rest of the evening floating around the party—munching on catered food, competing in cornhole, and people-watching from afar. Now that the sun has finally dipped below the horizon, the gentle glow of fireflies illuminates the backyard with a glimmering twinkle.

Macie rests a hand on my shoulder, turning me toward her to gain my full attention. "Hey, Scar. I think Liam and I are going to head out soon now that it's getting dark. Do you want to come with?"

Looking around, I notice that the party is winding down. Guests are saying their goodbyes, and the backyard is slowly emptying.

"I think I'll stay for a little while longer. I can walk home from here."

Macie looks at me with an empathetic face, making it clear that she knows what's about to come next. She scoops me up into a hug. "Let me know when you get back home, okay? I'll bring over the junk food, and we can pop in an eighties movie. I'm thinking *Sixteen Candles*."

I manage a weak smile. "I'm definitely going to need it tonight."

Leaning in closer, Macie cups a hand to my ear. "And remember, just goodbye for now. Not forever."

"Just goodbye for now," I say. "I can do that."

I wave to her and Liam as they say their final goodbyes and make their way back into the house. With a deep breath, I scan the rest of the backyard, searching for Nathaniel. My eyes land on him as he says goodbye to a few of the other partygoers. As they leave, I make my way over, wanting to grab his attention before he's caught up in another conversation.

"There's the party host," I say. "I've barely seen you all night."

He spins toward me, running a hand through his hair. "Who knew being a host was this tiring? There are only so many 'great to see you's' and 'how have you been's' that I can handle before I want to lose my mind."

"Well, in that case, great to see you…how have you been, Nathaniel?"

He tilts his head. "Okay, you're the one person who can pull those questions off and make me actually want to answer them."

Grinning back at him, I place my hands on my hips. The backyard has emptied out, with only a couple of stragglers remaining.

"I know you must be exhausted from the party, and you probably still have packing to do." My chest tightens. "Do you want me to, you know, get going soon?"

He shakes his head almost immediately, with a hint of alarm in his eyes. "No," he says. "Stay a little while longer?"

I grin at the idea that he would even have to ask. Before I can respond, Nathaniel points at the stone pathway leading toward the front of his house. "What do you say we go for a walk?"

"Go for a walk?" I ask. "I can't let the graduate leave his own graduation party."

His mouth twists into a smile. "You know, I am the graduate, which means today is kind of my day. And since today is kind of my day, I was really hoping you'd agree to go on a walk with me."

I giggle at his persistence. "All right then. Let's go, grad."

With that, he grabs hold of my hand and begins leading me along the stone path. Our fingers intertwine as he pulls me along, guiding me forward. I assume he's going to let go once we reach the front of his house, but he doesn't. He just squeezes my hand even tighter, like he wants to hold on for as long as possible.

"You seem especially into hand-holding tonight, Nathaniel Wilder," I remark.

"Hey," he raises his wrist, bringing his watch closer to my face. "I only have a couple more minutes before my parents notice I've busted out of my own party. I want to get in as much hand-holding with you as I can until then."

CHAPTER TWENTY-TWO

I squeeze his hand back. "I won't object."

We continue to walk side by side, our footsteps echoing along the pavement. Looking over my shoulder, I realize that he's leading me to the same park we had visited the other week. The setting looks completely different tonight from what I remember. The park is backlit by the glow of adjacent streetlights, the atmosphere calm and quiet. The last time we were here, I thought I was about to say goodbye to Nathaniel. The irony is that, this time, I actually am. I'm not sure which is worse.

Nathaniel guides me over to a bench near a tree. Sitting down, he pats the seat next to him in invitation. I follow suit, tucking my dress underneath me as I join him.

With that, Nathaniel extends his arm around me and pulls me to him. Instinctively, I rest my head on his shoulder, allowing his body to support the weight. Like the push and pull of a current, I feel his shoulder move up and down with each breath he takes. We don't say any words, and we don't move. We just sit on the bench in the middle of the park, reflecting.

After a while, he lifts his head and looks at me. The night is dark enough that I can't see his face in detail, but I can make out his silhouette.

"Scarlett, I want you to know how much I'm going to miss you." His voice is low. The sound of my name on his lips makes my stomach roil. Turning toward him, I notice the streetlight casting a gentle glow over his features. "What do we do about us?"

His words leave me weak. I feel like I can barely breathe.

"I wish you didn't have to go," I whisper, my voice wavering, "but you're going to have such an exciting life in New York. A new city, new friends, and new experiences. I can't hold you back from that and all that you're going to accomplish." Blinking my eyes, I try to suppress the mist forming in them. I wish someone had warned me that saying goodbye could be this hard. How is it that "goodbye" can be tossed around so easily and yet impossible to say when it truly matters?

"And I don't want to hold you back either," he whispers. "Especially from your senior year and all you have ahead of you."

My heart is heavy. As I think about it, a strange thought dawns on me. "You want to know what stinks the most about all of this?" I ask.

He tilts his head in my direction. "What?"

"Well," I hesitate, unsure how to explain my mental comparison, "in a strange way, it almost feels like you're dying."

Shaking his head, he laughs. "I hope I'm not about to die anytime soon, unless you know something I don't."

"With death, there's the finality of it. People get to say goodbye, knowing the ones they care about are gone permanently."

"Okay, I see your point," he chuckles. "But where are you going with all of this?"

"Well," I pause, my throat constricting, "it sort of feels like I'm saying goodbye to you, but you're going to go on living this completely separate life from me. And I'm going to wonder what that life's like. And how different it would be if I were in it. And if I'm ever going to see you again."

His eyes grow soft as he looks back at me with comprehension. "Scarlett," he breathes, "I know how you feel. I'm going to be doing the same with you, too. I'm going to be wondering how you are, and what you're up to, and who you're with."

At his words, I feel a tear condense, trailing down my face with a wet stain. "How do we do it then? How do we let each other go, at least for now? How do we stop ourselves from the constant wondering?"

Nathaniel grows quiet, holding my gaze. "Maybe it's okay to let ourselves wonder."

I tilt my head, trying to understand.

"At first," he continues, "it might be tough, even unbearable at times.

But slowly, it's going to get better. We'll make it to the point where it doesn't hurt anymore. We'll feel proud thinking about each other, because we'll see how far we've come and how we wouldn't have gotten to that place without having met each other, regardless of what happens."

Blinking back the tears in my eyes, I stare at him, stunned by the firm reassurance in his voice.

"When I wonder about you, what should I imagine you doing? Tell me what will make me happy when I think about you."

He pauses. "For now, imagine me standing on stage at the Oscars, giving a heartfelt speech after winning the award for Best Actor. I'll thank the Academy for recognizing my cinematic excellence and all of the people in my life who have had faith in me."

"Okay," I chuckle. "When I think about you, I'm going to imagine you're following your dream of becoming an actor. That you're up there on stage accepting an award for doing what you love most."

"And what about you, Scarlett? Tell me what to imagine you doing when I think about you."

I think about where my ultimate passion lies and decide to go with the answer that comes naturally to me. "Imagine me creating beautiful clothes for retail brands and working with famous runway models. My designs will be so groundbreaking that I'll be featured in acclaimed magazines, like *Vogue* and *Harper's Bazaar*."

Nodding, Nathaniel laughs. "Alright, then. When I think about you, I'm going to imagine you as the most highly sought-after fashion designer in the country."

Pulling back from Nathaniel, I look into his eyes. "Then, that's that. Whenever we think about each other, we'll just wonder about our dreams for each other."

"Wonder about our dreams," he repeats, digesting the words as they roll off his tongue. "I like that."

"And who knows. One day, if I get into FIT, and you're at NYU—and we're both in the same city…."

"Then maybe we won't have to wonder anymore," he finishes my sentence.

As we sit in place, the headlights of a car shine into the distance. The car passes, illuminating our faces and then fading into the darkness.

Nathaniel glances down at his watch. "My parents are probably going to kill me. I never told them I left."

It's as if he just replaced my sunshine with dark thunderclouds, and I get the sinking feeling that this is the moment. The fateful, but inevitable, moment I've been dreading—the one where a piece of my heart is about to get ripped out of me.

"How do we do this?" I whisper, my voice barely audible. "How do we say goodbye?"

Nathaniel releases a long, pent-up breath. He tips his head up to the sky. "I've never said a goodbye like this before, so I don't even know where to begin. The only thing I can think of is going step-by-step."

"Step-by-step," I repeat back to him. "Well, I guess that's better than all at once, because I don't think I'm capable of that right now."

Nathaniel pushes himself off of the bench and extends a hand to pull me up to standing level.

My legs feel weak beneath me. "What's the first step, then?"

He moves closer, until he's only inches away.

"First step. I'm going to put my arms around you and hold you as tightly as I can."

Nathaniel pulls me close, wrapping his arms around me until I'm fully pressed against him. I feel the warmth of his body as I rest my head against his chest, listening to the thrum of his beating heart. With each moment that passes, the tension from my muscles dissolves.

Leaning down, he brings his lips close to my ear. "Second step. I'm going to tell you that I can't imagine what this year would have been like without you in it."

My voice catches in my throat as I release a shaky breath. "I don't think I can imagine what next year will be like without you in it." I echo his words back to him.

"Third step," his voice wavers, "we're both going to start moving backward." With care, he pulls away slowly, releasing me from his grasp. My body instantly feels colder, as if he's the only one who can evoke warmth in it.

With his eyes still trained on me, Nathaniel continues, "We're both going to start walking backward at the same time until we finally need to turn around."

With reluctance, I take my first step backward, watching as Nathaniel does the same. I keep my eyes focused on him, blinking back the swell of tears rising to the surface. I can't believe this is really it. This is goodbye.

I'm about to turn around completely when I hear him call out to me. "You didn't think I'd stop at the third step, did you?"

My body floods with relief.

"Fourth step," he yells, "I'm going to run back toward you..." his legs pick up speed as he breaks out into a sprint, "because I can't say goodbye without kissing you one more time."

I'm caught by surprise as he lifts me off of the ground. My body is suspended in mid-air, and my feet are dangling, so I wrap my arms around his neck. Slowly, he lowers me to him until our faces are inches apart. With a feather-light touch, his lips brush against mine, as if I'm made of glass, and he's afraid I might break. The sensation is equal parts bitter and sweet, like consuming the last bite of a chocolate bar that you know is almost gone. When he finally breaks away, I feel like a piece of me has broken off, too.

"Fifth step," he plants me carefully back onto the ground. "I'm going to set you down like this and say goodbye to you one last time."

My lips quiver as I try to regain the breath he stole from me.

"Goodbye for now, Scarlett," he brushes my face with his fingertips. "Wonder about your dream for me."

Before I can speak, he backs away and turns around. I keep my eyes fixed on him as he walks in the opposite direction, moving farther away.

Just as he's about to exit the park, he glances over his shoulder, looking back at me. With a nostalgic smile, he extends his hand and waves. It's a simple gesture—the type of wave you'd give to someone you're going to see again soon. With a soft smile, I lift my own hand in return and wave back, hoping that maybe sometime soon, I will.

One day, this chapter in my life might seem like a distant memory: a hazy picture no longer in focus. As we both go on living our lives, I might start to forget the little details: what he looks like, what he sounds like, what he feels like. After all, our relationship was a singular experience—as unique as a snowflake falling from the sky. At some point, every crystal dissolves, melting away. Yet this doesn't invalidate that, for a brief period of time, each beautiful pattern was the only one to ever exist.

As for Nathaniel and me, we may never be able to rewind to this exact point in time, but we won't need to. No matter where we go from here, we will still appreciate our time together and think about each other in the best way.

With a deep breath, I find the strength to turn around and walk forward. Wiping away a final tear, I smile to myself.

"Wonder about your dream for me, too, Nathaniel Wilder."

Acknowledgements

This book would not be possible without the support of my family. Mom, thank you for inspiring me every day with your passion, confidence, and drive. I look up to you as a business woman, leader, role model, and mother. You've never made my dreams feel unattainable, and you've helped me believe I can achieve anything if I put my mind to it. Thanks for being my "Hype Mom" and supporting me every step of the way.

Dad, you are one of my favorite writers and biggest creative inspirations. Thank you for fueling my passion as a kid by encouraging me to write short stories and submit to newspaper competitions. You were the first person to ever read this book, and although young adult romance is "not your typical genre," you still read my entire manuscript page by page and helped me make it the best it could be. You've taught me that "less is more" and not to use the big adjectives just because they "sound impressive."

To my favorite sibling, Noah. Since impressing our parents with your law school acceptance, I had to do something to try and compare, and publishing this book felt like the closest thing. I can't wait to see the talented lawyer you become and finally hear you use the phrase: "If you can sue it, you can do it." Also, thanks for agreeing to give my book a positive review if I buy you and your friends twelve-packs. I might take you up on that offer.

To my childhood friend, Catherine, thank you for always brightening my day with your kindness, warmth, and joyful spirit. You have taught me what true friendship looks like, and our 20-year one is one of my great privileges. I still expect to have sleepovers, take walks around the neighborhood, and make embarrassing Photo Booth videos even when we're old and gray.

To my high school friend, Deepti, this book would not be possible without your curiosity, creativity, and compassion. Thank you for pushing me outside of my comfort zone, like the semester we decided to try set design. Even though we spent a painstaking amount of time painting that trellis, it was one of my favorite memories, and I'm very grateful for you.

To my roommates, Emily, Jess, Ben, Clarence, Katie, and Piper. Thank you for willingly choosing to live with me and putting up with my unique habits. I hope you'll bond over that one-of-a-kind experience and remember my quirks for years to come. Thank you for the heart-to-hearts, deep discussions, and for knowing me better than most.

To my New Albany, University of Richmond, New York City, Ann Inc., and HelloFresh friends, teachers, professors, and coworkers. Thank you for giving me the opportunity to learn from such supportive and dynamic communities. You are all a part of my story that I'm continuously writing, and I can't wait to see what the next chapter brings.

To the Schaffir, Miller, Schlosberg, Hand, and Sigman families, I'm so grateful to have an extended family that stays close even when we live far apart. To my grandparents, Inabeth and Bill, Sandy and Kurt, thank you for bringing us together and instilling the importance of family within us.

To my editor, Shawn Simmons, and the Level Best Team: Thank you so much for believing in my story and helping to bring it to life. I appreciate all the work you've put into the publishing process to get this story ready for launch. It's been a delight working with you and my fellow Level Besties, and I'm so proud to be a part of this group.

A special shout-out to my agent, Cindy Bullard, who took a chance on me and made my dreams come true. Without you, I would just be a writer who likes to daydream. Now, I'm a writer who likes to daydream with my signature on a literary contract. None of this would be possible without you.

To my publicity team: Crystal, Grace, and Leilani—you are so talented at what you do, and I'm lucky to get to work closely with you. Just the street credit of saying "I'll have to check with my publicity team," is enough to evoke my gratitude. Also, thank you to BookSparks for the beautiful book cover. I still can't stop looking at it.

Scott, you have been my sounding board, cheerleader, and source of strength. It's only fitting that I'd consider writing a future book with inspiration from you. Thanks for sticking by my side even before I was a big ol' author and supporting my passion regardless of the outcome. Together, we're one step closer to living out our dreams of being "subtly" famous.

Annie Nybo, your developmental edits gave me the crash course in editing that I didn't know I needed and truly transformed my writing into the finished book it is today. Kristen Ricordati and Lauren Kay, thank you for your words of wisdom, even when I was a newbie who was just figuring it out. I appreciate the encouragement, and I look up to you as fellow young adult authors. Julia DeVillers, Sarah Ainslee, Leah Dobrinska, and Micki Bare, thank you for taking time out of your day to read my story and provide a blurb. It's been an honor to include your words with this book.

All my friends, family, loved ones, and anyone who has ever believed in me or encouraged me along the way, you don't know how much it means. Thank you from the bottom of my heart.

About the Author

Alison Schaffir is a social media strategist and young adult author living in New York City. A lover of contemporary fiction, Alison developed her debut novel, Your Dream for Me, fusing two of her favorite interests, fashion and theater, together. She graduated from University of Richmond with a major in business marketing and a minor in psychology. When she's not making up stories in her head, she loves indulging in Trader Joe's lava cakes, belting early 2000s pop hits, and spending time with her friends and family.

SOCIAL MEDIA HANDLES:
   Instagram: @alison.schaff.writer
   Twitter: @ASchaffir
   Medium: https://medium.com/@alison.schaffir

AUTHOR WEBSITE:
   https://alisonschaffir.wixsite.com/alisonschaffirauthor

CPSIA information can be obtained
at www.ICGtesting.com
Printed in the USA
LVHW041249050323
740959LV00002B/252